I0676232

The
$50 Million
Perfect Score

The $50 Million Perfect Score
A Financial Thriller
Mesa, Arizona

Copyright 2024 Rick Lindstrom
ISBN 979-8-9906240-1-6
ISBN 979-8-9906240-2-3 (epub)
First Edition
May 30, 2024

This is a work of fiction. All incidents and dialogue, and all characters with the exception of some well-known historical figures, are products of the author's imagination and are not to be construed as real. Where real-life historical persons appear, the situations, incidents, and dialogues concerning those persons are entirely fictional and are not intended to depict actual events or to change the entirely fictional nature of the work. In all other respects, any resemblance to persons living or dead is entirely coincidental.

The
$50 Million
Perfect Score

A Financial Thriller

Rick Lindstrom

Financial Thrillers by Rick Lindstrom

The $50 Million Perfect Score

Follow the Fortunes

Abduction

For Kim and our memories aboard the *A Train.*

Part I

Chapter One

Warehouse on Duwamish Waterway
Seattle, Washington
March 19, 2015

"Are you comfortable, Mr. Sims?"

Lucas Sims was not comfortable. Still in his business suit, strapping tape secured his wrists and forearms to the armrests of his wheelchair. Strapping tape also held his body to the back of the chair. His legs were not taped; it was unnecessary. He was paralyzed below the waist.

Scared, Sims didn't answer. Though uncertain, he had a good idea of the reason for his bondage. Just enough light filtered into the room for him to see he was alone with his captor. Looking down, Sims saw zip ties holding his wheelchair to four bolts set in a sheet of plywood. Sweat poured out of his entire body, and he bordered on panic.

In the thirty-six years since the accident, Lucas Sims had become proficient with the wheelchair. He had learned to wheel himself to the passenger door of his van and pull himself out of the chair onto the front seat using hand grips. From inside the van, he could reach down and fold the chair. Sims had developed a strong upper body and, though not easily, could swing the folded chair back through the sliding door.

A simple electronic system made it possible for him to open and close the sliding door from the front seat. The bench-style seat allowed him to maneuver himself and drive using the manual controls, common for those without the use of their legs. Earlier today had been different. He hadn't made it to the front seat.

Sims had been on his way to an afternoon meeting in Bellevue when a man in black grabbed him in the parking lot, taped his mouth closed, and bound his hands behind his back. The bag the man put over Sims's head had holes, allowing him to breathe but not big enough for him to see out.

His abductor carefully placed him in the back of a truck, recognizable by the hard floor and hollow noises. As fear set in and sweat dripped down his back, he had heard at least one voice, although he couldn't make out any words over the noise of the truck. He had no further memory of the experience until he found himself taped to his wheelchair in this dark room.

Now the bag had been removed and he could see. He moved his fingers; they were okay. And he could twist his head; that was about it. He maneuvered his hands, trying to loosen the tape. It proved futile.

Sims didn't recognize the large man in a gray business suit seated in front of him on an old, rusted lawn chair. It wasn't the same man who had grabbed him. That man had been shorter, muscular, and quite stocky, and dressed entirely in black, including the balaclava which covered his face.

By turning his head, Sims saw three windowless walls. There may have been a window behind him as a small amount of natural light permeated the space. The winter cold made him shiver, and except for the occasional squawking sounds of seagulls outside, the room was silent. He couldn't tell the time, but his body's clock said it was afternoon.

"Mr. Sims," the large man said in a strong, careful tone, like a stage voice. Although sitting, the man appeared to be well over 250 pounds and more than six feet tall. He wore a perfectly cut designer suit. "You have a business relationship with my employer, Mr. Bruno Cento."

"I'm sorry, but I've never heard of Mr. Cento," said Sims.

"But you do know Danny Haber, who is also known as Stubby, don't you, Mr. Sims?"

At that moment, fear took over and Lucas Sims became ill. Stubby was a bookmaker and a gambler, and Sims owed him money. A great deal of money.

As Sims swallowed to keep the bile from pouring out of his stomach, the big man spoke again. "Stubby works for Mr. Cento. Perhaps you didn't know that. Mr. Sims, did Stubby ever tell you how he came by that name?"

Stubby had only a thumb and two fingers on his left hand. Sims shook his head slowly and stared straight ahead.

He noticed the man occasionally glance toward the back corner of the room. *Was there a second person? The man in black?* He couldn't tell. He heard the seagulls again.

The big man continued speaking in the same strong voice. His eyes were two spots of black within an expressionless, white face. "Mr. Cento wanted you to know he appreciates your business. He understood you might have trouble paying what you owe him. He also knows one hundred thousand dollars is a great deal of money to you. It is a great deal of money to you, isn't it, Mr. Sims?"

Sims couldn't speak.

"It's a great deal of money to Mr. Cento too. That's why he's concerned you haven't paid him. Do you understand?"

Sounds spilled out of Sims's mouth, although they couldn't be described as words. He strained to control his body and think at the same time, though it proved to be difficult. Two seconds later, Sims lost the battle for control and threw up all over himself.

The big man spoke again. "I'm sorry you're not feeling well, Mr. Sims. But we won't be here long, at least we don't have to be. Mr. Cento suggests you go to your office tomorrow and tell Jacques Levesque you require one hundred thousand dollars. Mr. Cento is certain you will find a way to persuade Mr. Levesque to give the money to you, and you will have it for us tomorrow at five p.m."

Who was this man? How did he know about Jacques Levesque? Sims couldn't think. But for the first time in the past hour, he started to recover and realized he might get out of this—at least for today.

"Do you consider Mr. Cento's suggestion to be a good one, Mr. Sims?"

After several seconds, Sims managed to croak out a sound. "Yes."

"Good. You'll receive a call tomorrow at four p.m. You'll be told where to bring the money. All of it. And, Mr. Sims, Mr. Cento sends his great appreciation for accepting his suggestion."

Chapter Two

Wells Fargo Center
Seattle, Washington
March 20, 2015

People noticed Jacques Levesque. He commanded a room. In a group of people, he stood out in a way no one else did. Not even beautiful women. Genuinely friendly, he made people feel as if they were the most important person in the room. He was strong and convincing, impossible to disagree with.

Levesque was sure Lucas Sims would prefer to be anywhere else. Instead, he sat in his wheelchair in front of Levesque's massive desk in Levesque's massive office. Levesque was his boss, and Sims had just told him about what happened the day prior. About how he owed Danny Haber one hundred thousand dollars. About how the large man had intimidated him. And about Bruno Cento's "suggestion." He should have appealed to Levesque immediately after the abduction, but he lacked the courage. A day later, he had summoned the will, and Levesque listened quietly, not once interrupting.

Levesque contemplated what he had heard and what

to do next. "How long has this been going on?"

As chief financial officer, Sims was in a perfect position to embezzle funds. He might have used the company's money to pay the gamblers. No evidence existed but Levesque's question was a reasonable one.

Only a finance executive could remember details the way Sims could.

"It started two years ago. I used to bet twenty-five dollars every week on the Notre Dame football games with a friend at the Washington Athletic Club. I love Notre Dame, and I always bet on them to win. Then, we started adding games, and before long, one of us might owe the other two hundred or three hundred dollars after a weekend. We decided it would be better for our friendship not to bet against each other. We asked the locker room attendant at the club if he knew a bookie, and within two or three days, we met Danny Haber in the coffee shop where he hung out. Everyone knew him as Stubby."

Sims continued to tell how the number of games increased and how the bets grew. "Over the next couple of years, I bet more and more football games and added basketball and baseball."

Levesque remained impassive.

"You know how sports gambling works. The bookies get an extra ten percent on losses. Even if you win half the time, you'll lose money. The higher your bets, the more you'll lose. Over time, it's almost impossible to win. I probably knew that before I started, but I thought I was smart enough to beat them." Sims slumped in his wheelchair.

Jacques Levesque had never gambled but understood

what Lucas said, especially the part about the bookies always winning. He also understood the ten percent concept and knew how quickly that advantage accrued to the bookie.

With a heavy sigh, Sims took a deep breath and looked around the room, as if seeking an escape, then went on. "Most bookies settle with their clients on Tuesday if the bettor has a losing week, or on Wednesday if the bettor has a winning week. The bookie collects from the losers first and pays the winners later. Because of the ten percent concept, the bookies rarely collect less on Tuesdays than they pay out on Wednesdays. Once Stubby and I knew each other better, he often carried the settlements over into the following week with no cash changing hands."

As Levesque listened, he almost seemed to be in another place, although he paid close attention.

Sims continued to tell his story in remarkable detail—how the increasing action and increasing wagers led him to a critical decision point. "Before long, I was betting around a thousand dollars a game, and the weekly settlement was in the range of ten to twenty thousand. I stayed close to even. Then, I had four bad weeks in a row, and Stubby wanted his money. I owed him close to fifty thousand. Ulrika and I had enough in our cash accounts, and because I manage all the household finances, I got the money without her finding out. I went to the coffee shop and paid Stubby."

"Why didn't you quit?" Levesque asked. "You were putting everything at risk."

Sims's forehead glistened with sweat as he told his story. "You're right. I knew I'd let things get out of hand,

and I bordered on addiction. But I also knew I hadn't reached that point. After seriously considering quitting, I made my decision. I increased my bets to three thousand dollars a game.

"I won three weeks in a row, and when Stubby paid me off on Wednesdays, I was ecstatic. Sports gambling is an all cash business, and it thrilled me when he handed me a McDonald's bag with twenty thousand in cash inside." Sims's hands fidgeted in his lap. "My good luck didn't last."

Levesque stared right through Sims as if he weren't there. His thoughts were elsewhere but Sims didn't notice as he talked on.

"I had another four-week losing streak. I lost over eighty thousand. I took the last fifty thousand from our family bank accounts and gave it to Stubby. I still owed him thirty."

Even though Levesque always kept his office cold, sweat soaked through Lucas Sims's shirt. "I needed to win the thirty thousand back. If only I could win that money, I promised myself I would be finished with Stubby and quit gambling forever. I knew I could do it if I just won enough to break even again. That was three weeks ago."

Sims's story sped up as he explained his logic for his continued betting. "I spent the entire next week studying the schedule of football and basketball games for the following weekend. I had decided to put more effort into my selections than ever before. I must have looked at two hundred games and studied the past performance of the teams. I considered whether they were at home or on the road, looked at the weather forecasts, read about injuries, and checked all the handicappers' selections. By Friday, I narrowed my picks down to seven games. They were my top choices, and my confidence soared. I could win all of them. They were all pro football games to be played on Sunday."

Levesque could guess the next part, but let Sims tell his story.

"I planned to increase my bets, and I wanted to discuss it with Stubby in person. Saturday, I drove to the coffee shop and told him to raise my bets to ten thousand dollars a game for seven games. If I won at least five, I'd no longer owe him anything, and I would quit." The sweat stains on Sims's shirt were growing by the minute.

"Stubby didn't react in the way I thought he would. He said he liked me and felt bad for me, but that my idea wouldn't work. He offered to carry me for the thirty thousand until I could come up with it, at least for a little while, but increasing my bets to ten thousand was too risky and that he couldn't handle that kind of action himself. He'd have to go to bigger sources to find someone to take that size bet. If I lost, they would want to get paid—immediately."

Sims shook his head. "I gave him my picks for seven games. Ten thousand on each one. Stubby took the bets."

In almost a whisper, he went on, "I lost all seven, Jacques. Just like that, I owed a hundred thousand dollars. Only this time, I didn't just owe Stubby. I owed his partners as well. I barely had a hundred dollars let alone a hundred thousand. Stubby warned me I'd better start making payments immediately, but I couldn't. I didn't have anything. He told me his partners were not nice people and not patient either. If I didn't pay, they could hurt me. I couldn't do anything."

Levesque took in Sims's pale, sweat-drenched face and shaky hands. A bubble of sympathy started to grow but he tamped it down.

"I was sick every minute. They called the house and confronted me on street corners. They threatened to hurt me if I didn't pay. They even came here. Ulrika found out and went to her mother's house with the kids. Then yesterday, they grabbed me. I'm at the end of the line. I don't know which way to turn."

Levesque listened to every word as he mulled over a plan which had been taking root in his mind for several months. He could benefit from Lucas Sims's problem, an opportunity to exploit. He rarely felt or expressed compassion for anyone. He didn't know how. But this wasn't compassion, it was business and business has no feeling. He looked at Sims. "So, what do you want me to do?"

Sims remained quiet for a minute before answering. "Jacques, I'm desperate. They want the money today by five o'clock. They've threatened my family and me, and I've seen what they did to Stubby. You're my only hope. If I don't get them the money today, I'll be lucky if they just cut off my fingers."

Levesque winced internally but didn't let on he had been affected. "Why should I give you money? Just because these guys know you work for someone who is a successful businessman doesn't mean I have to put it up. I've paid you well over the years. What did you do with it all?"

Sims didn't answer.

"What's wrong with asking those guys you hang out with at the club?" Levesque asked.

"I've been to them. There's nothing. They say I have a gambling problem and don't want to lend me anything. I didn't want to come to you. But now, you're the only one left. I'm down to the last minute. If you don't help me, I'm . . ."

Levesque had known Lucas Sims for ten years. Sims had worked for him for six. As well as the company's chief financial officer, Sims was also a first-rate programmer. Jacques had come to respect Sims for his professionalism and his problem-solving skills. More than once, Jacques had considered making a proposal to Sims that involved questionable work. He never did because he knew Sims would turn him down and leave. He also didn't want it known he had less-than-legal plans under consideration. Even now, on hearing of Sims's four years of gambling and his problem paying the bookies, he felt confident Sims had maintained his integrity. Still, if someone threatened to hurt him, you never knew. Now could be the perfect time to bring up the idea. He decided to make a proposal.

"Lucas, you're in a bad spot," he said, as if Sims didn't already know. "I don't have a hundred thousand dollars lying around ready to give to anyone with a problem. I've worked hard to build this business to where it is, and I never gamble. Gambling is for losers."

He paused to let the words sink in. "There may be a way for you to earn a hundred thousand . . . and quite a bit more." He could see Sims concentrating on his every word. "Are you interested in hearing more?"

Sims nodded.

"You're a good programmer, Lucas. The best in Seattle, I believe. Even though you have staff doing that work for you now, you're still the best. I need special programming done. Programming that will alter what we're doing here at LeGrande Benefits. Programming about which only you and I will know." In the next minute, Levesque would find out if Sims would cross the line.

Sims squirmed in his seat. "What about my reputation? I'd be putting everything I've worked for at risk. What about my licenses?"

Levesque smiled. "What reputation? Your reputation as a gambler? It's a sad reputation. Putting everything at risk? You already did that, Lucas, and you owe a lot of money. Your licenses? Ask Bruno Cento to renew your licenses."

Sims had a hard time forming the words. "What do I have to do?"

Levesque had been fairly confident Sims would take the bait and accept his proposal, but he didn't let on. He'd give Sims the money, but before he did, he needed to assure himself Sims would go along with the plan.

"I can help you, Lucas. But if I do, you and I are going into business together—a business different from what we do today. You will revise certain programs to override systems we have already put in place."

Sims nodded in defeat.

"The condensed version is that our new programming will divert money we now administer for the insurance companies into our accounts. We keep that money, the gamblers won't hurt you, your family will come home, and you'll be better off in a few years than you otherwise could be in your entire career."

Levesque watched as various emotions crossed Sims's face—first relief, then dismay, and finally greed.

After a pause, Sims asked, "So we'll be partners?"

"That's right, Lucas. Partners."

"Fifty-fifty?"

"No, Lucas. Eighty-twenty." He stared at Sims. "In case you're wondering which one of us gets the eighty, it's not you."

Chapter Three

Colman Ferry Dock
Seattle, Washington
May 15, 2015

On Friday evening, a black Lincoln Continental, with license plates stolen an hour earlier, idled in the rain near the end of the line of cars. They waited to enter the 7:50 p.m. ferry to Bremerton at slip number 1 at the Colman Dock in Seattle. The driver knew this boat was always crowded, filling to its capacity of 140 cars, and selected it because the Kaleetan was the larger of the two ferries serving Bremerton. Minutes later, five weeks of careful planning for this moment rewarded him with a space for his car in the last row of the boat, exactly where he intended.

On the Kaleetan, the car deck was the lowest, a few feet above the water. The boat attendants on the car deck went to work as soon as the last car drove onboard, and the ferry was ready to leave the terminal. They closed a three-foot-high gate behind the last row of cars and placed large wooden blocks behind the tires of the cars at the back. Other than the gate, the parking level was open from the deck to the ceiling.

The driver of the Lincoln settled in exactly where he wanted to be, waiting as other drivers exited their cars.

Although not strictly enforced, signs encouraged car drivers and passengers to leave their vehicles and move up to one of the passenger decks. These decks featured food, drinks, comfortable seating, and a warm, pleasant environment in which to enjoy the one-hour ride. Most drivers and passengers moved to the passenger decks, the only exceptions being those wishing to stay in their cars and sleep. Because of the bitter cold, everyone else had gone up.

That was perfect for the driver of the Lincoln, who remained in his car and pretended to sleep. When the boat attendants hurried to a warm room, he was alone.

One-half hour into the crossing, he stepped out of his car and moved behind it. The big boat's engines created a constant deep hum at the stern end of the ferry. The man, secure in his belief that no one heard or saw him, went to work.

Because he had removed all the bulbs from the vehicle, no light came on when he opened the door or the trunk. Although muscular, he was not a tall man and could barely be seen behind the car if anyone had bothered to look. He wore black pants, a black jacket, and a black watch cap, making him virtually invisible on the dimly lit car deck. He knew where the security cameras were located and moved in a way that assured no one could identify him or his car.

A short bungee cord allowed the trunk to open only

enough for the man to remove his cargo and drop it on the car deck. Three-inch-wide duct tape secured a larger man's knees and ankles. His wrists were taped together behind his back. Tape over his mouth prevented him from speaking, though he tried to scream.

The man in black made every move with precision and exuded confidence. He showed no fear of discovery, and because of his strength, his work was straightforward.

He tied one end of a 200-foot rope to the cargo's ankles. He tied the other end to a deck cleat near the rear of the car. Still, no one saw them. The man in black whispered something into the cargo's ear and let out a soft laugh. He heard his cargo trying to scream as he lifted the large squirming mass over the three-foot-high gate and dumped him into Puget Sound. The man returned to the inside of the Lincoln to resume his nap.

When the ship's captain announced the boat's approach to Bremerton, the passengers returned to their vehicles. Twelve minutes later, the cars began to move out, and the Lincoln headed through the exit tunnel toward State Route 304 and south, out of town.

Thirty miles away, the man in the black Lincoln was confident and relaxed, driving south toward Tacoma where he connected with the interstate highway and returned to Seattle. With his work for the evening completed, he could go home, shower, put on fancy clothes, and go out for a night on the town.

Most boats in the Washington State Ferry System were known as double-ended ferries. The Kaleetan was a double-ender. They had interchangeable bows and sterns allowing them to move between terminals without turning around, thus saving time. Upon landing, the crews simply moved from one end to the other and the bow became the stern for the return trip.

The Kaleetan's captain walked through the upper passenger level from what had been the bow to the other end. The bridge at one end is identical to the other. He and his mate immediately prepared for the return trip to Seattle. Their nighttime pre-sail routine included a test of the headlights and searchlights at that end of the boat.

Almost immediately, the mate spotted an object floating in the water ahead of the ferry. Within minutes, crew members hauled a dead body from the water onto the car deck. It was tied to the boat by a 200-foot length of rope.

Part II

Chapter Four

Yacht Haven Marina
Lake Union
Seattle, Washington
July 15, 2019

Ross and Kim Taylor sat side by side in the quiet cockpit of their boat, relishing the last rays of sunshine reflecting off the buildings on the east side of Lake Union. The summer sun set late in Seattle, located at the west end of the Pacific time zone and in the far north part of the country. Though nearing ten o'clock, the water in the marina still mirrored the buildings' silver sheen.

Ross broke the silence. "I can't remember a more beautiful evening. We've been here, what, three years? And it never gets old. Coming here has to be the best decision we've ever made—except to get married, of course."

Kim smiled her agreement as she refilled their wine glasses. Three years ago, they sold their home in Phoenix and purchased a boat in Seattle to call their new home—a huge change at the time.

Tonight, the activity around the lake and the sounds of car traffic from the Aurora Bridge provided a pleasant background. At first they found the noise intrusive and annoying; now, they loved it. Soft music drifted up from inside the main cabin. John Coltrane.

Though late in the day, Ross still wore business clothes—what he called the shorts and t-shirt he always wore when doing boat chores. Earlier in the afternoon, he repaired a pump which powered the freshwater system. The pumps needed regular service, and he loved the work. During the time he and Kim lived aboard, he noticed most boaters loved to maintain their own vessels, at least the routine work. Even people who never knew where to find the breaker panel in their house or who couldn't change a furnace filter or a garden-hose gasket became experts on their boat. The marina tenants could talk forever about their boat projects.

"Do you ever second-guess yourself—about choosing this life?" Kim asked. They sat in the rear corner on the port side of the cockpit, her favorite place, where they held hands and looked out over the water.

"Never. I may have questioned myself when we first made the decision but not since we bought the boat. I don't miss a thing we might have been doing in Phoenix. Well, I guess I do miss the D-backs. I haven't caught on with the Mariners yet. And we were making good money."

Ross had held the position of chief executive officer of a life and health insurance company until a senior executive engineered a clever fraud. Although Taylor discovered the crime and the criminal, and recovered the stolen money, the chairman fired him in a petulant search for a scapegoat.

"But I'm grateful to trade the daily grind for what we have here," he said. They loved life aboard their boat and the city of Seattle. He squeezed her hand. "How about you?"

"I don't regret our decision, but I miss seeing all the wonderful things you've given me through the years— especially the music boxes. Those and all the little figurines mean so much to me. I know they're in the storage trailer, but I often wish they were here."

Ross missed them too but understood the tradeoffs of living on a boat. "You know, I've lived at nineteen addresses in my life. Nineteen separate places I've called home. A few were fabulous. Many were dumps. I remember every one of them, and this is my absolute favorite. If you'll agree, this will be our last home."

Kim agreed. They moored their fifty-foot boat, *Pura Vida*, at the north end of the lake. Lake Union attracted visitors and locals alike as one of Seattle's favorite destinations, especially around sunrise and sunset. Slightly less than one square mile, it was a small, freshwater lake located just north of downtown. Many places on the lake afforded a breathtaking view of the downtown skyline as well as the boats and bridges which surrounded it.

Seaplanes arrived and departed regularly from the south, and pleasure yachts from nearby Bellevue and Kirkland used it as a point of transit between Lake Washington on the east and Puget Sound on the west. Floating home communities lined the shores on all sides. From their slip at the Yacht Haven Marina, the Taylors enjoyed one of the best views of the Seattle skyline from anywhere on the lake.

"Is the water working again?" she asked.

"Yeah. The usual problem with a valve leak. All fixed. No more noise."

"Good. By the way, what did Chris want?"

Ross and Christine Bell had met for the first time almost fifteen years ago, back in the days when they were moving up the ladders of their respective companies. Both became CEOs—Christine for Great Chicago Insurance Company. Kim knew her through industry conferences, and the two were friends.

Soft sounds of water lapping at the side of the boat accompanied their conversation. Probably the wake from a passing vessel farther out in the lake.

"She asked if I was available to help her with a problem she's having. I appreciate her calling. She knows what happened to me in Phoenix and believes I got a raw deal. She's afraid she might be at risk for the same thing."

"You mean getting fired because someone else stole money?" Kim shifted in her seat to see his face better.

"Maybe. She told me Great Chicago had experienced unexplained losses for the past few years. They've looked at the problem from all angles and can't seem to figure out why they're losing money."

Many insurance company CEOs suffered from this problem at one time or another. "What does she want you to do?" asked Kim.

"She asked me to put a fresh set of eyes on the problem. They've been looking at various explanations on and off for over two years—all the obvious ones, at least—but still no answers. She hopes I might use my personal experience to shed light on what's happening."

He took another sip of wine. "It's not a minor problem

either. She estimates their profit has been at least ten percent below expected levels. For Great Chicago, that means their profit is down by fifteen to twenty million dollars a year for three or four years. It's a big deal. She sounded desperate."

"Do you really want to take on her problem? That's why we left Phoenix—to get away from just this sort of thing."

"I know. It does seem like a step backward. But it's a major challenge, and right now, she's facing it on her own. I could gain back much of the credibility I lost when Frank fired me."

Kim squeezed his hand. "Back when we first came here, you wanted to spend your time working on the boat and getting it ready for an ocean passage. Your dream. Have you forgotten that dream? Is the money that important?"

Ross contemplated Kim's questions. "No. And you're right. I wanted to spend all my time on the boat. But it's been hard to let go. I can't forget what happened. I hear Christine describe her situation, and I shift back to my old thinking. I want to outline strategies, evaluate alternatives, assign tasks, and solve the problem. I want to be effective for her and, if there is a bad guy, to find him. I'd like to recover my reputation."

Kim listened, leaning closer to Ross.

"After our call, I wanted to help her. As for the money, it's not a priority. We have enough to meet our needs and desires. Anyway, I won't know how much the assignment might be worth until I talk with her again."

Kim looked skeptical. "I don't know. This might be a

lose-lose. You saw how it ended for us at Arizona Life."
She paused. "What does she want you to do?"

"Well, she wants me to come to their office and hear
the details personally. The quicker, the better. She also
wants me to meet her staff." Ross stared out at the water,
now black. "It's an intriguing situation, and she could
be right. A new insight, a different perspective, might
produce an explanation. Besides, you and I haven't been
to Chicago together in quite a while. If she hires me, it
will no doubt mean a trip back to her office later in the
summer. It'll be fun for us to stay longer and see the city
again. We used to love it."

"That would be fun," Kim admitted. "I changed
my mind. You ought to do it—at least go and hear her
out. If she hires you, I'll move out of the office to give
you space while you're on her project." She referred to
a shared office they built into the forward part of the
cabin.

"I'll call her in the morning and set up my meeting.
You and I can decide together when I get back. I'll take my
lucky charm." The two smiled and nodded in agreement.

Kim changed the topic. "Did you see the King
County Committee to End Homelessness is holding a
rally on Sunday?" She worked with a group that sought
alternatives for the population who made the streets of
Seattle their home. "They're meeting in Pioneer Square,
and the mayor is supposed to speak. They plan to have a
couple of local bands. Will you go with me?"

It went without saying that Kim would attend, and Ross
agreed to join her. The two were constant companions
since meeting at an insurance industry conference in

1997. A reporter for the old *Seattle Post Intelligencer*, Kim had been researching an article on insurance company executives for her weekly column. They married three months later and would soon celebrate their twenty-first anniversary.

A breeze blew through, dropping the temperature several degrees. Ross picked up their empty wine glasses. "Why don't we walk up to The Rudder, grab a burger, and talk about something else? The kitchen should still be open."

A small commercial area just across the street from the marina served the boaters in Yacht Haven. Along with a small grocery store, a laundromat, a gift shop, and a boating supply store, The Rudder attracted boaters, locals, and the townspeople who wanted to be boaters. The bar featured a limited but excellent food menu.

"Can I go dressed like this?" he asked.

She laughed at his joke. "Do you think Crenshaw's going to complain?"

Ross and Kim reached the top of the marina and walked another hundred yards to the bar. They were regular customers, going when they didn't want to cook dinner on the boat—like tonight. They noticed their favorite bartender Crenshaw and took two seats at the end of the bar near him. He walked over.

"A guy somehow falls out of a sixth-floor window. As he hits the sidewalk below, a woman runs up and says, 'What happened? What happened?' The guy says, 'I don't know. I just got here myself.'"

Groans could be heard throughout the bar area.

"What can I get my favorite customer and her husband tonight?"

They laughed and ordered. Except for when Crenshaw brought them their food and another glass of wine, Ross and Kim spent the remainder of the evening talking about where to go on their next cruise. They never mentioned Great Chicago again, though both knew if Ross were offered the opportunity to work with them, he would accept.

Chapter Five

Wells Fargo Center
Seattle, Washington
Tuesday, July 16, 2019

Sweat poured from Jacques Levesque's body. He leaned against the floor-to-ceiling windows of his office and casually dribbled the basketball. Proud of his reputation as the only executive in America with a basketball court in his office, he just beat one of the talented young players working in his building. And to think, he'd turned forty-seven only two days ago. Jacques reveled in his success in the insurance business and as chief executive officer of LeGrande Benefits, Inc., but being known for the court made him even happier. His one-on-one opponent that afternoon passed by Lucas Sims as he wheeled in.

He never came in unannounced, but today, even though Levesque expected him, Sims knocked on the door repeatedly before being granted entry.

"I'm worried," Sims said as he rolled into the cavernous office.

Jacques Levesque displayed every inch and pound of his large size as he rolled the ball away and stood staring out through the floor-to-ceiling windows of the forty-first floor toward Elliott Bay. On a sunny day, Seattle stood out as one of the most beautiful cities in the world—especially on a day like today. Levesque stared in the direction of the Olympic Mountains, still snowcapped in July, but though an incredible view, he saw none of it. He returned his attention to the room and moved around his desk to tower over Sims in his wheelchair.

"Quit worrying, Lucas; everything's fine." He picked up a half-empty bottle of Gatorade and took a long drink. "The only chance of us having a problem is if you say too much."

Sims hesitated but finally spoke. "I know, but Great Chicago wants to come back and look things over again. I don't think they suspect anything, but I'm worried just the same. What would you like me to do?"

LeGrande placed most of the insurance business it sold with Great Chicago Insurance Company. LeGrande also stole money from them. Now, Great Chicago was asking to perform another audit.

As a rule, Levesque wouldn't let someone with Lucas Sims's worrying personality within two floors of his office, but he learned years ago that Sims possessed the sharpest information technology mind in Seattle, and Levesque fashioned a way to take advantage of that talent in a way to make him rich. Since Levesque saved Sims from dangerous people, the two had fashioned an extremely lucrative, though threatening, enterprise. He found it more than worth his while to put up with Sims's whining and worrying. Over fifty million dollars' worth, to be accurate.

Levesque attempted to be courteous, as much as it strained his nature. "Look, Lucas," he said softly, "let's go through this one more time. No one is going to figure anything out. It's not going to happen. We've put too many controls and sidetracks in place. Operation Perfect Score is foolproof. If they examined us for a year, they'd never find anything. And besides, by this time next year, it will be over, and we can put all of it behind us."

Once a week, Levesque ordered his office swept for transmitting bugs and had secretly installed a voice distortion device as a failsafe. He felt confident nothing they said in his office would be recorded.

"Why don't we just call it off now?" asked Sims. "We've already put aside more than enough, and besides, if we quit now, there's no way anyone is going to figure it out." As he spoke, Sims rolled his wheelchair closer to Levesque's huge desk.

Levesque wanted to run the scam twelve more months to meet his personal goal of eighty million, but Sims didn't need to know that. "I know how you feel, Lucas, and I'm about ready myself," said Jacques. "Let it go a little longer, and we'll unwind it in a couple of months. In the meantime, what do those people from Great Chicago want this time?"

"It's only one guy, Jacques. Hasse Olsson. Christine says he wants to check us out again. Olsson still has an idea that something is going on here that they're not going to like."

Great Chicago Insurance Company specialized in dental insurance and sold more than any other company in the United States. Christine Bell, their chief executive officer, maintained the business relationship with LeGrande Benefits personally. They collected over one billion dollars in premiums annually, and Levesque's company accounted for over three-hundred million of it. This made LeGrande Great Chicago's largest producer, by a wide margin.

"Who's Hasse Olsson?" Levesque asked.

"A Swedish auditor who works for Stockholm Fidelity. They're the bonding company for Great Chicago and are under contract to reimburse Great Chicago if their losses are due to fraud. They have a big interest in this. The last time he examined us, you were away. He spent several days looking into our premium accounting. I know that's not a problem area for us, but he could be getting closer."

Levesque looked at his watch. His schedule included a speaking engagement at a meeting of the Seattle Executive Association in an hour, and he wanted to be finished with Sims for today.

He moved back behind his huge desk and stared at Lucas Sims. "He didn't come close to finding anything when he came last month, did he?" Without waiting for an answer, he said, "Let's face it, he's fishing around and, I suspect, making a nuisance of himself at every one of Great Chicago's big administrators, not just us. Let him come here if he wants. We're not worried."

Sims still looked worried. "I guess you're right." He continued to stare at his boss.

Levesque saw desperation in his eyes.

Chapter Six

Alaska Airlines Flight 22
Seattle to Chicago
Tuesday, July 16, 2019

Ross Taylor didn't always fly first class, but today he had been lucky and given an upgrade. A close call, since only one seat remained as he waited the last fifteen minutes at the gate. But, thanks to a thoughtful no-show, he now sat in seat 3A, enjoying a cold beer. The trip to Chicago took almost four hours, and he planned to relax, read, and maybe write. He'd have time upon arrival to organize his meeting with Christine Bell.

He thought about Kim, whom he adored, and how his legs weakened the first time they met. It had been as though he lived his earlier life in black, white, and gray. When he saw her for the first time, everything turned to color. This morning, as he kissed her goodbye, she considered joining him on the trip. If Ross's meeting with Christine Bell resulted in an engagement, Kim would join him on the next trip.

Taylor anticipated an enjoyable lunch. Alaska Airlines

still provided a delicious meal and friendly attention, even in these days of boxed lunches and no service. Customers always received a satisfying choice of entrée and drinks. As he settled in for the flight, he mused about his career choice for almost thirty years—a business that, until his run-in with Frank Walsh, had treated him well. Since the fallout with Walsh, he had begun to reestablish himself—initially as a consultant and, recently, with increasingly complex fraud investigations.

He accepted all the work offered to him, and as if needing additional activity, interviewed for a position as an adjunct professor in the business department at Seattle Pacific University. They wanted someone who could impart practical knowledge, a behind-the-scenes look at how the insurance business really worked. Taylor thought the appointment would be fun and secretly hoped they engaged him. Always an optimist, he mentally composed a first-session student handout. Then he set his beer to one side, opened his laptop, and began to write.

The insurance business is by no means a new concept. Although commercial insurance developed into the form it takes today during the seventeen-hundreds, its roots go as far back as the eighteenth-century BC. Through the years, various forms of commercial risk-taking followed, which gave rise to the market we now know as Lloyd's of London.

Edward Lloyd ran a coffee house in London in which ship owners gathered and described the voyages their ships were scheduled to make. Risk takers, known as underwriters, offered financial protection against the ships' sinking or other losses such as by piracy—an early form of property insurance.

At the same time, societies formed in which members purchased shares each year in a pool. At the end of the year, the widows and children of those members who did not survive divided the pool according to their shared interest. These benevolent societies represented an early form of life insurance.

Today, the insurance business flourishes in every area of the world, and insurance may be purchased on any imaginable risk. But the insurance companies operate comparably and predictably. They all collect premiums, pay claims, invest their assets, and incur expenses. Regardless of the risks they insure, regardless of size, and regardless of location in the world, the fundamentals remain the same.

First, premium flow. Companies set premiums for their products with the goal of realizing a profit after they account for investment income, claims, and expenses. These premiums are carefully calculated and an error, in either direction, can be disastrous for the company. If the company sets premiums too low, they won't be sufficient to cover claims and expenses and may produce a loss. On the other hand, if they set premiums too high, the company won't be competitive with other insurers, and they will lose market share. The margin between success and failure is quite narrow.

Another key measurement of success is investment income. A sizable portion of the revenue to an insurance company is dividends and interest on the company's portfolio of assets. The company must invest these assets at little or no risk of loss, a very conservative approach. At the same time, sufficient investment income must be earned to assure the profitability of the company. This can lead some investment managers to seek higher yields through riskier investments. The difference between conservatism and excessive risk can be quite small.

Third, the company must pay claims—the greatest source of financial outflow. In a health insurance company, benefit payments made to people with claims, or to their health care providers, account for at least seventy-five percent of the premiums, often more. When an insurance company sets its premiums, it makes a careful estimate of the number and amount of claims it expects to pay. Any error in this estimate will result in premiums too low to produce a profit or too high to be competitive with other insurers.

The fourth and final component of outflow is company operating expenses. The company must carefully manage expenses to assure the assumptions that went into calculating premium are met. Insurance companies often succeed or fail based upon their ability to properly forecast and manage internal expenses.

That's all there is to it. Companies collect premiums, earn investment income, pay claims, and pay their expenses and what's left is profit. Of course, as in most matters, it's not that simple. Hundreds of factors come into play that can alter any of these variables. Any deviation can produce results for the company far different from those predicted. In this class, we will learn how that might happen.

Though it needed more work, Taylor liked his first draft. Students should quickly grasp the simple nature of the insurance business. But their fascination would be in learning the subtle deviations which produced unexpected profits or losses, subtleties that Taylor planned to reveal. He hoped to identify such subtleties at Great Chicago Insurance Company, his prospective client, to explain their unexpected results.

Lunch arrived. He closed his computer. His beer can empty, he ordered another. This might be a good time to contemplate Great Chicago.

Taylor already knew the company, with headquarters located on Michigan Avenue in Chicago, conducted its business all over the United States, and its only business was dental insurance. Dental insurance produced predictable and straightforward results. In exchange for the premiums they received, Great Chicago paid the dental bills of their insured customers. The company collected over three billion dollars in premiums every year, making it one of the largest dental insurers in the country. From that premium, they expected to earn around one-hundred-twenty million dollars in profit for their shareholders, around four percent before taxes. All in all, a rather boring business.

For Christine Bell, the results were anything but boring. Profits fell substantially below expected, and she didn't know why. Ross Taylor had been invited to offer an opinion. He had to prove he was the right person to find the answer.

Chapter Seven

401 N. Michigan Avenue Building
Chicago, Illinois
Wednesday, July 17, 2019

Anticipation filled Ross Taylor as he thought about his meeting with Christine Bell. As chief executive officer for Great Chicago Insurance Company, Christine maintained her office in Chicago with the majority of the administrative staff.

In its eighty-fourth year, Great Chicago benefited from its reputation as one of the oldest insurance companies in the United States. Its home office remained in the 401 N. Michigan Avenue Building in Chicago since the building opened more than fifty years earlier.

Ross had arrived at the Peninsula Hotel around eight o'clock the previous evening, after a thirty-five-minute cab ride from Chicago's O'Hare Field. Check-in took exactly two minutes. Only later did he learn the hotel provided complimentary limousine service for its guests.

Before showering, he called room service and ordered a hamburger and two bottles of Old Style for delivery to his room. Befitting the luxury of the Peninsula, his sandwich arrived on a bone china dinner plate placed in the center of a rolling table covered with a starched white linen tablecloth. The beer chilled in an ice bucket normally reserved for champagne. A red rose in a bud vase, which matched the dinner plate, completed the presentation. Perfect.

He knew from experience that traveling east always disturbed his sleep, even though it was only two time zones, so he went to bed early. A light breakfast in the hotel lobby dining room energized him for the twenty-minute walk to his meeting.

Taylor knew the city—was born on the North Side, only a few miles from the office he would now visit. Though his hometown, he'd been away from Chicago since he left after college. When he and Kim lived in Phoenix, they loved to visit every couple of years and take in the jazz scene—especially the Green Mill. If Christine Bell offered him something of interest, he and Kim could return together.

As he walked, Taylor thought back to his upbringing. His parents, his younger sister, and he had lived in a comfortable house five blocks south of Wrigley Field. He grew up a Cubs fan and went to high school only two miles from home at Lane Tech, where he played basketball and baseball for four years. During his senior year, his father found trouble with the law, forcing his mother and the two children to move to a less desirable neighborhood. It was a terrible time.

Fortunately, the University of Illinois awarded him a basketball scholarship. It started him toward his degree, and though cut from the team, the aid he received during his first year proved to be critical. On his own financially, he worked various on-campus jobs to support himself for the next three years.

Although studies, club basketball, and work kept him occupied, he still found time to develop two activities that were new to him—boxing and magic. Both were a surprise. Boxing never held any interest for him as a boy. But a friend and fellow student in the mathematics department trained as a boxer and introduced Taylor to the sport. Taylor watched him fight on occasion, and before long, the friend invited him to join a local boxing club. In short order, the club became his daily afternoon home. By his junior year, he fought regularly at the 175-pound level, with more wins than losses.

At about the same time, he saw a performance on campus by well-known Canadian magician Tony Eng. Fascinated, he began to fill any spare time with lessons from a local magician. He soaked up as much as he could about stage illusions and close-up magic, but he favored card magic. He learned fast and, as with boxing, soon performed at a high level.

During the summers, he stayed at home in Chicago with his mother and sister. It was then that he first developed his love of boats. He owned a car but rode his bike the few miles east to Montrose Harbor on Lake Michigan to admire the sailboats. Occasionally, a boat owner recognized him and took him out for an afternoon. He always knew that one day, he would have his own sailboat. Now, his sister Rose and her family lived in Buffalo Grove, a suburb northwest of Chicago, his mother, Cathy, lived with them, and he finally owned his boat.

This morning, his route to Christine's office took him south on Michigan Avenue, Chicago's Magnificent Mile—so named because of the upscale hotels and high-end retail shops along its corridor. The rent for office and retail space on these few blocks ranked among the highest in the United States. Taylor worked hard to ignore the glamour this morning; other things filled his mind.

As the elevator in the skyscraper rose toward the thirtieth floor, he glanced at his reflection in the mirrored walls. Taylor had succumbed to a certain degree of middle age, and his face displayed a fullness he didn't remember being there in his youth. He'd also added a few pounds although not enough to be called fat. In fact, at six feet, one inch and 185 pounds, his appearance could still be impressive.

His light brown hair remained thick, and a wave occasionally fell in front of his eyes. Except for that, he kept it cut short and trimmed close across his temples. Little could be done about the nose—a remnant of his basketball history. Kim told him she thought it to be her favorite feature on his face. He thought it should be his blue eyes.

His neatly pressed navy-blue business suit fit him perfectly. Overall, he considered his look to be friendly and professional.

Chapter Eight

401 N. Michigan Avenue Building
Chicago, Illinois
Wednesday, July 17, 2019

The elevator door opened into the lobby of Great Chicago Insurance Company, centrally located within the office suite. There were no windows. Even before seeing it, Taylor knew the environment would brighten when he entered Christine Bell's office. An enormous portrait of an unknown gentleman adorned the wall to his right, the only decoration in the lobby. He asked the receptionist the identity of the man, but she didn't know. She had only been with the company for three months. Amused by the response, he refocused his attention on one of the annual reports from a stack on the lobby coffee table. Just then, Christine arrived to greet him.

"Great to see you, Ross, and thanks for coming." She extended a hand which he shook, then she hugged him. Her warm greeting reflected their many years of friendship. "Did you have a good trip over?"

"Nice to see you too, Chris. Yeah, the usual. Four

hours of boredom, a quick trip downtown, and in bed by nine. I do like the Peninsula, though. Quite elegant. Thanks for the tip."

He always thought Christine bore a remarkable resemblance to Merle Streep as she looked in the late nineties. Flowing, reddish-blonde hair, pronounced cheekbones, and the same large-frame eyeglasses Streep frequently wore. Today she wore a gray, belted shift dress with a high collar and a black three-quarter-sleeve jacket. Even with her high heels, she stood at least seven inches shorter than Taylor.

"Let's go back to my office where we can get caught up."

As they talked, the two walked from the lobby through a long corridor of private offices to the end which opened into a large corner office. Unlike the lobby, this room afforded a beautiful view outside. She asked her assistant to please bring coffee.

The rays from the mid-morning sun warmed the room, and Ross envied Christine's surroundings. Even as a CEO, he never enjoyed an office this luxurious.

"Please sit down." Christine pointed to a long leather couch near the center of the large space. As he did, she seated herself in a matching chair opposite him. An antique oak coffee table separated them. In the large room, the presence of a fine area rug, exactly the size of the conversation area, created an intimate feel, as if they were in a smaller room. Perfect for discussing confidential business. A moment later, the coffee arrived.

"How's Kim? Is she still as beautiful as ever? Still running every day?"

"She's great. One of the magazines just published another article, her book is out and selling well, and she's working as hard as ever for the homeless in Seattle. I wish I had her energy. She thought about coming with me on this trip, but we decided to wait until the next time and do some sightseeing and shopping."

"Maybe you'll come back sooner than you think. At least, I hope you can help us, Ross." Christine Bell always came to the point quickly, one of the reasons for her success. And today offered no exception. "Do you have any objection to signing a confidentiality agreement? What I'm going to tell you is in the strictest confidence."

Ross fully expected a request to sign such an agreement. He quickly but thoroughly scanned the document she supplied and then signed it.

"Thank you. We have a situation here that needs outside eyes, and you may be just the one to supply them. I know all about what happened to you in Phoenix. Not your fault and no CEO could have seen that problem coming. Frank Walsh is well-known as a jerk, and I'm surprised you put up with him as long as you did. But somebody always must pay when a crime occurs inside a company. He stuck it to you. Maybe your experience can help us."

He nodded his understanding.

"In short, our profit isn't what it should be. You know our business. All we write is dental insurance, and we should be able to predict our profits within a small range. But we've been way off this year and can't figure out why. The last few years, the same thing although on a smaller scale." She paused to take a drink of coffee before continuing. "We didn't think much of it at the time it started. For the first couple of years, we considered it a fluke. But it's become worse."

Ross knew the business as well as Christine did, and he knew what he would do if he were in her place. "Give me an idea of the scope of the problem."

She went on. "We're a three-billion-dollar premium company. We expect to earn around four percent before taxes, between a hundred-twelve and a hundred-twenty-eight million on that premium. This year, if things continue in the second half as they did in the first, it looks like we'll earn around ninety million. Not a bad year by most measures but well below expectations for us and our shareholders. This is the fourth year of increasing losses." She stopped again to let the magnitude of her problem sink in for Ross.

Taylor always held Christine Bell in high regard. Extremely competent, she usually anticipated outcomes well ahead of everyone else when analyzing a situation. For her to be this uncertain puzzled him. "So, you're looking to fall short this year by close to twenty-five million, right?" he said. She nodded her agreement. He then asked, "What about the previous years?"

"It looks as if the unexplained losses were about the same last year and half as much for each of the prior two. As I said, at first, we considered it a fluke and didn't give it a great deal of thought. In hindsight, I should have jumped on this sooner, but it simply didn't seem like anything other than chance fluctuation. Now, whatever's causing the problem has cost us close to sixty million. Our board members have been aware of the problem since the beginning and supported my approach. But now they've made it clear they want an explanation and a corrective action plan."

She stopped again to let her words sink in, before going on. "Winston started his team working on this the first of the year, and they still don't have an answer. You know Winston Lester, don't you? He's our chief financial officer. He also oversees regulatory compliance. They've looked at all the usual suspects—pricing errors, claims payment errors, poor risk selection, premium or claim fraud by one of the outside administrators—and none of them shows anything unusual by itself. Of course, we've been checking our own work for so long it's possible there's something right under our nose that we're not seeing. If you take us on as a client, you'll probably want to examine us as well."

He said nothing but nodded again.

"I'm desperate, Ross. I need to figure this out quickly." Over the past twenty minutes, her expression had changed from one of warmth to fright. "The board has started to give hints that they think I'm in over my head, especially because I'm a woman. They won't say that, of course, but I've heard comments. The board is exclusively men, each of them over sixty-five. I can't afford to lose my job at this stage of my career. I'd like your help."

Taylor had a reputation as a dogged pursuer of fraud. He loved nothing more than unmasking someone who cheated an insurance company, causing policyholders to pay more for their insurance because of criminal behavior. He deserved his reputation as the best at figuring out those scams, and the industry considered him an expert. How ironic to be fired from his last job because of a fraud.

"Are you bonded?" he asked.

"We're bonded by Stockholm Fidelity. Hasse Olsson has serviced our account for years," she said. "Unfortunately, as you know, the bond is primarily there to protect us from fraud, not underwriting losses. We could make a claim if it turned out to be fraud but not if we were just having bad luck with premiums or claims. We've alerted Stockholm to the problem, but we've also told them we don't suspect wrongdoing. Olsson has stayed in close touch with us and visited the largest administrators we work with. If you want to talk to him, I'll let him know you might be calling."

Taylor stood to stretch. He looked past Christine, through the window behind her desk, out toward the great Chicago Loop, and thought about what she just told him. Her private office occupied the southwest corner of the thirtieth floor. From it, one could take in a breathtaking view of the city, its skyscraper skyline, and the water—in both directions. The Chicago River ran west along the north and west sides of The Loop and east toward Lake Michigan. A view of Lake Michigan completed the panorama.

"Incredible, isn't it?" Christine smiled, in spite of everything.

Taylor moved closer to the windows. Below were Michigan Avenue, the Magnificent Mile, and the Michigan Avenue Bridge over the river.

"It sure is. Kim and I love playing tourist in Chicago

and we especially enjoy the ride on the Wendella riverboats." The boats boarded passengers beneath the bridge. They cruised along the river and passengers were treated to a spectacular view of the skyline of skyscrapers and a ride through the locks into Lake Michigan.

Christine Bell's office, especially its fantastic location, exuded success, both hers and her company's. A perfect place in which to contemplate a business problem, as Ross Taylor did at that moment. He sat again and returned his focus to Christine.

"It sounds like you're in real trouble here, Chris. I'd need to do a deep analysis of the data to have a chance of finding something—particularly since Winston and his group have already done so much work. Most likely, it's pure bad luck, but we won't know any more until I have a look."

"Ross, I know my job and my career are in peril. In its last meeting, the board of directors made it clear that my future with the company was in jeopardy and that I should view this matter as the most important item on my agenda." She paused as if contemplating how to proceed. "I own stock options in Great Chicago which, when I can exercise them, should provide me with a reasonable net worth and a comfortable standard of living when I do decide to leave. Unfortunately, I can't exercise them yet and if my employment ended, I would have little financial security. So, from my narrow personal perspective, I want to find a solution to the problem. Quickly. I'm counting on you to provide the answer."

"Will I have access to everything I need?" Ross looked closely at her.

"Yes, you'd have carte blanche, Ross. Everything. I've already discussed this with the board, and they approve. I plan to alert everyone on my team that you're working directly for me and you should be given access to anything and everything. Finally, I'll make clear that whatever you asked for should be supplied as quickly as if I asked. Your work will be our top priority."

Taylor nodded but said nothing.

"I expect you'll want to examine some of our producers. We get business from brokers all over the country but the largest three also provide administrative services. I'll get you their names and alert their executives that you might be calling to arrange visits."

She paused again and scribbled half a page of notes before continuing. "We'll pay you twice your normal daily rate while you're on this assignment. If you find the answer, there will be a two-hundred-fifty-thousand-dollar bonus for you. We've tried without success to do it ourselves."

She paused once more, this time for effect. "And, if you find that the problem is one of fraud, we'll pay you two percent of everything you recover as a success fee. We have no reason to believe that it is fraud, but we don't rule it out either. We'll also cover any expenses you incur for yourself and for anyone else you feel you need to help you. Are you in?"

Ross Taylor did a rough calculation in his head. He normally billed two thousand dollars a day plus expenses. He thought he could make a preliminary evaluation in about three to four weeks. By then, he would know the potential for a solution. Fifteen to twenty days at two thousand dollars a day times two meant he could earn between sixty and eighty thousand dollars. For Taylor, this represented a particularly good payday. His engagements normally produced less, and the potential of a quarter-million-dollar bonus for success excited him.

"Your proposal is very generous. I'm in." He tried not to display the delight that raced through him. "Let's work out the details and get moving. I don't have anything that I can't set aside to help you."

She nodded to him. "This won't be easy. I need an answer. Fast. I can only give you a few weeks. If you don't have something by then, I'll have to look somewhere else."

Taylor nodded in understanding.

"With an assignment like this, where would you start?" Christine asked.

He pondered the question for a moment. "We'd start by confirming the problem isn't simply a matter of the premiums being inadequate. Or that your risk selection criteria are flawed. You've probably already done that, but I'll want to examine that possibility anyway. If that doesn't yield an answer, we'd begin to suspect criminal activity.

"If we conclude that we're dealing with potential fraud, we'll start with predictive modeling—examine your historical data over at least five years and compare it with our database. My experience is that customer tendencies and behaviors are especially predictable for dental insurance. Complete and reliable data from you will be critical."

Taylor took comfort in describing this approach to

solving the problem—an approach that proved valuable on many occasions in his past.

"Of course, the effectiveness of our predictions will depend on both the quality of your data and the validity of ours. To ease your mind, the database we'll use for comparison includes claims information for more than five million insured people for more than fifteen years. It's essential that your historical data is equally reliable and includes our required predictive information." Taylor warmed up and was in his confidence zone now.

"Sooner or later, we'll uncover variances between your data and ours. Those variances will reveal how the fraud is being committed. That will lead us to the source of the problem. And that, will lead us to who's behind it."

Satisfied with the answer, Christine said, "Okay, then. I'll get you a forty-thousand-dollar advance and round up as many of my team as are in today to join us to meet you. Winston can help you get set up with the encryption service we use. It'll be easier as well as safe."

She looked at her watch. "I'll make clear to them that you're critical to our success and they should give you their full cooperation. While that's going on, one of our staff attorneys can draft an agreement covering your engagement. Does that sound all right to you?"

It did. Now, could he meet the challenge?

Chapter Nine

Yacht Haven Marina
Lake Union
Seattle, Washington
Thursday, July 18, 2019

Ross Taylor started before daylight, leaving Kim in bed to sleep a little longer. After dressing, he went onto the foredeck to service the anchor winch. He loved this sort of work—at his own pace. He knew for months the winch needed work, yet he kept putting it off. Today, he decided, was the day. He scheduled all boat work in this manner. Besides, he knew from experience that it cleared his mind for business ahead.

Kim emerged from below with steaming mugs, and he sat next to her in the cockpit. They loved their morning coffee together on the deck. Days like this, with the sun already warming the air and no wind, were perfect. In another hour, activity in the marina and the noise it brought would be in full force. But not yet. So, they enjoyed the peaceful quiet, the fresh sea air, and their usual view of the beautiful skyline framing the south end of the lake. Only an occasional car sound from the Aurora Bridge above them interrupted the quiet. Life couldn't get much better

"How did Chris look?" Kim asked her husband.

"She looked tired, more lines on her face than I remember. But other than that, she didn't look any different from the last time we saw her."

"Is she holding up all right under this cloud?"

Ross shook his head. "I don't know. But it's a big problem and the stakes for her are high. I'm going to guess her unvested stock options are worth about six million dollars. She hasn't been in the position long enough to have full vesting, so if she were to lose her job over this, she'd probably lose out on most of the six million. That's enough to keep anyone awake at night. Me included."

"Do you have any ideas yet? Do you think you can help them? It's a great assignment for you, and you have an opportunity to make an enormous impact on her life."

He thought again about everything that took place with Christine Bell and the others at Great Chicago. After their meeting, she introduced him to three executive members of her team, including Winston Lester the CFO. All promised full cooperation. He asked for several sets of data that he needed. The encrypted files were already on his phone when he landed, allowing him to begin his analysis. They also worked out the terms of his engagement, and Christine gave him a check for forty thousand dollars. Overall, a good trip. Now, he needed to perform.

He thought aloud. "The first and most probable cause is bad luck. Bad years happen, and Great Chicago may have suffered from a string of them. But she said this has been going on for almost five years, so I doubt it's bad luck. I'll get Schlump to check that part out. If it's not bad luck, the most likely cause is they didn't set their rates high enough to cover the risk. Schlump can help there too." Schlump was a long-time friend and actuary who frequently collaborated with Ross on data analysis.

Kim nodded her agreement.

"They could also have a problem with their claims system programming and are routinely overpaying. The CFO and his team have been studying this problem and claims would be the first area they examined. They haven't found anything, but I might. That's where I plan to start."

Ross took another sip of coffee and continued. "She also told me they didn't consider a scam likely, but you never know. Someone may have altered programs internally and have been siphoning off funds. They've outsourced almost ninety percent of the back-office work to outside administrators. It's possible one of them is at the root of this. The usual way they do it is by diverting premium. Instead of sending the insurance company the entire premium they collect, they help themselves to a part of it. That's another place I'll be looking."

"Why don't they suspect fraud?" Kim asked. "Couldn't someone inside their company have a scam going?"

"I guess they don't see any of the obvious clues. Their premiums are at about the right level. None of their big producers has experienced a downturn in premium. Claims are higher but that doesn't always point to deception. You see, premiums are easy for Great Chicago to audit, so premium fraud is easy to detect. Claims are almost as easy to audit. Anyone running off with sixty million dollars through claims fraud would have to be a genius. I agree with you though. I'm inclined to think if it is fraud, it's coming from the inside."

Kim got up to refill their mugs. He watched her every move in silence. When she returned, he asked, "Have I told you how awesome you look this morning?"

"No. You've been too busy."

"Well, you're breathtaking."

"You say that to all the girls."

"No way. Why don't we take the morning off?"

"Get back to work, Buster. You've got a problem to solve." She kissed him. "What are you going to do first?"

"Well, if you insist, I'm going to take a macro look at the data I have. I don't expect to find anything right away, but I'll get an idea what more I need from Great Chicago to dig deeper.

He thought for a moment then added, "You know, I appreciate her calling on me. Frank Walsh fired me because of an internal con, and she knows it. She's in the same place. If someone is stealing from her and she doesn't find the source and recover the money, she'll lose her job, her reputation, and her retirement security. She's trusting me to see that doesn't happen."

Christine Bell faced serious consequences.

"Every time potential insurance fraud comes up, I think of my dad," Ross said. "None of us could ever conceive of the idea of his deceit. He gave us no clue. He lived the life of a working guy, like everyone else in the neighborhood, although a little more successful. Kind, gentle, loved his family, worked hard, kept the bills up to date, looked forward to the weekends. We seemed to have a good life. I wanted to be just like him. Then, one day, he didn't come home, was sent to prison, and we were forced to move. We didn't know what would happen next. I'm still not over it."

Neither of them said anything. The topic always brought sadness to Ross.

Changing the subject, Kim asked, "Do you ever regret we didn't sue Arizona Life? You would have presented a convincing case."

"I agree. I thought about it again on the flight to Chicago. But, no, I don't regret it. A lawsuit could have tied us up with them for years and who knows how it might turn out. It could have cost us a ton of money to bring the suit. Besides, I like our life now and don't want to waste time in depositions and filings, or worse, sitting across from Frank Walsh. Good riddance."

After a while, they took their empty coffee cups and went below deck to enjoy breakfast together. Sunlight poured in through the windows surrounding the main salon, and the boat gave off a light and airy feel. As usual, jazz played softly in the background. Oscar Peterson. A beautiful boat on a beautiful lake—a wonderful place to live, and Kim and Ross made the most of it. They enjoyed vegetable omelets with fried potatoes, and Kim volunteered to clean up.

Ross set aside his earlier memories of his father and Frank Walsh as he ducked into the office.

Taylor couldn't bring himself to think of the rooms on their boat as staterooms; that sounded too haughty for him. He preferred to think of them as cabins. This office was his pride and joy. Originally a V-berth, craftsmen spent almost three weeks turning the larger of the two cabins into a modern, floating office. A wrap-around desk, which he shared with Kim, replaced what originally was a bed. The comfortable upholstered swivel chair, mounted to the opposite wall on movable brackets, could be pushed aside when not in use.

From this office, they could concentrate on their respective projects. The sharing part worked quite well despite earlier concerns their work schedules might conflict. Although both were usually busy on some work project, Ross occupied the office more often. Today and for the near future, he had first claim on the work area.

The office included a compact combination wireless copier-scanner-fax machine, two laptop computers connected to secure wireless internet through the marina, and two business-only cell phones. On one side, two thirty-inch, wall-mounted, smart flat-screen televisions were in continuous use. One displayed CNBC for the financial news, the other general news. Each could be used for data projection from the laptops when a project required enlarged viewing. Both TVs remained on mute.

On the opposite wall, shelves formed a library for work papers, thumb drives, and a limited number of books, while two eight-inch analog clocks—one set to Seattle time and the other set to the time of whichever client either of them worked for now—occupied the remaining space.

Ross Taylor considered this an office equipped every bit as well as any executive office. He noted two differences, however. First, he sat in a desk chair on a boat rather than in an office building. Second, he wore shorts and a t-shirt instead of a suit. *Major differences,* he thought.

"Ross," Kim interrupted handing him another cup of coffee, "I didn't want to bother you with something now that you're working on a big assignment. It's probably nothing, but another email came from that guy, the one who saw me running a couple of weeks ago." Three weeks ago, an email arrived with embarrassingly lewd suggestions. At the time, they shrugged it off as a prank.

"What did he say this time?"

"Same stuff but more explicit. He said I looked more beautiful than ever. Especially loved how I fit in my pants. Has great pictures. Couldn't wait to rub me with his hands."

Taylor was fuming.

"It's creepy, Ross. I'm not afraid, but at the same time, it's unnerving to know this guy is watching me—violating me with his eyes. It's weird. It makes my skin crawl thinking about it, and I want it to stop. This time he said he watched me on the Burke-Gilman Trail just north of here. The other time, Green Lake."

"I'm going to put a stop to it. Don't worry. Send me a copy of the email and let me know if you hear from him again." Taylor no longer wanted the coffee, furious at the story Kim told.

"Ross, just one more thing before you get started. You know the homeless rally I mentioned? Don't forget to put it on your calendar. They've changed it to two weeks from Sunday."

"Got it," he said. In truth, the event wasn't even in his calendar, but he didn't mind going. Though he didn't have the same passion for the homeless Kim did, he knew the importance of the rally to her. With that, he settled in with his coffee, the reports, and the data drive he received at Great Chicago. He planned to work long hours during the next few days.

As would Jacques Levesque.

Chapter Ten

Wells Fargo Center
Seattle Washington
Friday, July 19, 2019

Jacques Levesque did everything with confidence. But despite this, he did so in an understated manner.

He wore fashionable clothing, but not top-of-the-line designer brands. He entertained in an elegant fashion, but not overly elaborate. He drove a year-old Lexus SUV. When traveling, he alternated between first class and coach, not wishing to draw attention to himself through an extravagant lifestyle. With one exception: his unusually large office with a unique feature.

His company, LeGrande Benefits, leased the forty-first and forty-second floors in the Wells Fargo Center on Third Avenue and Marion Street in Seattle for the company offices. Unlike many other such companies, LeGrande conducted its routine business operations in only one-half of the leased space. Levesque's personal domain occupied the other half.

His private office dominated the northwest corner and enjoyed an expansive view of Elliot Bay, the harbor, the shipping terminals, and the spectacular Olympic Mountains. The office's configuration set it apart from other large executive offices. In place of offices and cubicles, half the space was a basketball court.

The office measured sixty feet along the west side and forty feet along the north side, an enormous space. The basketball court extended two stories high and forty feet by forty feet on the floor. It allowed for half-court play, free throws, and up to three-on-three games. Unbreakable floor-to-ceiling polycarbonate windows kept the ball and bodies in play. Players new to the baseline of Levesque's court, seeing the ground from forty-one stories up, often confined their play to the perimeter.

Jacques played basketball in high school and made the team as a first-year student in college. Though he rode the bench in college before quitting, he still could play and always accepted if someone offered a one-on-one challenge. He made sure anyone he met heard about the court in his office and how he could still dunk the ball at age forty-nine.

The other half of his space contained his office and meeting area. His huge desk immediately drew attention. Set in the corner of the room offering the best view, it measured in feet, not inches: twelve feet wide by nine feet deep with a semi-circular opening cut into one of the lengths. Here sat his oversized, stuffed, leather swivel chair. This configuration put him in the center of his work area, and seven people could be seated at the desk. To further emphasize his prominence, Levesque ordered the desk raised six inches and located his chair on a six-inch elevated platform.

When a group gathered, he didn't conduct a meeting so much as hold court. Sitting there now, looking past Lucas Sims, he wondered how long they would continue the scam before shutting things down.

Lucas Sims said, "Chris Bell called me this morning. Hasse Olsson, the bond guy, won't be coming to audit us. She's hired someone else. His name is Ross Taylor. I'm to expect his call and give him whatever he needs."

"What do you know about Ross Taylor?" Levesque asked. He knew of Taylor and some of his background but preferred to hear a complete report from Lucas.

"He's a management consultant who specializes in insurance fraud," Sims began. "He works only for insurance companies. Before going into consulting, he held executive positions, including as chief executive officer of Arizona Life. His companies were always successful, and until being fired from Arizona Life, everyone who knew him held him in high regard. In fact, they still do."

"Why did they fire him?"

"It probably shouldn't have happened. During his career, he developed a keen awareness for fraud, almost like a sixth sense. He could often sense a problem or something going wrong well in advance of the financial control people, and he knew how to get to the root of a deception quickly. At least he did until someone beat Arizona Life out of almost ten million dollars. An insider, but Taylor figured it out. The guy went to jail, and the company recovered all its money, but Taylor lost his job because of it.

"That happened a little over two years ago. He decided

to drop out of corporate life and spend more time with his family. In his case, he meant it. From what I heard, he and his wife live around here, and he spends his time enjoying life and looking into problems inside insurance companies. She's a freelance writer."

Sims paused to consider his next words. "My sources tell me this guy is as shrewd as they come. Ross Taylor can discover the cause of a problem quicker than it takes someone to create the problem. I would be ecstatic if he never came around here. But it's going to be hard to keep him away. We've got to be careful about what we say and do. He could cause us real trouble."

It took very little to put Levesque in a foul mood. Today, it started early. The rain and cold, which began last night, became worse. Then, someone parked their car in his private parking place. To top it off, the homeless advocates were demonstrating again outside the building, blocking his path into the coffee shop, and the rain soaked him.

His phone rang. One of his three phones: black, white, and red. Black and white on his desk. Red in his desk drawer. All were small cellular phones with the latest features and applications. The black phone, his office number, rang most frequently. On it, he conducted company business, spoke with his executive assistant, and occasionally suffered through a conversation with an employee other than Lucas. He used the white phone for personal calls from friends, Aubrey, and close business associates. A limited number of people knew that number. The only people who even knew of the existence of the red phone were Lucas Sims, Christine Bell, Felix, and the jeweler. No one else. No exceptions. The red phone rang.

"Yes," he said as he picked it up. His mood brightened. The jeweler.

"Mr. Levesque, this is Ira Stone. I have your diamond. A beautiful five-point-three carat, round, ideal cut, D color, flawless as you requested. Just under four-fifty." By four-fifty, Stone meant four-hundred-fifty thousand dollars. "I'll have it ready for you on Tuesday afternoon. I'll bring it over."

"Perfect." Levesque thumbed the phone off. The call took nineteen seconds.

Jacques always experienced a thrill when Stone called, almost as big a thrill as when he first let his fingers caress gems. Now, though, he returned his attention to Sims. "Lucas, why don't you go ahead and schedule a meeting with Taylor? He'll be starting from scratch. Maybe we can find a way to lead him in the wrong direction for the time being. We should be able to push it out far enough to be close to finished with our little business. Agree?"

Whether Lucas agreed or not made little difference to Levesque, and Sims knew it. "Of course. I'll set it up and let you know when."

The meeting over, Sims turned the chair around and wheeled himself out of the office.

Ross Taylor was a serious threat.

Chapter Eleven

Wells Fargo Center
Seattle, Washington
Friday, July 19, 2019

Felix Contador wasn't an ordinary office building receptionist. Not a security officer with a badge and a handheld radio clipped to his belt. Not a retiree looking to supplement a pension. Rather, the public saw him as one of the best-dressed and happiest thirty-year-old men they ever met. Everyone in the building knew him by name, and he knew them.

Every weekday morning, he provided information and directions as the lobby receptionist in the Wells Fargo Center, the building that housed the offices of LeGrande Benefits. His wardrobe stood out as varied and as fancy as that of any executive in the building. Often, he appeared to have just stepped away from a *GQ* photo shoot, and on other days, he looked like a rock star. Today, he wore a three-piece, light gray, pinstripe suit with a pale blue shirt and an off-white tie which perfectly complemented the suit. Though they were hidden from view beneath his desk, Felix also wore black Ferragamo shoes.

Not a tall man, he possessed the well-muscled look of someone who spent a great deal of time in the weight room. His tailored clothes fit him perfectly and the men who worked in the building looked at him with envy. The women looked at him with a different emotion. A close look revealed almost coal black hair, eyes nearly the same color, and a youthful face. And he always smiled.

But his real trademark: sunglasses. No one could remember seeing the same pair twice. He claimed to own over two hundred pairs and could almost make it through a year without repeating. He always wore them when he arrived and when he left. He often wore them at his desk, as he did today. He owned every imaginable style, frame color, and lens color. Today, they were a semi-traditional design by Gold & Wood with gray oak frames and gray lenses and were among his favorites.

People wondered how he could afford to dress the way he did. Because he only worked mornings, the building occupants thought he must have a separate high-paying job in the afternoon. And they would be correct, in a way.

Felix enjoyed the reputation as a highly skilled individual, an independent contractor. A fixer. Not leaking faucets or squeaky door hinges. He fixed personal problems, and he did so in the afternoons and evenings. If a person experienced difficulty, say, collecting a debt, Felix might be just the man to consult. If someone couldn't locate cocaine, Felix might be able to find a source. Or, if one needed an errand run that required more physical strength than most men have, Felix was at their service. And he was paid well for these services. So much so that he probably earned more money than many of the higher-paid executives in the Wells Fargo Center.

Jacques Levesque employed Felix often and for varied purposes when circumstances called for someone with his talents. Felix could always be counted on as dependable and effective. And, despite his well-mannered and refined appearance, Felix Contador could be a dangerous man. Levesque knew something else about Felix which he kept to himself.

Chapter Twelve

Wells Fargo Center
Seattle, Washington
Friday, July 19, 2019

Jacques Levesque strode across the street. His lunch, taken alone in a quiet booth at the Metropolitan Grill, his favorite place to think, was already a memory as he contemplated Ross Taylor and what he might be looking for. The Met occupied the southeast corner of Second Avenue and Marion Street, directly across the street from his office. He rode the covered escalator from the street up two stories to the building lobby. While there, he decided to stop and visit his safe deposit box. His second time this week.

"Hello, Violet," Jacques said to the teller assigned to the safe deposit vault. Anyone not close to him or who didn't do business with him thought him a charming and caring man. They would be mistaken.

But Violet didn't know that and cheerfully returned his greeting.

"How are the studies coming?" he asked, pretending to be interested.

Violet Baxter-Granville came to the United States from England as a teenager and now studied to become a US citizen. She told Levesque how thrilled she was when the bank told her she could work as a teller with her Green Card.

"I'm doing pretty well, and I feel I understand the information. I'm scheduled to take the civics test next month and have it over with." As if her accent were not enough, her pronunciation of "scheduled" immediately betrayed her English heritage.

Levesque wished her well.

"I can tell you the names of all the presidents," she offered.

"Not right now, Violet. I'm in a bit of a hurry."

Violet stood out among the other young women, impossible to overlook. She stood six feet three inches tall and weighed roughly 150 pounds—unusually tall and unusually thin. She kept her long hair styled in a mix of tight curls and tendrils. As if not already sufficient to set her apart from everyone else, her hair featured two colors—purple on the right, orange on the left. Her favorite colors, she said. Today, she wore a long-sleeved, floor-length peasant dress that matched her purple hair.

Levesque could only shake his head.

"Will you want to use your box today, Mr. Levesque?" Violet recorded the names of customers wishing to gain access to the vault and their safe deposit boxes.

"Yes, thank you." He signed the form she slid across her desk. Jacques maintained his business banking relationship with a branch of Wells Fargo Bank, located in his building, and retained a personal safe deposit box with them as well. Ira Stone's call this morning filled him with excitement and motivated him to visit his box.

The relationship with Stone began as an experiment. Levesque had located him through the internet. But, after a short time, Levesque realized he needed Stone. The third generation of a family of diamond dealers, Stone knew all aspects of the business, especially the sources of the high-quality diamonds which Levesque sought.

Violet escorted him into the vault. "Will you require a private room today, Mr. Levesque?"

He said he would, and the two of them moved toward the section which included his box. He gave her his key, she added hers, and opened the door to the box.

"You can use any of the rooms on the left, Mr. Levesque." She handed him the box. "I'll be right outside if you need me."

He didn't even hear her as he moved toward the small room—barely five feet wide and only deep enough to accommodate a two-foot countertop and a chair. But, all in all, the room met Levesque's needs. He locked himself in.

The box was a typical metal safe deposit drawer. Dark green in color, about four inches high, twelve inches wide and almost two feet deep with a hinged lid. Not unusual for a safe deposit box. Unusual for its contents.

Levesque lifted the hinged top to reveal a smaller box, made of fine, highly polished mahogany. Nervous, fingers quivering, he removed it and placed it on the counter alongside the safe deposit box. The smaller box, about the size of a financial calculator, could fit in a standard suit coat pocket. It featured a pearl inlay in the shape of a round cut diamond embedded into the fitted lid. Levesque ran his hands over the wood, feeling its coolness and smooth surface. Beautiful by anyone's standards, like a priceless painting. His breath caught as he stared at the box, anticipating its contents. He brushed off a piece of dust.

Slowly, almost reverently, he removed the lid. The lid and box were lined with black felt. Inside the box lay the objects of Jacques Levesque's lust—diamonds. Large diamonds. And a considerable number. Levesque set the box on the counter. A black jeweler's felt along with a ten-power loupe and a pair of tweezers were in the back of the safe deposit box. Jacques placed them on the counter. He unfolded the felt and spread it out. Only then did he allow the contents of the wood box to trickle onto the felt.

Levesque experienced a physical rush as the diamonds slowly poured out. He became light-headed. His breathing rapidly increased. He couldn't explain his enthusiasm to feel the diamonds and found himself oblivious to any other thought or outside stimulus.

He saw more than three hundred, each at least three carats, many over six. They almost filled the box. He fingered them, picking up his favorites. He immediately recognized the first diamond he purchased in 2016. Even after accumulating these stones for over three years, every time he opened the box, he became almost giddy, more excited than the first time. They were like close friends.

But the diamonds themselves were not the source of his excitement. Rather, their value in dollars literally made him weak. Directly in front of him were diamonds he could sell for between forty and sixty million, and there were no bank accounts, no brokerage accounts, and no records of this accumulation. Just this small box of which only he and Aubrey were aware.

Murmuring quietly, Jacques continued to stare at the collection, mesmerized by what he saw. The thought of adding another large stone next week began his shaking again. After calming himself, he replaced the diamonds in the wooden box and returned it, along with the jewelers felt, loupe, and tweezers, to the safe deposit box. Enough for one day. He regained his composure, called Violet, and they replaced the metal box.

Levesque walked from the safe deposit box room into the lobby. His body still tingled from the experience in the vault. As he walked toward the west side of the lobby, he noticed Felix and waved to him. Felix smiled and waved back, although neither said a word. Just then, a visitor to the building distracted Felix, and Levesque continued walking toward the elevator that took him to his office.

He needed to see Felix soon.

Chapter Thirteen

Elliott Bay
Seattle Washington
Sunday, July 21, 2019

"I'm on a diet, Ross. Gotta lose ten pounds this month. Only fourteen to go."

Ross Taylor first met Schlump, a credentialed actuary, years ago. Schlump worked on assignments with Taylor's companies—always as an independent consultant and never employed full-time. On their first job together, Schlump developed the pricing manual for a new health insurance product Taylor was rolling out at Arizona Life. It was perfect, and the two had been pals ever since.

A first-rate analyst, Schlump could spot number patterns in reports and charts long before anyone else noticed them. If the data was accurate, he'd know more about a company in a day than the company knew about themself. Of course, if the data was inaccurate, he would see through that quickly and know there was a problem.

Taylor had called Schlump—no one used his first name, probably because few people even knew it—and told him about his meeting with Christine Bell in Chicago.

They agreed to meet to determine Schlump's interest and availability to help with the investigation. Ivar's Acres of Clams, one of Seattle's oldest waterfront restaurants, served as their rendezvous.

Already waiting when Taylor arrived for their two o'clock meeting, Schlump sat at one of the wooden bench tables that afforded a splendid view of Elliott Bay, including the Seattle waterfront.

He didn't dress for success. He wore a baggy, black windbreaker and baggy, black pants. It was difficult for Schlump to find baggy clothes, yet somehow, he managed to do so. He weighed four hundred pounds. His hair was long and unkempt, as one might expect from someone who visited a barber shop every January whether he needed to or not.

What looked like an Ivar's Full Boat—a ten-piece fish and chips platter—lay in front of him. Not much remained. Families of four often ordered this menu item, but Schlump could easily handle it alone. Taylor wondered if it was even Schlump's first platter. He might have been there for a while.

Taylor picked up a Diet Coke and joined Schlump at the bench table. He glanced at his watch. Exactly two o'clock. "Thanks for meeting me on a Sunday, Schlump. Looks like I haven't kept you waiting."

"No." Nothing could be accomplished by trying to make small talk with Schlump until he was ready. As long as he ate, food took precedence over anything else.

Taylor slid an envelope of papers over to Schlump who didn't seem to notice. Taylor just waded in. "How well do you know Great Chicago?"

Schlump finished chewing and laid down his fork. "A little. Chris Bell. She's strong. The company makes a lot of money."

A loud horn blew from one of the ferries approaching the Colman Dock a block south of Ivar's. Probably the boat from Bremerton scheduled to arrive at quarter to three.

"Right. Except, she tells me they've fallen short by around ten to fifteen million a year for the last several years. They've looked at everything and nothing pops out. They can't explain it." Taylor filled Schlump in on what Christine Bell told him about the losses and how her board warned her to get a handle on the problem and do something fast.

Though Schlump didn't say anything, Taylor could sense his interest. These were big numbers, and they often foretold big problems.

"I asked her about fraud, but she doesn't think so. They've done audits both inside and outside. I'd like you to look at the data. See if it could just be bad luck. Or maybe their rates aren't high enough. I'd also like you to contemplate how someone inadvertently, or deliberately, could implement systems to bring about these kinds of results."

Schlump never looked up from the remainder of his fried food, but he did nod. "I'll need a list of key people."

"Why do you need the list?"

"Background checks. You can learn a great deal through background checks. I know a guy who can find out anything about anyone."

Seagulls flew into the dining area and walked around

the floor at the men's feet. Tourists loved to throw french fries at them. Not Schlump. "Who do they get their business from?" he asked.

"From brokers around the country, but ninety percent of it comes from Consolidated Group Benefits, Argus Benefits, and LeGrande Benefits. By far, the biggest producer is LeGrande right here in Seattle. Production data is in the envelope."

Schlump nodded his understanding.

"It shouldn't take us too long if we split up the work. Are you in?"

Schlump nodded again.

"Anything else you want?"

"No." He folded the envelope and shoved it in his pants pocket.

Taylor had been at Ivar's for no more than twenty minutes. Knowing Schlump, and the absence of food in front of him, Taylor considered the business part of the meeting ended. He shifted topics.

"How's Trudy?"

"She's good. Still looks the same as the day we were married, unlike me. She always looks forward to these times when I'm out of the house. It's her chance to get in my office and straighten it out. She hates my office—says it's too messy. But it's not going to work today. I changed the lock last week." He chuckled softly.

"By the way, I hired a new assistant. Her name is Michelle McKenzie. She's an actuarial student at Seattle University, but she's already passed four exams toward her Associate. She comes in for a few hours on Tuesdays and Thursdays. She's great. Best of all, she's just as messy as I am, but after a couple of weeks, she knows where everything is. Now if I can just keep Trudy out of there, we'll be fine. Michelle can help me with this project."

They got up together. Schlump walked toward his car on the other side of Alaskan Way, oblivious to the traffic.

A guy in a convertible with the top down slammed on the brakes. "Hey, Tiny, get your head out!"

"Why didn't you go around me, jerk?"

"I would have, but I didn't think I had enough gas."

Schlump gave him the finger and continued across the street.

Chapter Fourteen

Yacht Haven Marina
Lake Union
Seattle, Washington
Tuesday, July 23, 2019

Ross and Kim Taylor tried, mostly without success, to have breakfast together every morning. At least, that's what they planned. It seemed a reasonable goal, given they lived on a boat in confined quarters, and both were entrepreneurs unencumbered by nine-to-five jobs. Still, their work pulled them in different directions and at different hours, so this morning differed from most. They enjoyed omelets and bacon together, discussed the news, and were now working on their third cup of coffee while the dishes soaked. They sat next to each other on the settee.

"It's time to get away," Kim said. "It's almost August, and we haven't so much as moved the boat out of the slip this year. Now we're taking on more projects. We have to be careful we don't fall into the trap we left Phoenix to escape."

Taylor agreed and said so.

The rain fell outside, but the cabin heating system in the *Pura Vida* kept things warm and dry below decks. The water pump he had fixed worked fine, but when he woke up, he stepped in a pool of water on the floor of the main cabin. The problem had required immediate attention, so Taylor invested a couple of hours in boat work before getting back to the Great Chicago project. Always something.

The Great Chicago assignment had been occupying almost all his waking hours, and for several days, he and Kim barely spoke of anything else. An annoying consequence of his choice of work, he usually took on only one project at a time, but those projects tended to require immediate and full-time attention. Great Chicago represented a perfect example.

Trying to get off the subject for once, he asked Kim, "Any good bites yet on your proposal?"

"A couple of magazines have responded," she said. "No commitments but at least a little interest. *Seattle Magazine*'s response seemed to be the most positive, although that may be because the editor and I used to work together at the *P.I.* He always liked my work. I also heard back from *Alaska Airlines Magazine* and *Newsweek*. *Newsweek*'s looked more like a form response than personal. We'll see."

Kim Taylor, a freelance writer, sought a commission from a major publication to interview and write about a high-profile celebrity. Enough of her articles were in print that her name enjoyed a well-deserved reputation among the magazines. She was also known by her interviewees to be very understanding and fair.

"I don't know if they trust me to arrange the interviews I proposed. I told them I could probably set something up with Tiger Woods, Senator Warren, or Richard Branson. I've corresponded with each of them in the past. Even Bill Gates. I held a brief meeting with him once in my P.I. days, but I doubt he'd remember me. I could always interview the governor. He'll talk to anyone who gets his name in print. But none of the magazines are interested in him, unless, I suppose, there's a wild angle no one has covered before. Anyway, I'm sending out more inquiries today."

Kim dressed in all black this morning—a long-sleeved, high-collared thermal shirt and black leggings. At a slender five-feet nine-inches, she looked like someone twenty years younger than her forty-seven years. Taylor never tired of looking at her. Her naturally straight, light brown hair hung loosely around her face and down her back as she concentrated on how to convince a publisher. When she tucked herself into the corner of the settee where they ate, Taylor felt more in love with her than ever. A beautiful woman and the nicest person he ever knew. And not just him. Everyone liked her.

It had always been that way. She grew up as Kim Summers in Friday Harbor on San Juan Island a couple of hours north of Seattle. As a young girl, she didn't have time for writing. Only sports for her. She starred in volleyball, basketball, and distance running, and her teammates voted her captain of their teams. Her classmates elected her president. The writing came later.

"Did you ever want to do anything else besides write?" Taylor asked.

"I'd always planned to go to college, and I really wanted to go to the University of Washington. In addition to the quality of the school, because of its proximity to Friday Harbor, I could come home if needed but still be away on an adventure.

"In college, I first discovered my writing skill when I started receiving top grades for classroom writing assignments. I switched my major to journalism and joined the student newspaper. After about a year, they gave me a column and assigned me to write about interesting students and faculty. I found ways to get my interviewees to open up about themselves, often revealing things no one knew about them. After a while, my column became the first thing most students read when they picked up *The Daily*—the newspaper of the University of Washington. During that period, I made up my mind about a career. And here I am, looking for someone to write about."

"You should write your own story."

"Not interesting enough."

"I don't know. If some publication likes your proposal, it might not be long before you became syndicated."

"That's a long way in the future."

"Yeah. But eventually, you'll be asked to author a story about yourself. Why not start now, while you're waiting to land your next gig?"

"I'll think about it."

An idea came to Taylor. "What about the guy I'll be meeting with at LeGrande Benefits—Jacques Levesque? He's the one with the basketball court in his office. I'm scheduled to see him in a couple of days. I could size him up as to whether he seems interesting enough for you."

"That's a possibility," she said. "You're right. He's not well known. I'd never heard of him by name until you told me you were going to see him. But the basketball court, I knew about. We'll talk about it after you meet him. How's the project moving along?"

"We have all the data now and are in the preliminary analysis phase. Premium adequacy, unusual claims, pricing errors, that sort of thing," Taylor answered. He'd also been outlining his approach to the next level of the problem if the preliminary analysis didn't yield results. "So far, every possibility is open. We're still trying to rule out bad luck. That's what Schlump is working on right now. Actuaries can see patterns quickly. Then again, it might be something more. There could be fraud going on. That elevates the problem from unforeseen business losses to criminal activity. A big jump.

"Either way, there'll be travel involved, and Christine is in a hurry to get resolution. I only have a brief period of time. Schlump and I are going to be busy."

Kim listened intently.

"I've discussed my preliminary plan with Christine. She wants us to start with the external parties. She's satisfied her CFO Winston Lester and his team have examined internal operations sufficiently to rule out internal fraud. As soon as Schlump is convinced this is something more than just bad luck, he and I plan to audit the three agencies. He'll go to Kansas City and Atlanta. I'll manage LeGrande here in Seattle and, if necessary, Great Chicago. She's set up a meeting for me with the people at LeGrande for next Monday."

They were silent for a few moments.

"Ross, sorry to change the subject, but I heard from the stalker again. Same message. This time, he saw me yesterday at Green Lake. No threats, just lewd suggestions."

Ross Taylor instantly felt deflated. He had completely forgotten his promise to do something about this, for the love of his life. Instead, nothing. Embarrassed, he couldn't even look at her. "I'm so sorry, Kim. This should be my most important assignment. Instead, I'm concentrating on Great Chicago. I'll get to work right now. I will fix this."

"I know you're busy, and it just slipped your mind. I know you'll take care of me. You're my hero."

They were interrupted by a knock on the side of the boat and a dog bark. Kim walked to the cockpit's sliding door. She stuck her head out and saw one of her favorite people standing on the dock under her umbrella. "Hi, Liz. How are you? How's Brutus?"

Liz and her boyfriend Jim lived aboard a small trawler four boats to the east of the *Pura Vida*. They worked for the marina, servicing boats and doing odd jobs. Though twenty years younger, Liz and Jim hung out with Ross and Kim occasionally—most often at The Rudder. Brutus was a retriever of indeterminate color.

"We're great overall, although Jim is sick today. He's been in bed since last night. He's supposed to be changing Mrs. Fletcher's oil this morning. I'm subbing for him, and Brutus always walks up to your boat when we come out here. Mrs. Fletcher asked me to say hi to you. She hurt her hip and hasn't been getting around much lately."

Mrs. Fletcher lived on a boat exactly opposite the *Pura Vida* on the outer dock.

"Anyway, just wanted to say hello. You doing any cruising?"

"It's nice of you to stop, Liz. Funny, we were just talking about that. No, we're just hanging around Seattle for the time being. Both of us have projects going, but we hope to head north into the islands later in the summer. If we can get away, we're going to island hop for five or six weeks starting the end of August. It's the perfect time to be up there. We just have to push ourselves out."

Kim tossed Brutus a treat from a box she kept for that purpose. From experience, he expected it and barked again. She exchanged goodbyes with Liz and went back below. Ross's phone was ringing.

Chapter Fifteen

Yacht Haven Marina
Lake Union
Seattle, Washington
Tuesday, July 23, 2019

"Hello, Schlump." Taylor had emailed Schlump the data on Great Chicago only the day before, but it didn't surprise him that Schlump phoned so soon. Schlump knew how to relax, but he also could work for long stretches. This must have been one of his long stretches. "You got anything?"

"It can't be bad luck, Ross," he began. "No way. Dental insurance is one of the most predictable of all insurance risks. There's almost no risk. In most cases, if an insurance company loses money on dental insurance, it means they weren't charging enough premium. But Great Chicago's premiums are just about where they should be."

Taylor knew that Schlump must have put in a great deal of work to reach that conclusion so quickly. Actuaries require a mass of data, and he knew from having seen it that Schlump's office resembled a war zone. Though living well into the twenty-first century, Schlump refused to analyze data on a computer screen. He refused to work with anything other than hardcopy printouts and his scientific calculator. Most likely, he had hundreds of sheets of paper on the desk and floor of his office.

"If it's not inadequate premiums, what is it?"

"I'm not there yet. Just hear me out. After I evaluated their premiums, I took a high-level look at claims. Most claims are for routine visits like cleaning and x-rays. Others are for fillings. Some are more serious like root canals or crowns. The point is, the proportion of claims for these procedures is predictable. At Great Chicago, the proportions are exactly as expected. There's nothing unusual. They're not having bad luck in claims either."

Taylor contemplated what Schlump said. "If they're charging the correct premiums and the claims are coming in as expected but they've lost fifty million dollars, it has to be a fraud. There's no other explanation."

"I agree. Somebody has rigged a system somewhere in the overall process and is skimming—big time. What do you want to do?"

"Well, when I met Christine, she gave me carte blanche. I could go anywhere and investigate anything. It seems to me that we should start with the obvious places—her own home office and the three big benefits brokers."

Schlump agreed.

"How does this sound? I've already met the team at Great Chicago, so I'll look into them. I'll also take LeGrande here in Seattle. You begin digging into Consolidated and Argus. We'll start by outlining an audit plan for each location. To save time, we'll use the same format we used the last time. As soon as we hang up, I'll call Christine, get her okay, and ask her to give us the necessary introductions into the brokers."

"Sounds good. I already know people at Consolidated and Argus, so I can get started as soon as you tell me it's a go." He waited until he thought Taylor had finished processing the information then added, "Remember that list of key people you gave me? My friend Tony Postiglione dug into it for me. He's a genius at ferreting out information no one else can find. Everybody's clean except one person. The CFO Winston Lester has a record. I'll email you the details."

Taylor was dumbstruck. This news amounted to a major development. He wondered if Christine knew.

"That's great work, Schlump. Can you ask your guy to dig into one more thing?" He described the problem with the guy stalking Kim. "I know there's a way the identity of an emailer can be worked out from an address. Maybe he can find out who this guy is, and I'll pay him a visit. And, Schlump, ask him to hurry this up. It's important."

"I'll get right on it. Just text me the email address."

"One other thing. Christine promised me a bonus if I found the money. In addition to the usual hourly fee arrangement you and I have, I'll pay you one-hundred thousand dollars out of that bonus when they pay me."

"Thanks for your generosity. Until now, my day hasn't been going so well."

"Why? What happened?"

"Well, I went to the cleaner to drop off some pants. The lady said, 'Sorry, we don't do curtains.'"

Chapter Sixteen

Wells Fargo Center
Seattle, Washington
Tuesday, July 23, 2019

Lucas Sims sat in front of Jacques Levesque's huge desk at a few minutes after ten a.m. He, Oskar Kungen, and Nina Petaluma had been summoned to Levesque's office, and Levesque had just sent Oskar for more coffee.

The four were reviewing year-to-date sales results for LeGrande. Although Lucas, Oskar, and Nina weren't responsible for sales, Levesque wanted everyone in senior leadership to be aware of all aspects of the business. In similar fashion, he earlier apprised the sales team of the financial results. Oskar sat in on everything.

Lucas loathed these meetings. First, they were boring. He never learned anything he didn't already know. But the real reason he hated them: he couldn't stand being in his wheelchair beneath Levesque's elevated desk. He suffered from a keen awareness of his physical disability—confined to a wheelchair while Levesque attempted his slam dunks. And because of Levesque, he became a criminal as well. Now he just wanted to give up.

His thoughts distracted him. How did an ordinarily "good person" turn into a scheming criminal? How much did it take? Not much apparently. There's a fine line between reality and the illusion that certain illegal acts are okay. And that fine line is movable. People who are otherwise moral can be seduced to step over that line.

Lucas Sims hadn't always spent his days in a wheelchair, although to him, it often seemed that way. An active athlete through high school in Davenport, Iowa, he suffered a catastrophic injury. As a pole-vaulter, his pole broke during a jump. He fell back into the box and broke his neck. Only after four years of treatment and rehabilitation could he perform the major activities of daily living from his wheelchair.

At the time of his injury thirty-eight years ago, an experimental procedure existed which might have returned mobility to his legs. Sims's parents' insurance plan denied coverage. The family couldn't afford the cost, and by the time the insurance company approved one of the countless appeals, the doctors could no longer perform the surgery.

Paralyzed below his waist. For life.

That experience fueled a distrust and hatred of insurance companies that continued today. It made his decision to defraud Great Chicago easier.

At fifty-five years of age, in part because of the pressure the crime piled on him, he began to give in to a decline in his physical appearance. Added weight, thinning and graying hair. His skin sagged, and he looked older than others his age.

As Sims sat with Nina, Jacques Levesque changed subjects. "Christine Bell from Great Chicago is sending a different auditor. She didn't say why, but instead of one of her people or that bond guy Hasse Olsson, she's sending Ross Taylor. He'll be here on Monday. Lucas knows who he is."

Just then, Oskar ran in with the coffee. A recent MBA graduate, he served as protégé to Levesque. For perhaps the first time ever, Jacques thanked him and welcomed him back to the meeting.

Lucas gave a summary of Ross Taylor's background for Nina and Oskar's benefit and to refresh Jacques's memory. Then he added, "I don't understand why he's coming. Winston Lester, their CFO, came here last year, and Olsson barely a couple of months ago. This Taylor guy has a reputation for being a shrewd investigator."

"We don't have anything to worry about, do we?" Nina asked, looking back and forth between Levesque and Sims. She served as chief legal counsel for LeGrande Benefits, with primary responsibility for regulatory and legal compliance. In her first high-level corporate job, she demonstrated a remarkable work ethic while maintaining her enthusiasm. As a licensed attorney and officer of the court, her career would be in jeopardy if she even suspected a crime without notifying the authorities.

"No, we're good," Jacques said. "Every insurance company we represent audits us. Great Chicago is no different—except that we're by far their biggest producer. We send them almost three-hundred-fifty million dollars in premiums every year. So, to satisfy themselves and their board, they spend a great deal of time auditing our systems and books. This visit is not unusual."

Lucas Sims couldn't meet Levesque's eyes.

Levesque went on. "What I'd like you to do is make copies of all our major contracts—both in hard copy and on a thumb drive. I know Taylor will want to review them, and you might as well get a head start and be on his good side. Don't skip anything. Lucas, you put together hard copies and a thumb drive of all the documentation for our basic premium and claims systems. That'll get him started. He can let us know what else he needs later. I'll get the sales team to assemble activity and sales logs along with their contact lists. He'll need those too."

He slapped his palms together. "Is there anything else any of you want to discuss further?" No one said anything. "Then, let's get ready for Monday. Lucas, would you mind staying a while longer?"

Nina and Oskar left. To Lucas, today's meeting seemed less intense than most meetings in Levesque's office. Maybe because the others were in attendance. Or maybe because neither knew anything of the fraud Jacques and Lucas were perpetrating. Either way, the environment felt different. Then, Levesque reverted to form and shouted for Oskar to bring them sandwiches.

With Nina and Oskar gone, he spoke softly to Lucas. "I want you to use Operation Perfect Score on the claims system for Guaranty General just like you did for Great Chicago. We should maximize our take for the next few months. Then we can shut things down."

LeGrande placed a small amount of business with another dental insurance company called Guaranty General. The arrangement was identical to the one with Great Chicago, only smaller.

"Are you sure you want to do that, Jacques? I don't think it's a good idea. It will just raise the chance of another audit and the probability of someone figuring out what we're doing. I don't like it. Let's just take what we have and call it quits." Lucas, already bending under the pressure of the Great Chicago investigation, feared the consequences of yet another one.

"Listen, Lucas. Let me worry about what's a good idea. You just do your job, and I'll hold the Guaranty General people off. Do the programming then go to that IT conference in Milwaukee you were talking about. You can even pay a quick visit to our friends at Great Chicago while you're that close. It'll make us look good."

Lucas's nerves were telling him the end was near. He couldn't tolerate this much longer. He didn't think of himself as an evil person. Life thrust him into a transformation from a normal, law-abiding human being into a calculating embezzler. For four years, he lived with the conflict. Yes, he hated insurance companies, but not so much that he had ever considered embezzlement. Now, even the money Jacques owed him would not comfort him. He needed to do something soon.

Levesque dismissed him with a wave of the hand. As Lucas wheeled himself out, Oskar walked in with the sandwiches. "Mr. Stone is here to see you."

Jacques told Oskar to send him to the library and see that they were not disturbed.

When Jacques walked into the library, Ira Stone said, "Hello, my friend. Shalom." Stone greeted Levesque as a fellow Jew, even though Levesque no longer practiced the faith. Almost as tall as Levesque and a bit heavier, Stone wore a plain black suit, a white shirt without tie, a black kippah, and a full beard. He looked like what he was: a diamond dealer.

"Hello to you, Ira. You're looking well. For a minute there, I thought we were meeting on West 47th Street." Levesque referred to the diamond district in mid-town Manhattan in New York City, one of the largest retail diamond districts in the world and the largest in the United States.

Stone began his career in diamonds as an apprentice in his father's and grandfather's retail store. He came to Seattle in 2005 after a falling out with the family over expansion. They wanted to expand; he didn't. He opened his own small, appointment-only shop on First Avenue and prospered.

"Please, show me what you brought, Ira."

Stone carried a small briefcase. He opened it and removed a piece of black felt folded in quarters. He unfolded it into an eighteen-inch square and placed it on the coffee table. Then he removed an envelope from the breast pocket of his suit jacket.

As he did so, Levesque noticed what appeared to be the butt of a handgun. He couldn't be certain if Stone deliberately orchestrated the movement. Maybe just an accident. His eyes shifted back to the envelope.

From the envelope, Stone removed an even smaller envelope. In fact, three thin sheets of paper were folded into a packet in such a way as to keep its contents safe. Diamond dealers knew these as parcels. He removed a diamond from the parcel and laid it on the felt.

"Incredible." Levesque stared at the stone. He knew from experience that Ira Stone allowed him to pick up the diamond, but at that moment, he remained content just to stare at it.

"Here. You hold it." Stone picked up the diamond with tweezers and passed it to him along with a jeweler's loupe.

Levesque brought the diamond near his eyes. The sparkling gem measured a little less than half an inch across the top. He never stopped being amazed at how valuable such a small object could be.

While he studied the stone, Levesque's hands shook. "Tell me about it."

"As you can see, it's a round cut diamond like a majority of those you've purchased in the last couple of years. It's an excellent cut, meaning it has been cut to ideal proportions to maximize the brilliance and sparkle. It has a weight of slightly more than five point three carats. It's D color, meaning that it has virtually no color. There are no blemishes. Look carefully inside the diamond. It has flawless clarity with no feathers, clouds, pinpoints—no inclusions whatsoever. And no cutting errors. Jacques, it's as close to perfect as you can get."

Levesque continued to be mesmerized. He never tired of looking at diamonds, holding them, and most important, possessing them. Through the loupe, he looked for flaws but could see none. He moved the stone. Though colorless, flares of dazzling colored light shot out from the diamond. He agreed. Perfect. "The price?"

"Four-hundred-seventy-five thousand dollars."

After a brief pause, he said, "Done."

The diamond belonged to Levesque.

Retrieving cash from his office safe and going through the process of counting and recounting $475,000 in $100 bills with Ira Stone took the two men almost an hour and a half. When they finished, they said their goodbyes and Stone left the office. He supplied no diamond certification. Levesque trusted him and didn't need one. He looked at his watch and saw that the bank vault would still be open. He headed for the elevator.

Jacques Levesque felt nearer than ever to the South of France.

Chapter Seventeen

Yacht Haven Marina
Lake Union
Seattle, Washington
Tuesday, July 23, 2019

After he finished his call, Taylor thought about the shock Schlump delivered into their investigation. A criminal in Great Chicago. Christine's CFO no less. Did she know? If so, why didn't she tell him?

His phone chimed—a text message from Schlump. A copy of the report from Postiglione. He went into his office to study the latest information.

According to the report, Winston Lester graduated from Northwestern University in suburban Chicago with bachelor's and master's degrees in accounting and finance, performing near the top of his class at both levels. Shortly after his graduation, however, he ran into a problem with the law. He falsified documents to obtain a loan for a start-up business venture. After he received the loan proceeds, the bank discovered the misrepresentations and called the loan while, at the same time, notifying the authorities.

Lester repaid the loan at once, and no charges were ever filed. Nonetheless, Winston Lester carried a burden on his personal record that followed him wherever he went.

The report went on. After the problem with the bank, but prior to joining Great Chicago, he held non-executive financial positions exclusively—positions not requiring extensive background checks. In each, his performance was rated exceptional. Then Great Chicago hired him. There, the report ended.

Taylor called Christine Bell's private number. "Chris," he said when she answered, "I have some information you need to hear." When she didn't respond, he continued. "Winston Lester has a record of bank fraud." Again, he waited.

After more than a moment of silence, Christine responded. "I know, Ross. I'm sorry I didn't tell you while you were here. I made a mistake and should have told you. It affects your assignment and how you organize your investigation. Let me try to explain."

She went on. "About ten years ago, we were searching for a replacement for an assistant treasurer position at Great Chicago. Among the applicants, Winston stood out. He impressed all of us as clearly the best candidate we interviewed. Filling the position did not require board of directors' approval, so I offered him the job.

"He requested to meet me in person, ostensibly to discuss terms of his employment. I agreed, and he came to my office. Before we started, he said I needed to know something about him not revealed on his resume. He described the problem with the bank loan. He told me about the personal circumstances which led him to the misrepresentation and how he regretted it. He described the remorse he felt at the time and still did and that he'd understand if I changed my mind about hiring him.

"My immediate reaction—end the discussion. I thanked him for coming and he left. But I thought long and hard about everything. If we searched for another month, we'd still not find a better candidate. His resume included more education and skills than we ever contemplated for the position. Plus, he confessed to me voluntarily. So, I decided to give him a chance.

"I called each of the board members and told them the story. I told them I wanted to hire him but also sought their opinions. Every one of them said to go ahead and hire him. None of them told me directly that I might be out of a job if Winston turned out to be trouble, although I completely understood his hiring to be a career-ending risk.

"He performed exceptionally, and when the job of CFO opened, the board offered him the position. Of course, we couldn't forget his history, and when the shortfalls started to occur, we immediately thought of him and ordered an internal investigation. We could find nothing, certainly no basis to consider Winston a suspect. But now that you know everything, perhaps he should be one of the first places you look. I'll leave that up to you for now."

Christine's story about Winston Lester matched the report from Postiglione. Taylor expressed his confidence to her that his file contained everything he needed to know and agreed to move his internal review of Great Chicago up to sooner rather than later.

"Thanks, Chris. I'll take this into account and let you know my next steps." He hung up, stunned at the turn of events.

He and Schlump needed to focus on the data to get a better handle on how the losses were occurring. The *how* part, more than anything else, would direct them to the *who* part of the puzzle. He decided to continue as planned.

Chapter Eighteen

Yacht Haven Marina
Lake Union
Seattle, Washington
Wednesday, July 24, 2019

The basketball games on the courts at Green Lake were great this morning, and Taylor's shooting eye just kept getting better and better. The neighborhood players could hardly believe what they saw from this old guy. Then the rain came, and the court became too slick to play.

On his way to the *Pura Vida*, Taylor's phone rang. Schlump.

"I just heard from Tony Postiglione about the guy you wanted him to look into. I'll email you the report. It should give you everything you need." Schlump hung up without another word.

Fifteen minutes later, Taylor climbed back on the boat and immediately went into his office to read the report. He didn't know how Postiglione did it. He didn't need to know. From what he could see, the guy provided a complete demographic package on one Hubert

Meyerhoffer: address in Wallingford just north of the marina, along with a complete work and family history, and a photo. In five minutes, Taylor knew more about Meyerhoffer than he did about Schlump.

He heard Kim come down into the main cabin from the cockpit, returning from an hour-long run. "Kim, here's something you'll want to see."

She looked at the report on the screen. "Hubie Meyerhoffer! That creep. Is he the guy following me around?"

Taylor nodded.

"I'm surprised he's still alive. It's just like him to do this."

"You know this guy?"

"Oh sure. I knew him about twenty years ago. A lackey over at the *P.I.,* he never could do anything well. They just kept trying to find a place for him where he couldn't screw things up too badly. I don't know why they were afraid to fire him. He used to torment all the girls in the days before Me Too and female-abuse awareness, and he went well beyond flirting. He'd say lewd things, proposition the girls for sex, that sort of thing. For some reason, he targeted me more than any of the other girls.

"I remember him being a big guy then, but as far as I know, he never put a hand on any of the girls. And he always looked like a mess. Pants too big—even for a big guy. Shirts partially unbuttoned and smelled like he'd worn them for three days. You could smell him from ten feet. I haven't seen or heard of him in years."

"Is he the kind of guy who sends emails like the ones you got?"

"Oh yeah. He's just the kind. We didn't use email as much twenty years ago, or he would have used it then. Now that I see his name, I'm not at all surprised. He must have seen my picture on one of my articles; the credits always include my email address. But I'm surprised he reads anything I'm published in. And why me and why now?"

"I'm not sure that matters. I'm going to see that he stops."

"What are you going to do?" Kim asked.

"I'll need to show him that it's not all right to do what he's doing. He lives in the area and has seen you around the marina and at Green Lake—each time in the morning. The report from Schlump says he works nights at Husky Stadium. He probably hangs out around the lake on his way home from work. I'll bet he's been watching you for months and only recently worked up the nerve to use email. Do you think you could still recognize him?"

"Unless he's undergone a major change in appearance, like lost or gained a hundred pounds, I'd recognize him instantly. I especially remember his head—small compared to the rest of his body, and his hair grew only on the top, not the sides. He's hard to miss." She paused, thinking about Hubie Meyerhoffer for the first time in twenty years. "If you do see him, what will you say to him?"

"You're the love of my life, Kim, and I'll do anything to protect you. Whatever it takes. In my experience, in situations like this, it's not what you say, it's the way you explain it. In the case of Hubie Meyerhoffer, my explanation should be brief, and he'll understand. For now, let's decide on the best way to lure him out."

Chapter Nineteen

Western Oregon and Washington
Friday, July 26, 2019

"I used to love this trip, Jacques. It seemed like such an adventure at first—making the rounds. Now, it's just not the same. We haven't enjoyed this trip at all." Aubrey Reddy sat in the front passenger seat of Jacques Levesque's Lexus LX, her ever-present camera in her lap. They were wrapping up the second day of their three-day trip.

"It's going to get better, darling. One day soon, we'll be in the South of France enjoying the beauty of the Mediterranean. We won't even remember today. There's a fabulous chateau and spa near Nice where we'll stay while we look for a home. It's called the Chateau Saint-Martin. We'll live in luxury, eat the best food, walk in the warm sand. You'll never want to leave."

She loved the sound of it, and she loved Jacques Levesque. "It sounds wonderful. When I first learned photography, we used large landscape photos to learn composition and camera settings. The Mediterranean scenes were my absolute favorites. I'll look it up when we get home. Have you ever been there?"

"No, but my friends have. They say it's like nothing they ever experienced. The food is to die for."

Jacques and Aubrey were a couple and had lived together for the three and a half years they knew each other. Her beauty, green eyes, and long red hair attracted him the first time he saw her. She knew he was still attracted to her. They continued to drive.

"How long do you think it will be before we go?" She glanced in his direction as she asked the question. Aubrey loved Levesque deeply and wanted to be married to him. Levesque first made his promise to take her to France almost two years ago, but recently, she wondered if he meant it. Her heart wanted to believe him. When she allowed her mind to take over, doubts crept in.

"Sometime soon—maybe this fall," he said. "I don't want to talk about it around the office until you and I have all our plans in place. I don't want Lucas or Nina to worry about their futures unnecessarily."

Aubrey's mind wandered back to the first time they made the rounds to the banks. They "played make-believe" as Jacques put it. Over a period of six days, the two opened accounts in thirty different banks in five cities. They opened each account in the name of a different person. Felix arranged for a driver's license, social security card, and other identification for each name. Half were printed with her picture. The others featured Jacques's. When they told the bankers they were dentists and planned to make deposits between twenty-five and forty thousand dollars per month, the bankers were always enthusiastic to have them as new customers.

The whole process struck her as odd at the time. Her life's experiences did not prepare her for fabricating stories to bankers. She suspected they might be breaking the law, but Jacques convinced her of their legitimacy and that they weren't doing anything illegal—all part of his insurance business. She even began to get excited about the "make-believe" aspect and thought of them as latter-day Bonnie and Clyde. She set her suspicions aside.

Before meeting Levesque, Aubrey Reddy's business and worldly experience was limited. Her father abandoned the family shortly before her eleventh birthday, and she had helped her mother raise her two younger sisters. Even while at Seattle Pacific University studying psychology, she continued to live at home with her mother.

A boyfriend talked her into leaving college to travel with him. At first, she loved it, being independent, but she tired of waiting tables, driving a cab, and trying to sell her pictures at open-air markets to pay their room rent. After a few months, life turned into a grind. One day, the boyfriend disappeared, and Aubrey returned to Seattle.

The bank in Jacques's building hired her as a bookkeeper, her first real job. She excelled and became a customer service representative in the public part of the bank. The bank recognized her above-average intelligence and her problem-solving skills and put her into a fast-track program for career development. It was then that Jacques first saw her, and she soon became his girlfriend. Then, his "assistant."

At first, they scheduled road trips to the banks regularly—occasionally together but mostly separately and at different times. The bankers came to know them as good customers, dentists who received insurance claim payments for dental services and transferred those deposits monthly. Good business for the banks.

During the past couple of years, the number of bank trips slowed. Now just once every six months or so. On this trip, they were in the banks for a very short time — barely more than a "Hello, how are you?" She had to be careful to remember the name associated with each bank she visited.

In the early days when they traveled together, in addition to visiting the banks, they also made stops at upscale jewelers in each city. Jacques purchased high quality diamonds on those trips. He told Aubrey the money came from bonuses paid by the insurance companies he represented, money he was investing for his retirement. She knew of his success in business although she didn't understand the insurance business. But it always sounded exotic—especially the part about the diamonds.

The diamond shopping always perked Aubrey up. She felt certain he would one day give her a large diamond in a fancy ring setting—especially after he took her to his safe deposit box and showed her his collection. Lately, he had stopped shopping for diamonds on these trips. And no ring for her yet.

She wanted to ask him more about his plans to get away to the South of France but thought better of it. Not now. Clearly, his thoughts concentrated in some other place. Instead, she asked, "Where are we staying tonight?"

"Oskar booked us a suite at The Nines."

"In Portland?"

"Yeah. It should be nice. They have an extremely popular dining room. We'll be home tomorrow night."

"Which banks will we see tomorrow? We haven't visited as many as in past trips."

Jacques thought for a moment. "I'm doing more and more transactions electronically, honey. I like to stay in personal touch with the banks, but it just isn't as necessary as it used to be. We'll see four tomorrow—three in Portland and one in Bremerton—then get the ferry home. We could spend the weekend here, but I have to get ready for my meeting with that Ross Taylor guy that Christine is sending to check us out."

At the mention of the ferry, they fell into silence, both reminded of an earlier trip aboard the Bremerton ferry.

Chapter Twenty

Green Lake
Seattle, Washington
Saturday, July 27, 2019

Green Lake was a small, freshwater lake just a mile and a half north of the Yacht Haven Marina and Lake Union. Less than one-half square mile in area, it featured a running track around the perimeter of the lake. Roughly two and a half miles long, the track attracted all levels of runners. This morning, Kim Taylor warmed up on the track.

She told Ross that she felt no fear. Not quite true. Now that she knew who was watching her, she started to wonder about her safety. What if, during the intervening years, Meyerhoffer graduated to more serious habits than just making lewd remarks? More dangerous, physical pursuits. What if he was a rapist or a killer? Her eyes darted from side to side behind her sunglasses, trying to spot him. And she needed to know that Ross ran near her as she jogged along the track.

Taylor came separately in an Uber and now jogged on the same track, at his own pace, about fifty yards behind

Kim. They planned to stay in visual contact without speaking, and Kim agreed to use a prearranged signal in the event she saw Meyerhoffer. Both were in great physical condition, so they could keep this routine up for at least an hour and a half if necessary.

Kim deliberately dressed to stand out on the track. She wore her hair in a ponytail under a yellow baseball cap. Her t-shirt and shoes were a complimentary bright red, and her ankle-length yellow running tights matched her cap. If Meyerhoffer were there that morning, he would have no trouble picking her out.

Taylor shared his anxiety about the plan with Kim that morning. He already second-guessed their idea to entice Meyerhoffer to show himself; Meyerhoffer might be a real threat. But Taylor agreed to let the whole scene play out and make decisions on the fly.

He stayed as close to Kim as he could without making their plan obvious. He saw no reason why Meyerhoffer should recognize him, but as a precaution and so not to stand out, he dressed in shades of gray.

Every so often, Kim stopped, stretched, and allowed Ross to pass her. They didn't acknowledge each other. Then, further along the track, he stopped to stretch, and she passed. Because there were others on the track as well, running in both directions, it would be difficult for anyone to conclude that Kim and Ross Taylor were associated with each other in any way. They were just two more runners on the track. Nervous runners.

Forty-five minutes into their plan, Kim flashed the sign—both arms above her head, hands together in a stretching motion. Ross noted the man on the park bench ten feet to the right of the running track. No doubt about it. Meyerhoffer. Just then, the man lifted a camera to his eye, appeared to take a picture, and quickly brought it down.

Though only hearing Kim's description and seeing Postiglione's picture, Taylor knew. Kim continued to run at her pace putting distance between herself and the two men. Taylor ran a short distance further then stopped to stretch again. From his vantage point, he saw Meyerhoffer, barely fifty feet from him. Adrenaline poured into his blood, and his heart rate increased as he anticipated what might happen next.

After a short while, Meyerhoffer got up and walked toward the parking lot. Kim's description of him fit perfectly—even after twenty years. His weight remained the same, and his head was disproportionately small with hair only on the top. He dressed like a slob. There could be no mistake.

Taylor moved ahead at an angle, the parking lot only a short distance away. As he closed the distance between Meyerhoffer and himself, he noticed a characteristic missing from Kim's description: Meyerhoffer's face featured an asymmetrical look, as if unbalanced. Almost frightening. He reached the parking lot before Meyerhoffer. There were no other people nearby.

As a rule, Taylor didn't seek violence, nor did he seek confrontation. But neither did he fear violence or confrontation. In fact, when confrontation presented itself, he welcomed it. When he first took up boxing in college, he questioned his decision. He didn't fear being punched, but boxing didn't give him satisfaction to punch someone else either. Until his fourth fight.

He fought against a guy he knew to be a real jerk, who flaunted his size and arrogance and was a bully as well. Taylor quickly uncovered the larger guy's weaknesses and beat him thoroughly until the referee stopped the fight. That day, he discovered he liked hurting people he didn't like. It made him feel good. Energized him.

He didn't like Hubie Meyerhoffer.

Taylor looked forward to the next few minutes. Near the side of the parking lot, he stretched again unobtrusively and watched as Meyerhoffer walked toward an older model van. He walked in Meyerhoffer's direction, still stretching. As he came closer, he noticed that Meyerhoffer continued to wear the camera around his neck. Probably took all the pictures he wanted then would head home to enjoy them. They reached the van at the same moment, and for the first time, Meyerhoffer noticed Taylor. He waved a passive greeting then looked away and opened the door.

Taylor spoke in an even but confident tone. "Mr. Meyerhoffer, you don't know me. My wife is Kim Taylor, although you may have known her as Kim Summers. In any case, you are never going to look at her again. You are never going to email her again. You are never going to have anything to do with either of us again. If you ever see either of us, you will turn and run away that instant. I hope you understand."

Meyerhoffer drew a fist back and started to say something, but Taylor, already in motion, hit him flush on the left eye socket. As Meyerhoffer started to go down, partially supported by the van, Taylor recovered then hit him again with the same right hand—this time on the left jaw. Meyerhoffer lost consciousness before he hit the ground.

Taylor removed the memory card from the camera and put it in his pocket. The camera looked to be an expensive Nikon, so he removed it from around Meyerhoffer's neck and smashed it on the pavement, paying particular attention to the lens and the electronics. As a finishing touch, he stepped on both of Meyerhoffer's hands and ground the fingers into the pavement with his full weight. The time of the entire event: fifteen seconds.

Taylor walked slowly across the grass to the next parking lot where the Uber still waited. The Uber was a diversion—in case he had been seen. He didn't want to be connected to Kim. The driver, sound asleep, awoke and expressed his gratitude for the fare previously paid and the large tip Taylor now handed him.

No one observed what happened or noticed them as they drove away. Taylor knew Kim would follow close behind in her car. He looked forward to throwing his arms around her, telling her how much he loved her, and assuring her that she wouldn't be hearing from Meyerhoffer again.

On the ride back to the marina, Taylor began to think again. He felt certain their problem with Meyerhoffer was finished, but perhaps someone else hired him to intimidate or harass Kim? What if he wasn't just some creep who stalked women?

Chapter Twenty-one

Wells Fargo Center
Seattle, Washington
Monday, July 29, 2019

The entrance to the offices of LeGrande Benefits on the forty-first floor of the Wells Fargo Center looked more like a Swiss bank than a Seattle insurance agency. There were no floor-to-ceiling glass doors, no corporate logo, and no list of officers' names. Only a single-panel, dark-stained oak door and a three-inch by eight-inch polished brass plate set into the oak wall paneling to the right. It said *LeGrande*. Under the plate, a small, easily overlooked button.

Early for his nine o'clock appointment with Jacques Levesque, Ross Taylor tried the door. Locked. He pressed the button.

Approximately fifteen seconds later, a young man opened the door. "Good morning, Mr. Taylor. I am Oskar Kungen, Mr. Levesque's executive assistant. Please come in."

The invitation seemed more like a warm welcome

into a home than an office, an altogether new business experience for Taylor.

The small lobby measured barely twenty feet on each side and, similar to the greeting he received, was unlike any waiting area he ever encountered. No receptionist, no table stacked with annual reports, and no staff scurrying around. It reminded Taylor of the private library in the luxurious home of his former chairman.

In addition to the entry door, one other door led out of the room. Otherwise, the windowless walls were covered with mahogany bookcases filled with what were, no doubt, old volumes. Three overstuffed dark red, leather, wingback chairs, three lamp tables with matching lamps, and a triangular coffee table sat in the center of the room. Each chair was located an equal distance from the table. A Persian rug completed the décor of an extremely comfortable space.

The lone item on the table was a silver coffee service. Steam drifted out of the spout. "Mr. Levesque will be with you in just a moment. Please make yourself comfortable, Mr. Taylor. May I pour you a cup of coffee?"

When Oskar Kungen left, Taylor wandered to one of the bookcases to peruse its contents while he waited for Levesque. He knew the technique of forcing a visitor to wait in order to gain a business advantage, and he expected Levesque to do just that.

Instead, at exactly nine o'clock, Jacques Levesque walked in. "Good morning, Ross. We're glad you're here. I hope you don't mind my calling you Ross. After Christine told me about you, it seems like I've known you for years." He displayed a warm and welcoming smile.

Levesque impressed Taylor with both his stature and looks. Slightly taller than Ross, he estimated Levesque to be around six feet two inches and weigh at least 220 pounds. He exuded the confidence of a successful business executive.

"Thank you, Jacques. I'm glad to be here as well, and you can certainly call me Ross. Oskar made me feel right at home."

Levesque motioned for Taylor to take one of the chairs, and he sat in one of the others.

As he filled a cup with coffee, Levesque said, "Oskar has been with me for two years. He's an interesting guy. Most executives have an assistant with the traditional skillset—organizing, scheduling, time-management, communications—the usual things. I decided a couple of years ago that in addition to those skills, I wanted someone who aspired to be a CEO—someone who wanted and possessed the talent for a job like mine. Instead of recruiting from a staffing company, I recruited from recent MBA graduates. Oskar has to do everything a traditional executive assistant does. He schedules my travel, maintains my calendar, prepares correspondence, and sends flowers to my fiancé. You've been a CEO; you know how it is."

Taylor knew exactly what Levesque spoke of and was fascinated. "Is he good at it?"

"The best I've ever had. But, in addition, Oskar is learning how to be a CEO. He sits in on almost every meeting I have. If I have a conference call, he listens. He reads every report I get. He attends performance reviews. When I travel, he goes with me. His schedule is grueling—I couldn't do it anymore. But he's only twenty-seven; he soaks up everything and he's thriving. No Dow Thirty company executive has an assistant as talented as Oskar. Someday, he'll run a major company."

"This concept should be a business school presentation," Taylor said. "I'll bet if you approached the U, they'd be happy to have you as a guest lecturer. And the students would love it."

"You're probably right. The business school students aren't thinking about jobs where they have to run and get their boss a sandwich. In Oskar's case, he could have gone to work on Wall Street or in any of the major cities. He's that smart. But he's perfectly satisfied following me around, suffering through my rants, and getting my coffee. Anyway, welcome to LeGrande."

Taylor's briefing on Levesque by Christine Bell and the great deal he read about the man prepared him for the business they expected to discuss but not for Levesque's personality. He had been prepared to thoroughly dislike Jacques Levesque. It turned out not to be so easy. Relaxing in this comfortable setting, he found Levesque to be quite engaging and easygoing—almost likable.

"I know you probably want to get to work," Jacques said with a smile, "but I thought it might be useful for us to get to know a little more about each other before you dig in. I'll show you around the place when we've finished here. Believe me, it's not all like this beautiful room.

"We use our library, as we call this room, to greet our important guests and for brief client meetings. Otherwise, our company is the same beehive of activity and function as any successful insurance agency. What can I tell you about LeGrande or me to help you get started?"

Taylor had been anticipating this question since he left the office of Great Chicago almost two weeks ago. Christine asked him to investigate what might be a criminal activity, and he needed to proceed carefully.

"Well, let's start simple. How did you come to be running a wildly successful insurance agency like LeGrande?"

"LeGrande hasn't always been this successful. When I came to work here twenty years ago, I knew nothing about insurance. I'm from the east coast. Queens, New York, actually. I graduated from Brown and hacked around in various jobs before I decided I needed a change of scene. I came to Seattle on a whim.

"I needed to find a job. I interviewed for a position as a sales rep for Northwest Dental Benefits. My only interview. They were brokers for all the major dental insurers. They offered me a job and I took it. Almost immediately, they sent me out in the street to call on businesses and try to get them to buy dental insurance for their employees. They paid me on a commission basis."

Taylor appreciated Levesque's history. He started in commission sales himself years ago and remembered the pressure to make sales and the exhilaration when he did.

Levesque went on. "I didn't know anything, but I loved the freedom. I made mistakes, but I soon caught on to what it took to be successful in sales. I was a natural. I could sell to anyone. I could sell anything. We wrote so much dental insurance business neither the insurance companies nor our staff could keep up. We hired more assistants. We hired more back office. We still couldn't keep up.

"I quickly figured out that I could as easily sell a big client as a small client. I started targeting big business, and soon, I landed my first huge client: Boeing. We barely let the ink dry on that contract when I signed the Western Conference of Teamsters. Then the State of Washington employees. I became a hero and made more money than I dreamed of."

He paused to reflect. "I didn't always have it so great. My father worked as a bookkeeper. He took pride in his profession and his work. I think he pleased his bosses— at least until he got laid off. Let go in a reorganization about three years before he planned to retire. The big impersonal corporation screwing over the little guy when he least expected it. I always resented that company and hoped, someday, to gain revenge for him. Of course, they told him he'd be the first one called back when things improved, but they never called. Retirement for him and my mother didn't turn out nearly as comfortable as they hoped for.

"But like all fathers, he wanted me to have it better. He wanted me to be an accountant, a CPA, so I couldn't suffer the fate he did. He thought being a CPA meant protection. Unfortunately for him, I didn't have the slightest interest in being an accountant."

"What did you want to be?"

"I wanted to be a musician. But I couldn't play anything. I tried piano and guitar lessons. I didn't get it. I stunk. Then I thought I could be a concert promoter. Right after college, I found a new band and convinced them I could promote their careers and make them famous. I didn't make them any money, and I lost my own.

"Then, I came to Seattle, and it all worked out for me. But my dad made me aware of his disappointment. He strongly disliked salespeople. Thought they were all a bunch of hustlers who lied, cheated, and stole just to make a sale. And he reminded me to be wary of big corporations. He died before I became successful here."

Levesque's story fascinated Taylor.

"So here I was. Writing a ton of business and making a ton of money. The owners of Northwest Dental Benefits, my bosses, decided to make me a shareholder. They gave me a small percentage of the stock. I felt like a big shot. I started taking part in the company planning and sharing in the profits. And I continued to sell. Costco. Microsoft. State of Oregon employees."

Taylor could tell that Levesque took pride in his accomplishments and enjoyed telling this story.

"In 2010, they made me chief executive officer and gave me carte blanche in all decision-making. Because of our rapid growth, our offices became too spread out, and we were inefficient. At a time when other companies were decentralizing their operations, I consolidated our offices into this building. We do everything right here."

As he said that, Levesque swept his right hand to indicate the entire area of the LeGrande offices.

"You've probably heard about the basketball court. I'll show you that before we're finished. The other owners were initially reluctant to spend the money on what they considered frivolity and my ego getting the better of me.

But, over time, I think it has more than paid for itself in publicity.

"I got us into the benefits administration business. Previously, we were strictly a sales organization. We'd make a sale, and the insurance company took over. They paid us a commission, and they did everything else. We proposed to perform more administrative work for them, and they accepted. First, we just billed and collected premiums from our customers and passed those premiums along to the insurance companies. Later we started paying commissions to agents, then claims. We could perform these functions better, faster, and cheaper than the insurance companies themselves, and before long, we were administering all the business we sold."

Taylor's interest was suddenly piqued. "How many companies do you administer for?"

"Just two. Great Chicago and Guaranty General. Chicago, by far, is our biggest client. The insurance we write through Great Chicago represents ninety-five percent of our administration business. Their service is great, and their rates are usually the lowest. We only use Guaranty General when a customer fails to meet Great Chicago's underwriting standards."

Taylor could only shake his head in awe. "Impressive, Jacques. That's an American Dream story." He paused, then asked, "How did Northwest come to be known as LeGrande?"

"I've always wanted to celebrate my French heritage. My parents took a last-minute holiday to Paris just before my expected birth. I arrived prematurely while they were there. Born John Samuel Levy to Morris and Rachel

Levy of Queens, New York, on Bastille Day in 1972. So, when the other stockholders of Northwest gave me permission to change the name of the company, I settled on LeGrande. It sounded cool and it sounded French."

"Is that why you changed your name?" Taylor asked.

Jacques smiled. "I changed my name during college. I was Jack Levy for my first twenty years. I have been Jacques Levesque since. The French thing again."

None of this came out in the briefing Taylor received from Christine Bell. "Do you have favorite places in France?" He and Kim had loved Paris and the French countryside when they vacationed there in 2014 and often talked of returning.

"I have dual citizenship, but I haven't been in France since a week and a half after my birth. I plan to go there—perhaps permanently—when I'm ready to retire. I think about France all the time.

"But enough about me for now. Before I show you around, tell me how we can be of help to you in your work for Great Chicago."

"The problem is simple, Jacques. The solution may be complicated." Taylor explained the issues facing Christine Bell and the importance of finding a resolution. He outlined the various possibilities that he and Christine explored and how he intended to investigate LeGrande.

"In no way should you take my being here as a suspicion of LeGrande. Christine has suggested we start with the agencies which also perform benefits administration. My associate and I will be visiting each of their three largest administrators. Thanks to your personal success, LeGrande is the largest of the companies doing administration for Great Chicago. And because I live in Seattle, we're beginning here.

"Christine is reasonably certain the profit shortfall at Great Chicago is the result of mispricing of their products, not any kind of fraud. We are investigating that possibility. We haven't seen any evidence of mispricing, but we still hope she will be proved correct. In the meantime, though, we wanted to get started with the external audits. If an irregularity or fraud is taking place, she wants us to find it."

Both coffee cups had remained untouched since they settled in half an hour earlier. "Christine has told me you've been exceptionally successful in uncovering insurance fraud, Ross. Any examples you want to share?"

"One stands out—primarily because we recovered every dime the guy took. Did you ever hear of the Frankenstein matter? It made the front page of the *Wall Street Journal.* Maybe you remember him. Frank Stein. But it didn't take long for us to refer to him as Frankenstein, and the press picked up on it. I still do."

Taylor could tell that Levesque was anxious to hear more.

"Over a period of about three years, Stein fleeced our company out of almost ten million. My assignment: get to the bottom of it. It all happened ten years ago. We were certain he had taken money but needed to prove it."

"What did you do?"

"When we and the police raided his offices, his attorney showed up and threatened me personally. He all but assaulted me and said he'd personally put our company out of business and bankrupt me. But we got what we came for, all of his records. Three months later, after we finished our investigation and obtained depositions, I sat in the same lawyer's office. Without saying a word, he handed me a certified check for ten million dollars drawn on Stein's bank. One of the best days of my life. I didn't say another word to him, but I had a satisfied smile on my face as I accepted the check."

Levesque smiled and slowly nodded his understanding.

"We got all our money back. We were through with him, but the feds weren't. They prosecuted him for wire and mail fraud, and he did a little more than six years. Of course, while he enjoyed the hospitality of the federal government, his other insurance companies performed audits and found similar, although not as large, discrepancies. By the time of his release, fines bankrupted him, his insurance licenses were revoked, and his wife dumped him.

"I felt a great deal of satisfaction with how it turned out. Funny thing, just when you think you've heard it all, I get a call one morning. 'Hey Ross. I'm out!' It's Frank Stein—like he's my best buddy. He wants to get together for drinks and talk about old times. You can't make this stuff up."

"Did you meet him?"

"I thought about it for a while. He tempted me because he's such an interesting guy. But I also knew I didn't want to be around someone who stole my company's money and lived the life he did. Basically, a dirtbag. If not for me and my team, he'd be sipping margaritas someplace warm with his feet up. Instead, he's broke, his company's broke, and he's crawling around looking for another mark. No, I didn't meet him."

"Incredible." Levesque couldn't take his attention away from Taylor. "What turned you onto the Frankenstein fraud in the first place? Bank account records?"

"I've been involved in unravelling seven insurance frauds—three in my own company. They were all different, of course, but in one way, they were all the same. In every case, they utilized great technology, almost foolproof. The systems those guys developed were first class. Routine audits were unlikely to turn up anything. A few created 'secret' bank accounts. But those were uncommon."

At the mention of secret bank accounts, Levesque's interest intensified.

"In every case, a small but obvious feature of the scam showed up. Great technology, but not great enough. The scams still required people, and people made mistakes. Sometimes it took us weeks, even months, to uncover that mistake. But we always did. And when we finally found it, it had always been there staring us in the face and was enough to break the matter wide open.

"In the case of Frankenstein, I'll put it in simple round-number terms. My company knew him well, and we all liked him. We contracted with him to be one of our administrators. He'd collect, for example, one million dollars in premium from his agents but only submit nine-hundred thousand to our company. The remaining one hundred thousand, he diverted to a private account. His sophisticated systems rationalized the nine-hundred thousand premium as being correct, and our audits didn't uncover the fraud. At least for a while."

Levesque hadn't moved since Taylor started this story.

"He set the trap for himself when he paid his agents their commission. He owed them commission on the full million they submitted, not the nine-hundred thousand he reported collecting. Normally, we don't perform a detailed audit on commissions, and Frankenstein knew that. But, in this case, based on a hunch, we did. With that simple discrepancy, it didn't take us long to put the whole puzzle together. We recovered almost all our money, and he wound up doing time in Marion, Illinois."

"That's quite a story, Ross. It must have been especially satisfying to you. And your board equally so." Levesque stood and motioned Taylor to follow him. "Come on, I'll show you around."

For the next hour, Levesque led the way through a series of office units. "This is sales. That's underwriting. Around the corner is finance. Upstairs is claims. You get the picture, like every other insurance company you've been in."

When Ross started to get bored, Levesque said, "I have one more place to show you."

He opened an unobtrusive door, and they stepped into another world—Levesque's basketball court. It even smelled like a gym. Levesque picked up a ball and tossed it to Taylor who winced slightly from his sore right hand. He tossed it back and forth between his hands, dribbled a couple of times, and tossed it back to Levesque.

"You ever play?" Jacques Levesque asked.

Ross Taylor was a star in high school, but even as a scholarship player, he failed to stay on the team at the University of Illinois after his first year. He could still teach the younger players lessons, and he spent at least two mornings a week at Denny Playfield and Green Lake. The local boys all wanted him on their team. "I used to but not much anymore. Too old, I guess. You?"

"I played in college, Yeshiva. Quit when I transferred to Brown. I try to get a game in up here every day. Guys in the building come up on lunch break. Can you believe it? I can still dunk." He dribbled toward the basket and took off. He jammed the ball into the side of the rim. "Let me try again."

He did, same result. He tried without success to hide his embarrassment.

Ross Taylor felt generous. "You'd have made it easily if you were wearing your Nikes. Next time." He could tell from Levesque's form that if he could dunk at all, he couldn't do it regularly.

"This has been a nice introduction, Jacques. I should only be here three or four days. Maybe we can even get in a little one-on-one. Just see me out, and I'll be back here to start tomorrow morning."

"Sounds good. I've made it clear to my team that they're to make available anything you ask for. While you're here, your go-to guy will be Lucas Sims. He's my CFO and knows everything about the company. Anything you need, you ask him. He'll show you where you can set up shop tomorrow. If anything you ask for is deficient, let him know. He'll get it fixed. We know your work is important to Christine, and we want your stay here to be efficient. I'll see you to the lobby."

The two men walked together to the main entrance where they said their goodbyes and parted company.

As Ross Taylor walked to the elevator, Jacques Levesque took out his small red phone and punched one digit. When Lucas Sims picked up, Levesque said, "I want to see you in my office. Now."

Chapter Twenty-two

Wells Fargo Center
Seattle, Washington
Monday, July 29, 2019

Lucas Sims learned long ago what Jacques Levesque meant when he said "now."

Less than five minutes after receiving the call, he rolled his wheelchair in front of Levesque's desk. "How did it go?"

Levesque removed his suit jacket and tie and tossed them in a pile on a nearby chair. He still seethed in anger at himself for not dunking in front of Taylor. He turned his attention to Sims. "So, so. He has an agenda, all right. He's going to be searching for fraud. And you were right about him. He's an expert."

Lucas felt ill.

"The good thing is, he's looking not just at us but two of Great Chicago's other administrators as well. He mentioned an associate but didn't say his name. I got the impression that both planned to examine us at one time or another. Christine told me he lives right here in Seattle, so we could be seeing him more than we want."

"Did he give you any idea what he'll be looking for?" Lucas tried his best to sound confident, despite his discomfort.

"He says they suspect it's mispricing, but I don't believe him. Christine wouldn't hire a fraud expert to investigate mispricing. After all, we don't set the prices—Great Chicago does."

Color started to leave Sims's face. "You know how much I hate insurance companies. They're a bunch of damn thieves. But I don't like how this is developing at all. It's time to wrap up and move on. If he gets any hint of the existence of Perfect Score, we'll go to jail."

Sims had wanted to close the operation for months, but now he was desperate. "We can't keep doing this, Jacques. Sooner or later, someone's going to figure this out. Give me my share and I'll disappear. I have nothing else. Ulrika couldn't forgive me for the money I lost; she took the kids and the house. She's filed for divorce. I haven't seen them for over a year."

Levesque gave him a patient smile. "Ross Taylor is going to be here for a few days, maybe a week. He won't get to see anything unless you give it to him. I've told him you are his only source for company financial information. He's going to be starting with the basics. Nina is putting together a collection of all our contracts. You give him premiums and claims. The contracts could take him a week. Even if he sets the contracts aside for later, he'll still get caught up in premium and claim basics."

Levesque became pensive, first staring at the ceiling then back at Sims. From his high perch, he intimidated the man in the wheelchair. "He'll be checking to see if we are remitting all premiums. Of course, we are. Then he'll audit claims. The things he'll be looking for first will check out, thanks to your Operation Perfect Score. But claims are dicier. If he ever gets closer to more serious matters, he either won't recognize it, close up shop, and be out of our hair, or we'll take off. Either way, we should be okay for now."

Lucas didn't buy Levesque's explanation. He agreed that they buried Operation Perfect Score so deep in the company's systems that no auditors, especially Taylor who wasn't even an auditor, could discover the scam. But he worried that a manual, whiteboard analysis could trip them up. Perfect Score covered every contingency he could imagine, but you could never be sure. There might be one simple factor they overlooked.

Levesque broke into his thoughts. "Have you overlaid Perfect Score onto the Guaranty General business yet?"

Lucas had been avoiding doing so for as long as he could. The Great Chicago inquiry posed enough of a threat without running the risk of stirring up suspicion in another insurance company. He had hoped Levesque forgot about Guaranty General. Levesque did not forget.

"No, I've been busy getting ready for Taylor's investigation. I didn't want to divert my attention from a more important matter."

"I'll decide what's important." He slammed his hand on his desk. "Get on it."

Sims stared out over the basketball court toward the view of the Olympic Mountains. He didn't care about the scenery but it allowed his mind to focus. "I don't know how much more I've got in me. Give me a date. When can I take my share and go? This Taylor guy sounds like the real deal."

"Are you still going to Milwaukee?" Levesque asked. "It might be a good idea. You can tell Taylor you've planned this trip for months. Suggest he take time off to do something else while you're gone. I'll plan to be away at the same time. It'll buy us a little more time. We'll split things up and close the scam when you get back. Forget about Guaranty General." Levesque wore a rare smile on his face.

Sims felt instant relief. He almost cheered. "Great idea. I'll confirm my plans and give you my itinerary. In the meantime, I'll keep Taylor busy with more data than he can imagine. Thanks, Jacques."

"And listen, Lucas, when this Taylor guy is with you, make it clear that if he somehow gives us a bad name, he's going to be facing the lawsuit of his life, or worse. You got that?"

He got it. At least an end was in sight.

Chapter Twenty-three

Wells Fargo Center
Seattle, Washington
Monday, July 29, 2019

Jacques Levesque needed a visit to the bank vault after his meeting with Lucas. Nothing buoyed his spirits more than seeing his treasure. Yes, Lucas and he were at risk of discovery. But when he held the diamonds in his fingers, studied their beauty, and experienced their power, he believed he could go on forever. He felt invincible.

He would not close off the scam when Lucas returned from Milwaukee. No way. His goal, though in sight, still eluded him. He needed at least another six to twelve months to accumulate what he thought he required. Everything according to plan.

Before leaving for France, Levesque thought he'd require about eighty million in diamonds. To date, the cost of the diamonds in his box amounted to slightly less than sixty million. Of course, others were entitled to their share, and when he did get to France, Levesque knew the resale market would force him to accept a steep discount from the intermediaries. Still, he expected to net nearly fifty million—certainly enough to live comfortably on the Mediterranean coast.

But that would have to wait. Today, he stood alone in front of the safe deposit box attendant in the bank. Instead of a floor-length dress matching her purple hair, Violet wore a black t-shirt and a micro-mini which matched her orange hair. Even Levesque, who was not easily impressed, thought she looked incredible. After filling Levesque in on her progress toward citizenship, Violet finally left him alone inside the bank vault in a private room, with his safe deposit box.

As if it were a ceremony, he removed the small mahogany wooden box and the black felt pad from the metal drawer. He pushed the drawer to one side and unfolded the pad, pressing it flat against the work surface. Satisfied, he opened the box.

Diamonds were cut using a specific formula to achieve optimal brilliance. Levesque expected the sparkle of his collection to dazzle him. But today, it almost overwhelmed him. The flash and fire pouring out of the small box looked alive, even in artificial light. Breath rushed out of his lungs.

Levesque pushed them around with his right index finger—rearranging them into smaller groups. Larger stones on the right, smaller on the left. He stared at them, in a trance.

When he first began to acquire diamonds, Levesque purchased smaller stones from local jewelers which allowed his inventory to grow quickly. He paid around fifty thousand dollars each. As he learned more about diamonds, he began acquiring larger and higher quality stones from private diamond dealers. Recent purchases averaged around four hundred thousand dollars each. The price of his most valuable diamond, a seven-point-five carat, round, ideal cut, D flawless? Over six-hundred thousand. He stared at it now.

Until three years ago, Levesque knew nothing about diamonds. Even today, though he knew more, he couldn't be called an expert, but he did know the basics. He knew, for example, that the higher quality cut of the diamond, the greater percentage of his purchase price he could expect to realize in resale. Thus, he now concentrated his purchases on round ideal cuts that were as close to perfect as he could find.

At first, Levesque considered keeping the proceeds of the fraud in cash. Simple, but problematic to conceal or move in substantial amounts. Bank or trading accounts were out—too easy for the authorities to trace. Diamonds, on the other hand, possessed qualities that were more subtle and important to him.

He knew diamonds weren't easy to value, and he understood the difficulty he'd face negotiating a fair price with middlemen when he wanted to sell. But he accepted those limitations. On the other hand, they required little space. His entire fortune could be hidden in a hollowed-out book. And diamonds were difficult or impossible to track—no record of ownership. You handed someone a diamond for cash or in payment for a product, and he owned the diamond and you owned the cash or product. No paper trail, no evidence, no nothing. And no tax on profits. For Jacques Levesque, diamonds were the perfect way to store his wealth.

The sound of his phone broke his concentration. The red phone. A text message from Felix.

Yes, I can. I'll be there at five.

He put the phone back into his pocket.

Levesque replaced everything in the box and called Violet. The two of them locked the box, and he left the bank, returning to his office. Though still exhilarated from viewing and feeling his diamonds, his meetings with both Taylor and Lucas worried him.

He needed to see Felix.

Chapter Twenty-four

Wells Fargo Center
Seattle, Washington
Monday, July 29, 2019

Felix arrived at exactly five p.m. He dressed better than most executives in the building and wore a pair of his signature sunglasses. Today, they were by Bulgari. He looked fresh, as if he were just starting his day.

Over the years, Jacques Levesque had become one of Felix's better customers. The work Levesque asked him to do tended to be well-paying, and Felix always respected his important clients. He came to Levesque's office through the side entrance. Only insurance customers used the library entrance.

Levesque was in gym clothes, shooting baskets, and in full sweat when Felix walked in. He had been on the court for a while.

Felix wrinkled his nose at the smell. "When are you going to upgrade that car of yours? Aren't you about ready for a Bentley or something nice like that? That Lexus is for an old man. Guy like you should be driving something like, let's see, one of the McLaren Ultimates, maybe a Senna or a Speedtail. What do you think? Want me to look into one for you? Couple of million should do it."

Felix employed the *always be selling* rule—unless on assignment. Then he was all business. So far, Levesque hadn't given him an assignment, so he remained in selling mode.

Levesque drove his Lexus SUV for a reason. It was consistent with a successful executive but didn't draw undue attention. He would love to have a McLaren Senna, but there were more important things. He might check out the Senna when he arrived in France. Today, though, he wanted to give Felix an assignment.

Jacques motioned for Felix to take a seat on one of two card table chairs normally reserved for players waiting their turn on the court. He grabbed a towel and took the other one. "Maybe next time, Felix. Today, I need you to gather information on someone. The man's name is Ross Taylor. He's been hired by one of our insurance companies to look at our books."

"Can he do that?" Felix asked. "I mean, just come in and ask for your private records?"

"He can if the insurance companies ask him to. It's part of the agreements we have with the companies. They get to send anyone in to check us out whenever they want to. The contracts require us to welcome them.

"I know everything about his business background and how he makes his living. I don't know anything about him personally. That's where you come in. I want you to check him out—where he lives, his family status, where he hangs out, how he spends his spare time, what's important to him, that kind of stuff. Full report. Usual terms."

"Sounds good. When do you need the report? The longer you give me, the more I'll get for you."

Levesque thought about it. "I'm pressed for time. He's starting tomorrow. I'll need something by Wednesday. See what you can do."

"Can do. Is this guy trouble for you? Do you need anything else? Anything at all. Just let me know."

Felix hesitated before sharing his next bit of information. "I hear Lucas may be gambling again. I called Stubby to introduce him to a new client. He told me about Lucas."

Jacques thanked him for the information.

After Felix left, Levesque went back to shooting baskets. It helped him think better. At first, when Christine Bell told him about Ross Taylor's assignment, he thought nothing of it. No one could detect Operation Perfect Score. Lucas Sims had introduced a sort of "trojan horse" into their operating system which caused the system to perform authorized and unauthorized functions simultaneously. Certain claims funds were being diverted into private bank accounts. Lucas continued to assure him that no one could find it and, so far, no auditors had come close.

Now, as he shot baskets, Levesque had a bad feeling about Ross Taylor. And Lucas Sims bothered him even more. He required close watching. Levesque knew Lucas was nearing the breaking point, and if he'd gone back to gambling as well, he could be a real problem.

Chapter Twenty-five

Wells Fargo Center
Seattle, Washington
Tuesday, July 30, 2019

Lucas Sims and Nina Petaluma were waiting in the library for Taylor when he arrived at LeGrande Benefits. A coffee service, presented in the same china as the day before, lay on the table. Today, a small plate of scones added to the high style. The room looked identical to yesterday, though no doubt, it had been thoroughly dusted and polished. Today, Taylor anticipated his assignment for Great Chicago Insurance Company.

"We're pleased you're here, Ross," Lucas Sims began. "Jacques insisted you preferred to be called Ross rather than Mr. Taylor. This is my associate, Nina Petaluma. She's our general counsel and chief compliance officer. I'm Lucas Sims, the company CFO."

They all shook hands, then helped themselves to coffee.

"Let's get started." Taylor repeated the introduction made to Jacques Levesque the day before. "I'll be performing the analysis from my office, so I'll be communicating with you primarily via email. You can use email or text to provide the data I'll request from you this morning. I don't expect to spend a great deal of time here except when a personal meeting seems warranted. I may want to discuss preliminary conclusions with you before I relay them to Great Chicago. I find those discussions are better conducted in person."

Sims and Petaluma nodded in agreement.

Taylor handed each of them a brief list of information sets he wanted. It included data on premiums, claims, commissions, administration fees, producer contracts, and cash receipts and disbursements related to Great Chicago, along with format instructions. He requested a specific format for the data because having it in that form allowed Schlump and him to sort using any parameters they chose.

After glancing at the list, Sims said, "Jacques has asked me to be your primary source of information about our company. I don't see anything on this list I can't get you this morning. Anything else you need, just email or text. We've set up a private, secure office for you while you're in our building. Feel free to come and go and use it as you please. Oskar will show you how to set up your security access and our email and text encryption process."

Nina handed Taylor a notebook. "I'll send you this by email as well, but we thought you might like an organized set of all our important contracts and documents. It includes our corporate organization papers, sales and administration agreements with our insurance company partners, and major client contracts. You'll also find officer bios and specimen employee and broker contracts.

We have engaged third-party vendors who do work for us such as software developers and human resource consultants. Those contracts are there as well."

This meeting represented a good start, and Taylor told them so. Both Lucas and Nina seemed more than willing to make his job easier. After exchanging minor questions and answers, Ross and Nina stood up to end the meeting.

Nina asked, "Why are you auditing LeGrande specifically?"

Taylor set his briefcase back on the table. "You both know why I'm here. And it's Great Chicago who's ordered the audit, not me. LeGrande is their largest producer and also administers premiums and claims on that business, making you their largest administrator as well. My partner and I are looking at everyone they do business with, not just LeGrande. And we're looking at Great Chicago internally. Be assured we aren't looking solely at LeGrande."

Lucas and Nina expressed their thanks for the background and assured Taylor of their intent to cooperate in any way possible. The meeting ended in less than forty-five minutes.

As he headed to the elevator, Taylor thought about Schlump's comment last week—that Great Chicago's problem couldn't be mispricing. If that were true, someone was stealing Great Chicago's money. And he might have just left a meeting with them.

Chapter Twenty-six

Yacht Haven Marina
Lake Union
Seattle, Washington
Tuesday, July 30, 2019

Thoroughly absorbed in his thoughts, Taylor turned off Westlake onto the Fremont Bridge near the marina. As he passed over the drawbridge, the bells started clanging, shaking him out of his concentration. The gates began to lower behind him but he didn't notice. Instead, he focused on Sims's and Petaluma's willingness to work with him. Encouraging. It might be a straightforward analysis.

The Taylors were assigned two spaces in the marina parking lot across the street from Yacht Haven, part of the slip rental agreement. Kim always parked her black Mazda Miata convertible at the end—less likely to get dinged by another car. Ross didn't share her concern and always selected the spot closest to the marina entrance. Today, he pulled his Toyota Land Cruiser into the first open spot.

He missed having a large garage. Phoenix had been dry, and the cars were always clean. Here, because of the gravel parking lot and the frequent rain, their cars were always dirty. Regardless, he felt good to get back to the marina.

As he walked onto the main dock toward the *Pura Vida*, Taylor noticed hundreds of seagulls circling the marina. It sounded as if all were squawking at once. One of the marina tenants had been fishing outside the locks and was cleaning salmon on the back of his boat. The marina rules prohibited fish cleaning, but Taylor didn't care, and he liked the guy. They waved to each other and exchanged a thumbs-up as Taylor climbed aboard the *Pura Vida*.

"Anybody home?" Taylor shouted down the companionway. He heard the usual jazz playing and hoped Kim hadn't left for her appointment yet. He wanted to have lunch with her and tell her about his meeting. But no response.

Alone aboard the *Pura Vida*, he went below and changed into clothes more suitable for an early summer afternoon on a boat before settling in at his desk.

Overall, he thought things went fairly well during the past two days at LeGrande. Yesterday's meeting with Levesque seemed cordial. Aside from the obvious confidence, Taylor saw nothing in Levesque's body language or heard anything in his conversation to lead him to any conclusions—one way or the other. Levesque projected success and was used to getting what he wanted. Of course, so was Taylor.

He felt good about Sims. Christine Bell heaped praise

on him as well. Her own CFO called Sims the best CFO they worked with and said that LaGrande's systems, which Sims developed, were better than most major insurance companies. Just how good they were would be revealed when Taylor started extracting data. Of course, now that he knew of Winston Lester's history, he wondered if he could rely on Lester's praise.

Between the notebook of contracts and the box of hard-copy data Sims gave him as he walked out, Taylor didn't need anything else to keep himself occupied until he received the emails. If Sims followed his formatting instructions, he could sort the data in any manner he wished, giving Schlump and him a clearer picture quickly.

He was impressed with the top three executives at LeGrande and not surprised at the company's success. He found it difficult to imagine a fraud coming out of LeGrande Benefits. Levesque should be making a great deal of money from the business. Just to be sure he covered all the bases, Taylor would ask Schlump to investigate their backgrounds more thoroughly. His friend Postiglione had already proved his worth twice. Schlump told him the guy could find anything, especially things that no one else knew.

His phone alerted him to an encrypted email from Lucas Sims. There were twenty-one attachments. He opened one at random. A list of all claims paid by LeGrande on behalf of Great Chicago during 2017. He noted that he could sort the list in any of dozens of ways including date of service, date claim paid, employer group, claimant name, or dentist name, and a few others. It appeared Lucas Sims provided them with exactly what he and Schlump hoped for. This seemed like a good start. He immediately forwarded the email to Schlump.

Now he'd divide up the work with Schlump, and they could begin their analysis. When the two conducted this kind of investigation in the past, they used earlier templates as outlines. It would still be necessary to contact the leadership at Consolidated and Argus to get Schlump on their schedule. That could wait until tomorrow.

He heard a knock on the side of the boat. He went up on deck and saw the dock attendant. "Hi, Liz. What's up?"

"Sorry to bother you, but I just want to apologize if Brutus kept you guys awake last night. Someone came on the dock during the night, and Brutus made a lot of noise. Then he got loose and chased the guy into the parking lot. Jim went up and heard a car but didn't see anything."

Ross didn't wake up once last night. "Didn't hear a thing, Liz. Brutus is our favorite, and if he barked, it must have been for a good reason. Here, give him this and thank him for keeping us safe." He handed her one of the dog treats they kept just for Brutus. "Maybe there's something on the security cameras at the marina office."

"I checked. They're out again. Nothing."

Could it possibly have been Derek?

He shook off the thought and thanked Liz for the information.

One more thing to do before heading up to The Rudder for a late lunch. He dialed Christine Bell's office number. No need for him to bother her on her private number if she were busy.

She answered on the first ring. "Hi, Ross. How did it go?"

Taylor reported on the success of his two meetings and the high quality of the data that Lucas Sims and Nina Petaluma provided. He told her to expect an updated status report on LeGrande at the end of the week. He also told her to expect his complete schedule for examining Argus and Consolidated by then as well.

She seemed satisfied. "I don't know if I emphasized strongly enough how important it is that we resolve this problem quickly. I need answers and I need them soon. And if you need to come here and investigate Winston's part in the operation, do it. But don't waste any time, or I'll have to get someone else to do the job. Are we clear?"

Taylor never doubted the importance of the assignment to Christine. She called him in the first place because she knew his reputation as the best at what he did. But he didn't remember her ever being so assertive, almost threatening. Maybe he should tell her to go find someone else.

Then, he thought, her concerns were not unreasonable, and she labored under a great weight of pressure. After a brief pause, he said, "Of course, Christine. You're quite clear. We're making good progress, and I'm coming to your offices next week to check out Winston and his operation personally. You won't be disappointed. I assure you I will know what happened to your money in a short period of time."

After they hung up, he called and left a message for Kim. He knew she scheduled an interview that morning and wouldn't answer. He told her he loved her and planned to be at the boat when she returned, then he walked up to The Rudder. He needed a break and a beer.

Crenshaw occupied his usual place near the end of the bar, wiping glasses. Taylor sat on the last stool, happy because he always hoped to find it unoccupied. Crenshaw walked over.

"Hey, Ross. A priest, a minister, and a rabbi are arguing about who's best at his job. To settle the matter, they each go into the toughest part of town, find a tough man, and attempt to convert him to their faith. Later they get together.

"The priest begins. 'When I found my man, I read to him from the Catechism and sprinkled him with holy water. Next week is his First Communion.'

"'I found a man under the tracks by the river,' says the minister, 'and preached God's holy word. He was so moved that he let me baptize him.'

"They both look down at the rabbi, who's lying on a gurney in a body cast. 'Looking back,' he says, 'maybe I shouldn't have started with the circumcision.'"

Chapter Twenty-seven

The Rudder
Lake Union
Seattle, Washington
Tuesday, July 30, 2019

The first thing that caught the attention of anyone entering The Rudder was the rudders. They were everywhere. Hanging on the walls. Hanging from the ceiling. Even serving as tabletops. The sign in front of the restaurant, according to popular legend, replicated the rudder from Blackbeard's *Queen Anne's Revenge*. It equaled the size of a double garage door.

Rudders were movable flat surfaces in the water at the stern connected to the steering wheel or tiller and moved side-to-side to steer the boat. Each of the rudders at The Rudder, except the sign in front, steered a real boat at one time. Now they were decorations.

Nautical-style chandeliers lighted the interior, and the place had a warm feeling. Multi-pane, floor-to-ceiling bay windows brought light into the front and the two sides. They were set only six feet apart so that almost every table had a clear view out. Most customers saw boats and the water of Lake Union. Any space on a wall not covered by a rudder displayed a different nautical theme—nets, glass buoys, or ship's lanterns. Rough-sawn wood planks created the appearance of ship's decks, but all eyes were ultimately drawn to the seven-foot statue of Blackbeard in the center of the dining room.

The lunch crowd had thinned, and only a few of the tables were occupied. The staff in the public areas all wore the same uniform. Navy-blue collared shirts with white buttons, navy-blue pants, black belts, and black leather hip-length aprons. The kitchen staff all wore cook-whites. The various uniforms created a highly professional look.

Ross and Kim had lunch at The Rudder the first day they moved aboard their boat at the Yacht Haven Marina. More than three years passed, and they had been coming here two or three times a week ever since.

From the entry, the dining area occupied the left two-thirds of the public space. The bar was on the right. As often as possible, Ross and Kim sat on the last two stools at the end of the bar. From there, they could see the entire restaurant and look out at the lake through the windows behind them. Frequently, they found "Reserved" signs on the bar in front of those stools when they arrived. The signs were for them, compliments of their friend and favorite bartender, Crenshaw.

Alone today, Taylor had moved the signs to one side when he came in and anticipated Crenshaw's first joke. It was one of Crenshaw's best, and in high spirits, Taylor ordered lunch. "Fish and chips today, Crenshaw."

"Speaking of fish and chips, a couple of priests just

opened a fish and chips shop up the street. One's the Fish Friar and the other is the Chip Monk."

Without waiting for a response, Crenshaw turned around and put in Taylor's food order. Then he brought him the Fremont Lush IPA he knew Taylor wanted.

"How's your much better half?" He leaned against the backbar and enjoyed a few rare moments of rest. "I can never figure out how somebody like you could land a girl like Kim. I should be so lucky. Is she as perfect as she seems?"

"I can't figure it out either, but I agree with you. She's at an interview right now with *The Puget Sound Business Journal*. She's trying to get an engagement to write an article for them about some prominent figure—she thinks she could get Bill Gates. Can you imagine that?"

"She doesn't happen to have a twin sister, does she?" It didn't seem to matter to Crenshaw that Kim and Ross were at least fifteen years older than he or that they'd been married for twenty-one years. Or that he already had a girlfriend. He meant well.

"Sorry. No such luck." Taylor decided to take advantage of a few minutes alone with Crenshaw. "How long have you been tending bar at The Rudder?"

"A little over eight years. The time sure flies."

"Have you always tended bar?"

"No. Actually, this is my third bartending gig. I grew up here and went to college with a plan to become a lawyer. I played on the golf team at Washington State, but I quit before finishing undergraduate. I went in the Army for three years—even got selected for Officer Candidate School. I thought about making a career of it but wound up staying as an enlisted man until I got out." He poured himself a club soda and resumed his place against the backbar.

"After the Army, I finished school at Chico State in California. I hated the place, but I only had three semesters to go, and they let me in. So, I put up with it. Had time to play all the golf I wanted and finished with a degree in finance."

"You have a degree in finance? What are you doing here?"

"I was good at it, Ross. I understood it all, and I knew how to apply it. Fidelity Investments, Wells Fargo, and Metropolitan Life all offered me jobs. There were others. The problem? I couldn't stand finance. I took the offer from Fidelity but that didn't last. But I've got a great story from that experience. Just a second."

Crenshaw excused himself and filled drink orders for a couple of new customers who were also enjoying the afternoon.

Minutes later, he returned. "I took the job as a financial analyst with Fidelity Investments in San Francisco analyzing stock market trends. Chained to a desk making around fifty thousand. Loved Fidelity, hated the job. No money to spend, I could barely pay my rent. That was early in 2010, about the time I started my first bartending gig at night to make ends meet. By then, I just wanted a decent job back here.

"I had a girlfriend in Seattle, and she'd give me money to fly up here every now and then. She'd fly to San Francisco to stay with me on other weekends. On one of my trips to Seattle, I met her brother who told me he had connections with Amazon. He and I hit it off immediately. He offered to get me set up in a job at Amazon in supply chain management for $120k starting on April first. I couldn't believe my good luck. I'd be living the dream."

Taylor could tell from Crenshaw's animation that he enjoyed telling this story.

"I quit the job at Fidelity and moved back to Seattle. While I waited for April first, because I had no money, I sold my car, slept on the floor of the apartment of a buddy and his new wife, and tended bar at night—my second gig. Then my girlfriend broke up with me. She got jealous of the fact that the girls who frequented the bar flirted with me."

"Were you broke at the time?"

"Yeah. I borrowed money from my mother, bought new clothes and a new briefcase, and got a haircut to get ready for the new job. I showed up on the first of April, rode the elevator to the brother's floor at Amazon, and presented at the receptionist's desk.

"The brother stomped out, irate. 'Who the hell do you think you are? You break up with my sister and expect me to get you a job? You're just a punk. A bartender. Get the hell out of here before I kick your ass.'"

"What'd you do next?"

"I couldn't breathe. I had no job. I had no money. I had no car. I owed my mother money for my clothes. My buddy and his wife were tired of me being in their small apartment, so I had no place to stay. I was sick and could barely move.

"I staggered onto the elevator in a daze. The door

opened at the ground floor, and the brother and about twenty other people yelled, 'April Fools' and screamed with laughter. They'd been putting me on.

"I knocked out three of his teeth and left him unconscious. Took me a year and a half to get the charges dropped. Been here ever since."

Taylor was speechless. He'd learned more about Crenshaw in two minutes than he had in the last two years. And he liked him more for it. "You're my new hero, Crenshaw." Then, almost as an afterthought, he said, "You know, I feel kind of like an idiot calling you by your last name for over three years, but I don't even know your first name. What is it?"

"It's Crenshaw. My name is Crenshaw West." He walked away again.

Taylor noticed that Crenshaw walked with a new limp as he worked behind the bar today. When he came back, Taylor asked, "What's up with the wheels?"

"I had to close up last night. So, I'm rolling the trash container out to the front and some jackass roared out of the marina parking lot without his lights. I barely jumped out of the way—tripped on the curb. Twisted my ankle. I'm all right though. I could still beat you to the corner and back."

"Sure you could." Taylor smiled as he finished his beer. "Do you still play golf?"

"Quite a bit, actually." Crenshaw dried drink glasses. "At least a couple times a week. How about you?"

"Not much since we moved to Seattle and onto the boat. I used to play a lot when we were in Phoenix. It fit right in with my work. Now, my sticks are in the storage trailer gathering dust. Maybe I'll get them out and give you a lesson."

"Fat chance."

Ross Taylor didn't mind eating his lunch and trading smack with Crenshaw at any time. Today, he appreciated Crenshaw more than ever, but he wanted to get back to the data Lucas Sims had sent. Christine wanted results and so did he. He paid his bill and stood up to leave.

"Thanks, Ross. I enjoyed talking with you. Say, someday, could you give me a tour of your boat? I've always wanted to sail, and I'd love to see it. I'll bring a bottle of wine."

Taylor told him to come anytime and thanked him again.

"If there's ever any way I can be of help to you, whatever it might be, please let me know. There might be something in my background you could use."

Taylor went back to the *Pura Vida*, remembering what Liz had told him about someone being on the dock last night.

Chapter Twenty-eight

Bainbridge Island Ferry
Seattle, Washington
Wednesday, July 31, 2019

The text message from Felix got straight to the point:
I have what you need.
Where do you want to meet?
Levesque responded:

2nd and Marion. In front of
the escalator. 10 minutes

Though anxious to hear Felix's report about Ross Taylor, he didn't want to talk about it in the office. The security system inside his company featured state-of-the-art electronics, yet with important things, you could never be too careful. They would take a walk instead.

He looked outside and couldn't see a cloud in the sky. With rare exceptions, Seattleites were enjoying some of the best weather ever this year. No need for a jacket. He rode the elevator to the main lobby and walked out the west exit.

The homeless were demonstrating again. At least two hundred—more than normal. A pack of them were riding up and down the escalator to the street, harassing the office workers coming in and out of the Wells Fargo Center. They weren't there every day, but it seemed like it. Sick of putting up with them, Levesque thought the Seattle police ought to do something to clear them out. Of course, they did nothing.

Felix waited at the bottom of the escalator. "Where do you want to talk?"

Felix must have left his job in the building lobby early, because he wore casual clothes—a black sweatsuit. But, true to fashion, he wore sunglasses. Today he sported OhO Sunshine glasses with light blue lenses. They featured unusually thick rims and temples. A black Mariners cap completed the ensemble.

"Let's walk toward the waterfront."

The two men walked around the demonstrators, crossed Second Avenue, and headed west toward the ferry docks. Levesque got to the reason for the meeting. "What do you have?"

"I talked to a couple of people who know how to find things out, and I did a little poking around myself. Ross Taylor is quite an interesting guy."

Felix removed a small notebook from his sweatshirt pocket and began his report.

"Born in Chicago, he's fifty-one years old. He played basketball in high school, just like you did, but not good enough to stay on the team in college—maybe because he went to a Big Ten school. He graduated from Illinois then picked up an MBA at Arizona State with an emphasis in accounting. You should know, Jacques, he's still a solid baller, even at fifty-one. He holds his own with the younger guys up at Green Lake and a couple of other parks at least twice a week.

"He also boxed on a club team in college. Did pretty well in his weight class. I only found one thing about him ever getting into any kind of scrape after finishing school, but it was a doozy. From what I heard, he and his wife were out for dinner during their time in Arizona. He went to get the car while she talked with a friend. When she walked out of the restaurant, two guys grabbed her and pulled her between the buildings. They wanted her jewelry and her purse. Taylor jumped out of the car and beat them to a pulp. Broke their arms."

Levesque remained silent. They were at the Colman Dock, approaching the Bainbridge Island ferry. The 3:45. Jacques gestured toward it.

Felix shrugged. "Why not?"

They bought tickets and walked onto the boat. A nice day, they walked up the stairs to the top deck, where they stayed on the rear, facing the city. By doing so, they were looking away from the sun and partially protected from the wind. The round trip took a little less than two hours, but there were more topics Jacques wished to discuss. The time would be well spent.

Felix continued his report. "On the business front, before coming to Seattle, Taylor worked for Arizona Life and Health Insurance Company as their CEO. The story is that he did an excellent job until someone stole money from the company. He discovered it and recovered the funds, but the chairman of the board blamed him and fired him.

"He worked there for almost ten years and, despite

his dismissal, could have gone to any of at least a dozen other companies if he wanted to, but he and his wife thought they'd earned enough money and wanted to take life easy and enjoy it.

"I've put all this in a written report that I emailed you just before our meeting." Felix looked down and read from his notebook, fighting the wind to keep the pages organized. "He met Christine Bell during his days at Arizona Life and Health. She attended a conference where he spoke about insurance fraud. He'd been a victim a few times and decided to make it something like his life's work to see that nobody ever got away with it again. After his speech, she followed up with him, and the two stayed in touch.

"His father actually swindled an insurance company, if you can believe that. Put up fake bonds as surplus, whatever that means. According to my source—let me read this—the company became extended on a block of annuities and went insolvent. The regulators discovered his involvement, and he did time. I don't know what all of this means but you probably do. It broke up the family, and my source tells me Taylor never forgave his father."

Felix continued, "He's married to the former Kim Summers. She grew up in Friday Harbor and is forty-seven years old. They have one child, a son who they haven't seen in years. Just took off one day during high school. I don't know why. Before she met Taylor, she went to U Dub and studied journalism and creative writing. She wrote features for the old *P.I.* then went into freelance writing. She writes magazine articles about famous people and recently ghost-wrote the memoir of a famous transplant surgeon. Reports tell me she's a real looker too."

Levesque looked away and contemplated the information Felix gave him. The picture he formed of Ross Taylor started to become clearer. More so than he expected. But he still needed to know more.

"Here's an interesting thing about them. They can afford to live just about anywhere they'd want in the Seattle area, but they live on a boat. At Yacht Haven Marina up at the north end of Lake Union. It's a nice boat, don't get me wrong. Over fifty feet, a sailboat. But it's not Mercer Island."

He paused and refitted his cap when it started to blow off in the wind. He adjusted his sunglasses. "The marina has a main dock which extends south from the shore about four hundred and fifty feet. Four shorter docks extend perpendicular to the main dock, each of which extends to the west about a hundred feet. It looked to me like there were from five to seven boats on either side of the smaller docks—maybe fifty or sixty in all in the marina. It was dark so I couldn't say for sure. Being one of the largest boats, Taylor's is at the end of the last dock—the farthest from the entrance."

"Knowing exactly where he lives might prove useful someday. What did he do before Great Chicago hired him?" Levesque wanted to have a better feeling for the risk that Taylor might pose.

"That's the most interesting part. He's extremely selective about how he spends his time. Since he left Arizona, Taylor has been doing occasional assignments for insurance companies. He's been at it for a couple of years. He knows the CEOs at dozens of them, and they all respect him for his understanding of the business. They call him regularly, and he takes the jobs he finds interesting. He must have found Great Chicago interesting."

By this time, the ferry landed in the Bainbridge Island ferry terminal. They didn't intend to get off. The *Wenatchee* was a double-ender, so it didn't turn around. The two men walked to the other end, so that they were protected from the wind when the boat started moving again. They found a private spot where their backs would be toward the sun, and they once again faced the Seattle skyline—now about ten miles away. They continued their conversation.

"Does he have any bad habits, any history he would prefer not to become public?" Levesque asked.

Once again Felix pulled his cap down and adjusted his sunglasses. "We couldn't find a thing out of the ordinary. As far as we can tell, he's never wandered away from his wife and never taken an illegal dime from the companies he's worked for. None of his insurance or securities licenses has ever been suspended or revoked. He doesn't use any drugs. He likes his beer and wine, but it doesn't seem to be a problem. He did have one speeding ticket, but that happened in high school. I'm afraid we couldn't find anything you could hold over him."

"That's good enough for now. I've got Lucas working with him at the office. Lucas won't give him anything to cause me any trouble. Taylor should be out of my hair in a week or so—three at the most. Christine Bell will be satisfied that we aren't the source of Great Chicago's problems."

The ferry crossed the halfway point on the trip back to Seattle. The late-afternoon sun reflected off the office building windows, and the waterfront commerce began to come into view, a highlight for the tourists. The two men didn't notice.

"Speaking of Lucas, how's he doing?" Felix asked, looking straight ahead. "Has he performed the way you wanted him to? That con we pulled on him back in 2015 should have a book written about it. You caught him hook, line, and sinker."

Levesque smiled. "He never suspected a thing. The idea of Bruno Cento sending someone after him scared him, and he couldn't think straight. He bought the whole charade. Cento probably never even heard of him. That guy you brought in played his part like an Oscar winner. I wound up being the savior. Lucas would have done anything to get my help. And he's done everything I asked him to. Even better than I hoped. We're running systems the IRS couldn't work through."

Levesque turned and looked back toward Bainbridge. He smiled to himself at the thought of what he had done, then returned his attention to Felix.

"But I'm afraid he's starting to get cold feet. He's always been sensitive about going off the straight and narrow, but lately he's become even more nervous. He wants out. He could be a threat. I need your help defusing that threat."

Levesque had paid Felix a great deal of money through the years they had known each other. Felix didn't know the details of what Jacques did for a living. Jacques paid him well, and he didn't need to know. Still, he might have suspected. After all, he had helped Levesque set up the fake strongarm man and provided the thirty sets of fake identification. Today might be the turning point.

Jacques continued. "Lucas and I have a business arrangement which I want to continue for at least another six months, maybe a year. He wants to pull out today. Of course, he can't just pull out on his own. I'm in complete control of that. No, I'm worried that he might decide to give up and talk to someone about what we've been doing—someone like Taylor or, even worse, the police."

Felix Contador's demeanor changed. Both men were quiet now, contemplating the conversation so far. The next few minutes would be crucial. What came next might change the relationship between the two men forever. Jacques Levesque wanted a problem solved, and he'd seen Felix's talent in action with his disposal of the strongarm man/actor.

"Lucas is going to Milwaukee next week. Here are his travel plans." Levesque handed Felix a single sheet of paper folded into quarters. "If something were to happen to him while he's traveling, it would definitely remove the threat I feel."

"Setting him up for a shakedown is one thing, Jacques, but hurting him or killing him is something else. I know I've done some things like this and normally I'd be the right person, but he lives in a wheelchair. I can't help you with this one." Felix looked straight ahead, not at Jacques.

Levesque let the words sink in before saying anything. Then he spoke. "Yeah, I think you will, Felix. This is important to both of us."

"Why is it important to me?"

"First, Felix, let me explain why it's important to me. Then we'll get to you. I have an especially lucrative business going. Lucas is an important part of it. If he decides he's finished, he'll either just walk away or, worse, tell someone about it. Either way, I'm in great jeopardy. But he's my only risk. If he's no longer a threat, I can keep the business going as long as I want.

"But, Felix, here's why it's important to you. You've been a big help to me through the years, and I've paid you well. No problems, no disagreements. But I need to keep our relationship that way. I need to know I can count on you—that you'll continue to profit from our arrangement. It'll be well worth your while."

"What if I don't go along with you? What if I say no?"

"I don't think you'll do that. Remember the guy we hired to threaten Lucas, the big guy? You never told me what happened to him. You didn't want me to know, and I didn't want to know. But I saw you, Felix. On the Bremerton Ferry. The night you dumped him in the water. So did Aubrey. We saw it all. And I have pictures." He paused. "Right now, I have no need to make those pictures available to the authorities. If you help me out on this matter, I'll give them to you."

Felix continued to look straight ahead in shock. His legs weakened momentarily, and he gripped the railing tighter. As quick as it came, the feeling passed. This news changed everything. For an instant, he thought about dumping Levesque in the water but then thought better of it. There were too many witnesses. Besides, his OhO

Sunshine video sunglasses were still in record mode. Mutually assured destruction. "Tell me exactly what you'd like me to do."

Jacques Levesque gave the order to Felix Contador to "take care of" Lucas Sims. He told him what he wanted, and he told him how much he would pay. Even Felix found the offer to be quite appealing. They agreed to the terms of the assignment. And all on the record.

By then, the ferry arrived in Colman Dock, and passengers and cars were leaving. The two men walked down the stairs and off the boat. No more words were spoken as they walked with the crowd toward Alaskan Way. They stopped briefly, and Jacques handed Felix a thick envelope. Without looking into it, he put it into the waistband of his sweatpants and disappeared into the crowd walking toward the south.

As he strolled away, Felix wondered if he should call Gerhardt Bergmann.

Chapter Twenty-nine

Yacht Haven Marina
Lake Union
Seattle, Washington
Thursday, August 1, 2019

Schlump sat in his usual place inside the main cabin of the *Pura Vida*—on the centerline, to keep the boat from listing to one side or the other. He and Ross were enjoying a mid-morning snack before getting back to work while the hard rain poured outside. They had spent the morning discussing LeGrande.

Schlump stopped eating for a moment. "Did you just make this, Kim? In my life I've never tasted such good bread. I'd love to take a slice or two home to Trudy." Schlump began eating his third slice of warm Swedish *limpa* bread, this time spreading it with butter rather than blackberry jam.

Taylor finished only his first, although equally impressed. "You'd say that about any food, Schlump. You should take care of yourself, like I do." As he said so, he lifted his shirt to display what a fifty-something man called washboards.

"So, you take care of yourself. Big deal. All that means is that someday you'll be lying in a hospital bed dying of nothing."

Typical banter.

Kim refilled their coffee mugs. "I got up at four o'clock, like I do every morning, Schlump. Takes about three hours. It looks as if you're enjoying everything."

"I can neither confirm nor deny your outrageous allegation. But I do applaud your commitment to fine food." Schlump continued to eat.

"Here's another loaf. You can take it home to Trudy." Kim handed it over with a grin.

In fact, the bread came from a Scandinavian bakery a mile north of the marina near Seattle Pacific University. The Taylors went there for the *limpa* and other treats at least once a week, and Kim had picked up two loaves this morning, but she wouldn't admit it to Schlump.

"Now, I have to get back to my preparation for a phone conference I've scheduled with the assistant to Richard Branson. They agreed to talk to me about an interview. You get back to work." Kim went forward into the office, hers to use this morning.

"Richard Branson," Schlump said. "How does she do it? He's one of the most recognizable people in the world. Do you think she'll get to meet him?"

"I don't know. But she's landed interviews with heavy hitters all over the country through the years. Jack Welch, Paul Allen before he died, Clint Eastwood. She interviewed me too."

"You don't count. You weren't important. Besides, we're talking twenty years ago. But Richard Branson. That's impressive. Keep me posted."

"I will."

"Say, was the information Postiglione got you on the stalker of any use?"

"You bet. I met with the guy. Explained to him how he shouldn't do that sort of thing. Then I emphasized the point. We haven't heard from him since."

"I'll tell Tony you put his information to good use."

"It's great to be working together again."

"I agree, Ross. You're the only one who ever understood me, and you don't understand me."

An authority on arcane data, he said, "You know, Ross, according to the actuaries, the statistics on sanity are that one out of every four Americans is suffering from a form of mental illness. Think of your three best friends. If they're okay, then it's you."

The two men reopened their laptops and began reviewing what they knew about the assignment to date. Two weeks of little progress since Ross's engagement by Great Chicago put them behind on his self-imposed schedule. On top of that, Christine Bell made it clear that she wanted results quickly or she'd find someone else. Time for him to crank up the intensity.

"Okay. Let me summarize what we've agreed on so far. You've been through a high-level review of the data, and you've concluded that Great Chicago isn't the victim of bad luck in their claims. I agree. Also, they accurately calculated the premiums they should be charging and are collecting those premiums. So, their problem isn't premium inadequacy. I agree with you on that as well.

"You also told me that, according to the data, the proportion of claims for preventive, basic, and major dentistry are all within their expected range. For example, nothing stands out like dentists abusing the system by upgrading to expensive porcelain crowns instead of cheaper metal crowns just because someone has insurance. Or the claims administrators changing the codes for services. It must be something else."

Listening carefully, Schlump nodded along. "That's a good summary. It should narrow our focus. Still, Great Chicago's losses are excessive. We're going to have to dig a lot deeper into the claims than we have so far. This is Thursday. I'll perform an in-depth analysis on the claim files between now and Sunday night."

"All right. And, just so you know, I confirmed with Christine that she told Argus and Consolidated to be ready to open their books to you. She promised you'll have no trouble with them. If you haven't already scheduled with them, they're waiting for you."

"Good. I've set aside next Monday and Tuesday to visit Argus in Kansas City. I'll go to Atlanta on Wednesday and spend a couple of days looking around and gathering data at Consolidated. I have friends at both places. They're both expecting me and have promised full cooperation."

Schlump passed a sheet of paper containing the names of his contacts over to Ross. At the same time, Taylor updated his note file.

"Sounds good. I've already started my analysis of LeGrande. I plan to do nothing else through the weekend. I haven't seen or heard anything at LeGrande to make me suspicious of them, but I want to know everything as quickly as possible.

"Lucas Sims is going to be out of the office at a conference in Milwaukee next week, so I've scheduled a visit with Great Chicago on Monday through Wednesday. Christine is certain that there's nothing going on internally, but I want to satisfy myself that the problem isn't inside their own company. She may be right, but in effect, she assigned her own financial people to audit themselves. We'd be fools not to check them out, especially knowing what we do about Winston. She agrees."

Taylor paused for a few moments, deep in thought. "Maybe we shouldn't discard premium fraud so quickly. One administrator I investigated collected premiums from every client but only forwarded the premium to the insurance company for about three-quarters of those clients. He took a chance by identifying a group of clients who he thought were unlikely to submit claims. For those clients, he just kept the premium for himself—effectively making himself the insurance company. When he did get claims, he paid them out of his own account. The insurance company didn't even know the clients existed. For the administrator, an extraordinarily lucrative scam."

"How'd you catch him?" Schlump asked.

"We reviewed the complaint files for his company at the State Insurance Department. We found complaints and resolutions for people who didn't show up as clients on our audits. It didn't take long to unravel the fraud."

"Maybe we'd better do some cross-checking," Schlump said. "I'll spend this afternoon on the LeGrande data. I'll look for claims that were paid for clients for which no record exists. It's a long shot but may be worth the time."

Taylor and Schlump decided it was time to part company. They finished their coffee and bread and put on their rain gear. Kim remained in the office with the door closed, so they didn't bother her. They moved into the cockpit of the boat where the rain continued to pour. Ross got off the boat—always tricky in the rain; the decks could be slippery. He didn't say it out loud, but he felt concern that Schlump might slip and fall. At four hundred pounds, Schlump would be a load to catch if he did fall. Today, guarding the loaf of bread, he moved like a gazelle.

Taylor enjoyed the rain. He wore his yellow rain jacket, pants, and hat which kept him dry. He saw no one else on the dock, so he decided to walk up to shore and take a half-hour loop through the neighborhood. He checked on their cars and walked over the Fremont Bridge and back.

He thought about the Great Chicago assignment. It took a long time to get started, and now he felt like they were falling behind his commitment. If the data pointed toward fraud, there were four logical candidates: LeGrande, Argus, Consolidated, and Great Chicago itself. So far, they were barely underway at LeGrande, and they hadn't even started at the others. If it was fraud and the criminals sensed him closing in, they would either disappear or retaliate. In either event, he stood to be the loser. He'd need to cover a great deal of ground between now and the end of next week.

Instead of stopping for a quick lunch at The Rudder, Taylor walked back along the dock to the *Pura Vida*. He found a note taped to a lamp from Kim. She would be gone until late afternoon, so he went into the office and opened his computer.

He hadn't noticed the black Lincoln Continental parked across from the marina that he had passed a few minutes ago.

Chapter Thirty

Wells Fargo Center
Seattle, Washington
Thursday, August 1, 2019

At the same time Taylor and Schlump were discussing strategy on Taylor's boat, Jacques Levesque sat in his office at LeGrande Benefits, contemplating his next moves. Nina Petaluma walked in.

A small woman, Nina stood barely five feet tall and weighed no more than one hundred pounds. She all but disappeared in the cavernous office and the oversized chairs at Levesque's desk. Levesque liked her and appreciated her hard work. Loyal to him beyond question, she sensed nothing below board going on at LeGrande.

"Have you heard back from Taylor yet?" he asked.

"Not a word. I gave him all the contracts like you asked, and he seemed satisfied. Nothing since."

Levesque pondered what she said. He wanted Taylor to waste as much time as possible on the contracts.

"I'm sure you'll hear from him eventually. When you do, I'd like you to propose meeting with him to go through those contracts in detail. Make sure he understands everything about our relationship with Great Chicago—our roles, responsibilities, history, how the cash flows, everything."

"I'll take care of it. Anything else?" Nina Petaluma didn't hang around for idle chatter.

"Do you know anything about extradition law?"

"Not since law school. I remember the basics. If you want to know something specific, I could research it for you. Otherwise, I have an old friend from school who works for the US State Department in criminal enforcement. She'd know. If you want me to call her, just summarize the issue and I'll do it."

"Thanks, Nina. It's nothing important, just curiosity. I'll let you know."

When Nina left, Jacques picked up his phone and called Lucas. "You all set to go to the conference in Milwaukee next week?"

"Yes. We've taken care of Ross Taylor for a while. He has enough data to keep him busy for at least two weeks. He knows I'm going to be out next week, so you won't see him at least until I get back."

"Good. Will you get a chance to see a Cubs game while you're passing through Chicago?" Lucas Sims grew up in Iowa and Iowans tended to be Cubs fans.

"I'm planning to travel over the weekend so I can get there a day early. I'll check in at Great Chicago on Tuesday morning. I'm planning to see the Cubs on Tuesday evening. They're in the same division as the Brewers, so I'll have something to talk about at the conference in Milwaukee on Wednesday and Thursday. I'll see you back in the office a week from Monday."

Levesque hung up. Then he left a brief voicemail message for Felix.

Chapter Thirty-one

Pioneer Square
Seattle, Washington
Sunday, August 4, 2019

Occidental Park occupied a beautiful tree-lined, brick-paved area within the Pioneer Square neighborhood of Seattle. Visitors and locals alike were impressed by the native totems and bronze statues of fallen firefighters.

The park was a vibrant part of Seattle on sunny Sunday afternoons like this one. Musicians played, children played, and baseball fans prepared for a Mariners game.

At night, it quickly lost its charm and became aggressive and dangerous. The homeless were responsible for the change in vibe.

The mayor finished speaking to a crowd of around seventy-five, and people were once again enjoying the music. Two bands—one traditional jazz and the other salsa—were alternating short sets.

There were two sides to the homeless argument represented in the crowd. One faction favored doing anything possible, at any expense, to supply living accommodations to the unfortunate people. Others resented that, even though the homeless took over large areas of downtown Seattle and were responsible for an unacceptable level of crime, the city leaders refused to do anything about it. Neither side gained any satisfaction today.

Ross and Kim Taylor were seated in folding camp chairs they brought. Though not deliberate, they were located fifteen feet downwind of a Mexican food truck. The aroma of tamales cooking proved to be irresistible.

"The mayor didn't have much new to say, did she?" Ross asked between bites. "The problem is just as severe as last year. Can you believe twelve thousand people are not sure where they will spend the next night?"

Kim's anger rose at the lack of anything of substance from the mayor. "I'm more than disappointed. This is a major problem, but none of the solutions being considered seem practical. Tiny house villages only go so far."

Kim referred to a plan to set up small villages of one-room houses on plots of unused city or church land. So far, about two hundred such homes were finished. The results were still being debated. "And I never hear anything about involving the non-homeless community of Seattle. You'd think they should have a place in the conversation. I know I want to."

"You're right," Taylor said. "Ultimately, they're the taxpayers, and they'll be footing the bill. I know the public isn't heartless when it comes to the homeless. They're sympathetic. They just don't go along with the proposed solutions that ignore the rights of everyone else. Every area of the city is a mess. I'm glad I don't have to make the decisions. I don't have the patience, and besides, we have enough going on in our lives."

They went back to their tamales and listened to the bands. The traditional jazz band's turn came, and it played "Royal Garden Blues." Even the young people were enjoying it.

Kim reached over and grasped Ross's hand. "I haven't seen that creep at the lake since you had your meeting with him, and the emails have stopped. Thank you for always protecting me. My world is better with you in it."

She finished her tamale. "Are you still leaving early tomorrow?"

"Yeah. It will give me time at Great Chicago tomorrow afternoon. I'll be there all of Tuesday and Wednesday morning. It will just be audit work. Christine won't be there. Of all things, she'll be here—meeting with Jacques Levesque. There's a chance she'll get back to Chicago before I leave, so I may get to see her."

"Will you have your lucky charm with you?"

Shortly after they were married, Kim gave Ross a tiny, framed picture of the two of them on their honeymoon.

"Of course. I never travel without it. It's more than just my lucky charm." His phone sounded. A text message from Lucas Sims.

Ross, need to see you in person when I get back from Milwaukee. Meet offsite. Important. Thanks.

Taylor showed his wife the message, and they looked at each other, puzzled. Taylor wondered why Sims couldn't just call. They folded their chairs and started walking back to their car. "I'll get home on Wednesday in the early evening. We can go to The Rudder for dinner."

Chapter Thirty-two

En Route
Monday, August 5, 2019
A travel day

Christine Bell left Chicago on a United Airlines flight
from O'Hare Field scheduled to arrive in Seattle
shortly before noon. She had called Jacques Levesque
late in the day on Friday and told him she needed to
see him. Ross Taylor left her a text message earlier that
morning to give her a status report. She felt she needed
to coordinate with Levesque, in person.

She needed to reassure him about the Taylor
investigation. Levesque and LeGrande Benefits were a
critical relationship to her, and she wanted it to stay that
way. To the extent Levesque might have been concerned
about Taylor's involvement, she could encourage him not
to worry.

Unfortunately, she couldn't reassure herself. A great
deal hung in the balance. Hiring Ross Taylor may have
been a mistake. Her board thought it a clever idea at
the time, but now she lacked confidence that they
were solidly in her corner. What if Taylor uncovered

a fraud? Would they fire her immediately? And if not because of a fraud, would they fire her for deteriorating financial results? Or would Taylor ruin her relationship with LeGrande Benefits? And if her problems at Great Chicago weren't enough, she recently learned that her husband was running around with another woman and going to leave her.

She planned to see Levesque in his office that afternoon and have dinner with him and his girlfriend that evening. She would return to Chicago on Tuesday, possibly in time to meet with Taylor. She didn't look forward to any of it.

Ross Taylor left Seattle in the early morning, which allowed him a couple of hours in the afternoon to gather data at the offices of Great Chicago. He hoped to see Christine before he left.

Taylor scheduled a meeting with Winston Lester and his team on Tuesday. Christine had texted Taylor and told him to tear the place apart if he wanted to. If anything pointed to Winston Lester, she wanted to know about it. Better to find out she'd made a mistake now than later.

As he flew east, Ross Taylor felt uncertain and unnerved. Was he on the right track? Did he know anything at all about the shortfall at Great Chicago? Did Winston Lester have something to do with it? Someone at LeGrande? Someone else? His list of questions grew. Could he be in over his head?

Recently, his thoughts strayed increasingly to Derek. Was he still alive? Nearby? And then he thought about Meyerhoffer. Taylor experienced a real high when he took care of Meyerhoffer. Too high? Did that indicate a problem? He needed something to go right, a breakthrough.

Lucas Sims looked out the window of his room on the right side of the train. He boarded Amtrak's Empire Builder on Saturday afternoon in Seattle and settled in to enjoy the two-day trip to Chicago. Whenever he traveled to Chicago, Minneapolis, San Francisco, or Los Angeles, he took the train. Not only were trains easier for him in his wheelchair, but he loved trains—especially their relaxed pace.

On this trip, he'd spend two days and nights on the train, arriving in Chicago late Monday afternoon. Amtrak offered an accessible room in each of its sleeping cars which accommodated passengers in wheelchairs. He could immerse himself in uninterrupted thoughts or simply sightsee. An attendant brought him a breakfast of pancakes, bacon, an omelet, and a pot of coffee along with three newspapers. Everything came on time and hot, and he tried to enjoy the food as the scenery just east of La Crosse, Wisconsin, passed by unnoticed. Too many thoughts were competing for space in his mind.

His schedule started with a visit to Great Chicago on Tuesday morning, and he looked forward to seeing his old friend Winston Lester. He knew Ross Taylor was also scheduled to meet with Winston. He wanted to talk to Taylor but planned to wait until he returned to Seattle. He still was undecided on what to do.

Sims needed this trip away. The pressure was building, and Ross Taylor's arrival at the company only made things worse. Every day, Sims thought about what a big mistake he made the day he asked Levesque to bail him out. He might have found another way to pay the gamblers off over time. Instead, he rotted inside—a criminal about to be discovered.

Before coming to work for LeGrande benefits, he had been employed by two other insurance organizations. In them, he watched peers receive grants of stock options which made them wealthy while he received none. In LeGrande, he had hoped to find the pathway to wealth he felt he deserved. The pathway to wealth emerged but not in the manner he envisioned.

Should he tell Taylor the truth when he got back or keep quiet and take his share of the diamonds and disappear? Ironic. Taylor on his way to investigate Winston Lester for a crime Sims committed.

And then he thought of Ulrika and their children. He'd gladly give back his share of the diamonds just to be with them again. Sims neared the breaking point.

More than anything else on this trip, he looked forward to the Cubs game. Although a frequent visitor to Wrigley Field, this would be Lucas's first night game and would be a good chance to take his mind off his problems, for a little while at least.

After that, on Wednesday morning, he would drive a specially equipped rental car up to Milwaukee to attend the IT conference. If everything went as planned, he'd catch his return train in Milwaukee on Friday afternoon, which got him home to Seattle late morning on Sunday. He would have plenty of time to contemplate everything between now and then.

The simple task of boarding an aircraft didn't apply to Schlump. A 400-pound man does not fit comfortably in a coach seat. Or a first-class seat. Schlump solved this problem by buying two adjoining coach seats in the emergency exit row and bringing a pillow. The added comfort and legroom were well worth the added expense. After early boarding, he relaxed in his makeshift arrangement on an Alaska Airlines morning flight to Kansas City.

Schlump had appointments at Argus Benefits later in the day and all day on Tuesday. He would travel in a similar fashion to Atlanta on Wednesday for meetings at Consolidated Group Benefits later in the week, returning home on Saturday.

Ross Taylor and he started working together years ago while Taylor ran Arizona Life and Health Insurance Company and again recently when Taylor became an independent consultant. The audit system they developed proved to be quite simple. It allowed them to specify the information they wanted for the clients to assemble. Except for establishing initial rapport with the client, they performed all their work remotely.

Schlump loved Ross Taylor. Through the years, Taylor hired him whenever a problem required the services of an outside actuary. On the rare occasions when Schlump's business lagged, Taylor brought him in on assignments just to give him the work. Now that Taylor worked independently, he brought Schlump in on every project. The two men forged a partnership that flourished because of mutual trust. Taylor trusted and respected Schlump and routinely gave him all the credit for the work they did together.

Schlump placed his lunch order. Actually, two lunch orders because he purchased two tickets.

Chapter Thirty-three

Capitol Hill
Seattle, Washington
Monday, August 5, 2019

Gerhardt Bergmann did not conduct meetings in places readily accessible to the public. He preferred more private settings. Today's board meeting took place in a seldom-used conference room in the Odd Fellows Temple on Capitol Hill. Though a resident of the United States since 1990, he never forgot his roots in the Ministry of State Security in East Germany. German citizens knew it better as the Stasi. They knew him as Oberst Horst Brundt and avoided him if possible.

Bergmann, the name he now went by, earned his reputation as a ruthless underground field operative, assigned to Warsaw, Poland, for the six years prior to German Unity. Before that, he commanded a counterterrorism team. When the wall came down, he took all the Stasi's money he could put his hands on and quietly moved to Estonia, then Sweden, before settling in Seattle. With three other GDR emigres and Stasi comrades, he used his considerable nest egg to start several businesses. One was an insurance agency specializing in insuring German-owned businesses.

Originally known as Northwest Insurance Agency, it expanded, and the name morphed into Northwest Benefits. Then, when the German owners started to specialize in dental insurance, it became Northwest Dental Benefits. When Jacques Levesque began bringing in great volumes of new business, they put him in charge, and he gave it the name by which it's currently known, LeGrande Benefits.

"Send Mr. Levesque in please," Bergmann directed his assistant.

Jacques Levesque received the same treatment as any visitor, notwithstanding his position as CEO or his being a shareholder. Bergmann kept him waiting.

"Good morning, Gerhardt." Levesque nodded greetings to the others as he took an open chair at the end of the oval table. His demeanor revealed his loathing for these meetings and the company of Gerhardt Bergmann.

"Let's get right to your report." Bergmann wasted no time. As the CEO, Levesque was used to being in charge, but Bergmann wouldn't give him that advantage in his meeting. He'd rather have him under the spotlight and on the defensive.

During the past ten years, Bergmann visited the offices of LeGrande Benefits in the Wells Fargo Center on only one occasion. The others at this meeting, never. They were virtual strangers to the company but very much Levesque's bosses. The board met quarterly and expected Levesque to present a status report.

Seated at the other end of the table, Bergmann didn't

present an imposing figure. Barely five and a half feet tall and around 170 pounds, he was the smallest man in the room. Yet, even at seventy-one years old, he possessed a persona that intimidated those around him—including Levesque. The navy-blue tailored suit, white shirt, and repp tie he wore exuded power. Bergmann smiled without warmth or humor. Just a smile. He looked at Levesque as if he knew everything. He looked evil.

Levesque gave a thorough and detailed report that covered sales, new business prospects, administration, business turnover, and what they most wanted to hear about, profitability. Because LeGrande made more money than ever, the directors were thrilled.

After Levesque finished his report, the board asked him about the Great Chicago audit and if he thought there were any risks. He said no. Not all the directors were as confident.

"Is it the same person as in the past conducting the audit?" one asked.

"No. They've hired a former insurance executive to investigate. He's not an auditor as much as he's an insurance generalist. He knows how companies run. His name is Ross Taylor."

"He's not the same Ross Taylor who beat the crap out of that slob Meyerhoffer is he?" Bergmann asked.

"Who's Meyerhoffer?"

"Some oaf one of our guys hired to take candid pictures of women exercising. He tells me there's a big market for that sort of thing. One of Meyerhoffer's targets turned out to be a woman he recognized from his past. He was getting some good pictures. Everything went fine until he wrote to her by email. Lewd stuff. Her husband, whose name is Ross Taylor, figured out his identity and put him in the hospital. Made quite a mess of him."

"Did we do anything about it?"

"What's to do? Meyerhoffer's a moron and should be kept on a leash. I told our guy to warn Meyerhoffer if he ever went near the Taylors again, I'd visit him personally."

"Are we sure it's the same Taylor?"

"I don't know. But if it is the same Taylor who's doing the audit, be alert. He could be trouble."

Levesque nodded but said nothing.

Then Bergmann added, "Please call me at once if you change your mind about the risk we face in the audit, Jacques, and provide us with the final report the minute you get it."

Overall, his presentation, with questions, took a little over three hours, bringing them to lunch time. Bergmann didn't order lunch served. He preferred to work straight through his agenda.

"A thorough and satisfying report, Jacques. Before you leave, the board would like to express its appreciation for the excellent work you're doing. We'll be conducting our usual performance appraisal and salary review at year end, but we want to show our gratitude now as well."

He handed Jacques an envelope containing a check for ten thousand dollars. Jacques Levesque had presented a forecast of profits for the year of almost nine million dollars. Nine million and they were handing him a bonus of ten grand. Levesque looked like a man who was considering turning the table over in their laps. Bergmann didn't miss the fury in Levesque's eyes when he looked at the sum. Nor was he surprised.

"Thank you, gentlemen," Levesque said. "You're quite generous." He looked coldly at each of them in turn as he put the check in his jacket pocket.

After Levesque left the room, Gerhardt Bergmann called out to his assistant. "Please send Mr. Contador in."

Felix entered from a private office, unseen by anyone other than the assistant. Having performed assorted services for these men for more than ten years, Felix Contador was not unfamiliar to the board of LeGrande Benefits. Over the years, because they were no strangers to intimidation and force, they found Felix's talents useful adjuncts to their business ventures.

For his part, Felix enjoyed being of service to these men. There were never any disagreements, they paid him well, and they were pleased with the services he provided. But he also served Jacques Levesque who, through the years, became a valued client. The potential for conflict that always existed now loomed as a reality.

"Thank you for coming, Mr. Contador," Gerhardt Bergmann said. "We've just heard a presentation from Mr. Levesque. Can you tell us anything about Jacques Levesque or LeGrande Benefits that we should know— things which Mr. Levesque would be unlikely to tell us?"

Felix shifted in his seat uncomfortably. He knew little about Levesque's business other than that he and Lucas Sims were conducting something underhanded. He didn't know any details. He doubted the board knew anything either, and he chose not to tell them. He also knew they were unaware of the con he and Levesque played on Lucas three and a half years ago. He wouldn't tell them about that either. He didn't want to tell them anything. Especially not his discussion with Levesque on the ferry. At length, he decided to give them something. "Do you know Lucas Sims, the CFO at LeGrande?"

When they nodded, he went on. "I hear he's gambling. It's not the first time. Three years ago, he got in deep— over a hundred grand. According to my source, it's not a problem yet, but you never know."

"Does Mr. Levesque know?" Bergmann asked.

"I told him last week. He'll know what to do."

"Anything else you want to tell us about? Maybe about Mr. Levesque?"

Felix stared at Bergmann and shook his head.

"Thanks, Mr. Contador, and thanks for coming." Bergmann's experience taught him when people were not telling him the truth. Felix Contador wasn't telling him the truth. "Call me if you remember anything you think I should know. Anything. It would not be acceptable if you were to forget something. Do you understand, Mr. Contador?"

Felix always understood Gerhardt Bergmann.

Chapter Thirty-four

Chicago, Illinois
Monday, August 5, 2019

Ross Taylor loved being back in this great city—
Chicago. He had been born on the North Side, not
far from the Peninsula Hotel where he once again stayed.
He loved making the rounds of the homes he had lived
in with his parents as he grew up, but it had been years
since the last time he did the tour. Maybe on his next
visit.

Tonight he dined in-room again. This time, Chicago-
style pizza, delivered from Pizzeria Uno or Uno's as
many Chicagoans called it. Plus, three bottles of Old
Style from hotel room service. Settled for the evening, he
replayed his day.

His earlier flight was smooth and on time. He took a
cab from the airport directly to 401 N. Michigan Avenue
and arrived at Winston Lester's office around two-
thirty. It turned out, Lester's schedule contained several
conflicts, so they spent limited time together, but the
available time paid dividends to Taylor. Lester supplied
him with everything he asked for and introduced him

to every member of his staff. During the introductions, Lester emphasized to each of his team members the importance of Taylor's visit and that he expected full cooperation from everyone. Of course, Taylor knew that could be a phony setup but chose to accept Winston's order as sincere.

At one point when the two men were alone, Winston said, "I know why you're here, Ross. This is the first place you should look, but you won't find anything going on internally in our company. We're either doing a poor job of running our business, or someone is stealing from us. If it's the latter, it's most likely one of the three large administrators. We've looked into them, and our bonding company, Stockholm Fidelity, sent Hasse Olsson and his group to audit. Nothing."

Lester had prepared detailed reports on the operations of LeGrande, Argus, and Consolidated, and the three administrators. He gave them to Ross Taylor, both in hard copy and by encrypted email.

Taylor planned to email these to Schlump when he arrived back at his hotel.

Before they parted company, Lester took Taylor aside. "I want you to be as thorough as you've ever been on any investigation. Christine has given hints that she's concerned that I or members of my team may be responsible for the losses you're examining. I've become a suspect. I owe a great deal to Christine, and I'll do anything for her. I need her to know the problem is not internal, that I'm not stealing from our company. She and Great Chicago have my absolute loyalty. I'm counting on you to clear me in her eyes."

As Taylor enjoyed his pizza and beer, he thought about insurance fraud. The industry recognized Taylor as an expert; that's why Great Chicago hired him. He thought a strong possibility existed that someone was stealing from Great Chicago.

Members of the public frequently disliked insurance companies. They saw them as takers, not givers. They collected your premium but didn't pay your claims. Taylor knew firsthand that wasn't the case, but it remained a perception. Insurance companies were legitimate businesses that provided great value and were not in business to take advantage of the public. Just ask the person whose house burned down and had it replaced by the insurance company. Or a family who received a million dollars in life insurance when the breadwinner died. Despite that, some people committed insurance fraud just to "get even."

More frequently, the reason insurance companies were targets for fraud was that they held a great deal of money. Why rob a convenience store when you can steal millions from an insurance company? Of course, to do that, the criminals must be shrewd. It was no simple matter to steal millions of dollars from an insurance company. The companies didn't have millions of dollars of cash laying around for a masked robber. Criminals intent on insurance fraud needed far more ingenuity.

But Taylor knew that shrewd criminals were tough to catch. Often the fraud went on for years undetected. By the time someone discovered the crime, the criminals would disappear unnoticed. With Great Chicago, he was suspicious, but he needed to consider all possibilities.

Taylor started in the insurance business almost thirty years ago. He had been remarkably successful, proud of his accomplishments, and grateful for the people who helped him along the way. He also showed pride in the industry that supported him and his family. He bristled at any suggestion that insurance companies were less than honorable.

Most insurance company executives were hardworking, principled, honest individuals. Still, he also knew that bad actors were in the business who should be caught and punished. He hated with passion anyone who stooped to fraud.

That passion reminded him again of his father. Charles Taylor made his mark in the insurance business in the sixties. He became a life insurance and annuity agent for a small company in Nebraska and was assigned the territory which included Chicago, where he lived with his family. A grandmother made him the beneficiary of a small inheritance which, along with his basic compensation, paid the expenses of his young family. He took his commission compensation in the form of stock.

Through the years, he continued to excel in insurance sales and accumulated more and more stock. Eventually, he became one of the company's larger shareholders. When the board offered him the presidency, he was elated. Although he owned a substantial part of the company, he wanted more. He wanted to become truly wealthy and saw a path through greater stock ownership.

His only problem: he didn't have any money to buy more stock. He found the solution by forging municipal bonds. Through a confederate—a skilled lithographer in Gary, Indiana—he produced five million dollars in bogus bonds. He used them to buy more stock from the company. With Charles as the company's CEO, the company treasurer saw no reason to look carefully at the bonds. In the sixties, insurance companies still held physical paper bonds in the company safe.

Everything went smoothly until the company hit a rough period. Interest rates dropped, and the reserves required to support the insurance policies became inadequate. A careful regulatory audit uncovered the counterfeit bonds, and Charles Taylor went to prison. Worse yet, the company became insolvent, and the policyholders suffered personal losses.

The news shattered Ross Taylor's life; his father was a criminal. During that time, Ross came to appreciate how devastating a financial fraud can be to policyholders. People had trusted their money to his father's insurance company only to be cheated out of what they were promised. In recent years, Ross made it one of his business goals never to allow such a crime to take place within a company he was part of. He hadn't been completely successful, but at least he uncovered every fraud, the criminals were punished, and the customers made whole.

So far, though there were unanswered questions, Taylor saw no reason to suspect criminal activity within Great Chicago. Yet, situations like this required him to think critically. If Great Chicago had been the victim of a carefully planned crime, there were four likely candidates— the internal team or someone at one of the three major agencies which also administered premiums and claims.

After his visit this week, Taylor would know a great deal more about the internal team at Great Chicago. In the case of the three agencies, it would take a little longer. Their relationships to Great Chicago were complex and the analysis contained more variables.

These administrators sold dental insurance policies to exceptionally large employers and union groups and provided administrative services to Great Chicago. They billed and collected the premiums. After deducting their commissions and administrative expenses, they sent the net premiums to Great Chicago. Finally, they also paid the claims on behalf of Great Chicago. They did everything except take the insurance risk.

Tomorrow, Taylor planned to interview everyone on Winston Lester's staff. Schlump provided him with a profile of every executive and director-level employee at Great Chicago. His source uncovered details even trained detectives overlooked, and the information was invaluable as he prepared for his audit of the systems.

He checked his emails. Nothing important. Then texts. Nothing important there either. He considered yesterday's text from Lucas Sims. What could Sims want to discuss in person that couldn't be done sooner by phone or text?

Chapter Thirty-five

Metropolitan Grill
Seattle, WA
Monday, August 5, 2019

"What a marvelous dinner, Jacques, and it's been wonderful seeing you again, Aubrey." Christine raised her wine glass in a salute while the three enjoyed the end of a pleasant evening.

"How did you keep this place a secret from me all these years?" Although Christine Bell visited Jacques Levesque in Seattle at least twice a year for the past five years, tonight marked her first experience at the Metropolitan Grill, a classic Seattle steakhouse. The Met recognized Levesque as a regular.

"Sorry, Chris. Perhaps the surprise made the wait worthwhile. Anyway, it won't be long before things turn around for you, and we can come back here to celebrate. Your problems should soon be behind you."

Jacques's smile gave Christine some level of comfort. She had spent the afternoon in the offices of LeGrande Benefits going over optimistic sales projections for the next two years with Jacques Levesque. If realized, both companies could anticipate outstanding profitability.

They had also discussed Ross Taylor's investigation. Christine went out of her way to assure Levesque that she expected nothing to come of it. She told him he only had to put up with the questions of an outsider for a couple of weeks.

"I agree with you. We've turned the corner," Levesque said.

Christine sipped her wine and set down the glass. "How did your board meeting go this morning?"

For the fifth consecutive year, LeGrande Benefits earned the number one spot as Great Chicago's largest producer. Because of that, Christine kept in touch with everything that could affect the relationship. By paying close attention, she had learned that Levesque did not have a particularly cordial relationship with the other owners, despite the massive amount of profitable new business he brought into their company.

His response betrayed none of that. "Fine. The usual posturing, but nothing out of the ordinary. They did want to know everything about your audit. They don't like the idea of audits. Remember, they're former East German communists. Communists don't get audited. But they won't be a problem."

Christine waved her hand to dismiss the subject. "But we've already spent enough time talking business today. What good things are going on with you two?"

"We intend to do some traveling sometime soon," Aubrey said. "We've been pretty busy around the area for a couple of years, but we have a plan to go to the South of France, probably later in the year. Jacques hasn't taken a vacation in quite a while, and I've never been to Europe. It'll be a wonderful getaway for us both."

Christine leaned into the conversation now that the talk of business was over. She liked Aubrey a great deal.

"I'm also back into photography," Aubrey said. "I used to be a freelance fashion photographer just after I dropped out of college. I took pictures of everything. People, trees, the waterfront, baseball players, zoo animals—everything. And I loved it! I specialized in a few things, mainly candid shots of people. My customers were the fashion designers, but I couldn't make enough money. Now that I have more time, I've started where I left off—taking pictures of everything. This time I'm going to make it. I'm sure Jacques is surprised that I don't have a camera with me tonight."

They laughed softly.

When Christine looked at Aubrey, she thought of herself at a younger more carefree age. "I envy you, Aubrey. You're following your dream, and you have such romantic plans. Stick to that dream and those plans. You never know when something might happen to push you off your path."

"But, Chris, how could you envy me? You have everything a woman could want. You're at the top of your industry, and you made it as a woman. You're respected. You're highly paid, *and* you're beautiful. No, I envy you."

"Thank you, Aubrey. Those are truly kind words. But one thing I have learned in my career is . . . write this down . . . not everything is what it seems. Remember that." She smiled the smile of a friend and sipped her wine. But she felt anxious inside.

Levesque remained quiet. The women spoke so candidly with each other, with such openness and trust. He looked fascinated. In his world, everyone kept everything a secret. Or told outright lies. But these two women, virtual strangers, were in tune with each other like old friends.

Levesque paid the bill, and the trio walked to a waiting limo. After dropping Christine at the Olympic Hotel, Levesque checked his phone for the first time that evening. One text, from an unknown number.

Confirmed?

Levesque typed, *Confirmed* and hit send.

Chapter Thirty-six

Chicago, Illinois
Tuesday, August 6, 2019

Unbelievable. Lucas Sims couldn't find the words to describe how thrilled he felt to be out of the office and in Chicago.

The meeting with Winston Lester that morning had been cordial, and they concluded their routine business quickly. They decided to enjoy lunch together and talk about other things. From the 401 N. Michigan Building, Sims could easily wheel himself the short distance to the Sheraton Grand Chicago where he stayed and where the two men chose to eat. Scattered clouds allowed the sun to warm the air, so he and Lester enjoyed the outdoor promenade dining along the Chicago River.

Sims planned to take the rest of the day off and said so to Lester. "I'll wander around this neighborhood for a while then head up to Wrigley Field. Tomorrow, I'll drive to Milwaukee for that IT conference. I had hoped you were going too. Some great speakers are on the program, and I love the German food in Milwaukee."

Lester agreed. "It should be great. But with what's

going on here and Christine suspecting me, I can't afford to be gone even for a couple of days. Let's plan for next year. If I'm still here."

Sims nodded grimly.

The Chicago waterfront differed from Seattle's in subtle ways. Like Seattle, birds were everywhere. Here, however, there were no seagulls with their annoying squawking. Only pigeons, and the pigeons didn't squawk. The freshwater river had a different smell from the seawater around Seattle. Sims liked it; it felt like home.

Lester broke into Sims's thoughts. "If you're going to take the rest of the day for yourself, I have a suggestion. Have you ever ridden one of the river cruise boats?"

Sims said he hadn't.

"It's worth doing. You'll see Chicago as you've never seen it. All the great buildings, the bridges, and Lake Michigan. And you'll get a history lesson. Everything in about an hour and a half. I try to do it at least once a year. Never get tired of it."

Sims appeared to be listening but wasn't. He was thinking about the man speaking, for whom he held genuine affection. How ironic. Lester was under suspicion for a crime Sims committed.

These days, his life at LeGrande bordered on the unbearable. He had violated every principle he ever established for himself. He had transformed himself from an ordinary "good person" into a scheming criminal. His life was coming apart.

Although, through the years, he had overcome his bitterness at being confined to a wheelchair with its feeling of helplessness and rarely thought of himself as disabled, he was unable to pardon himself for his crimes. Only his hatred of insurance companies partially eased him through the emotional wounds he inflicted on himself.

Yes, he would soon be free of the mental burden. Jacques promised him that in their last meeting. That helped, and he'd have his money as well—more than enough to get along wherever he decided to hide. *Stolen money*. Without his wife and children, he didn't have a clear idea of where he might go, where he might be safe from prosecution. Did he even want to leave Seattle?

He looked at his phone. Nothing urgent. He looked at his texts. What had he been thinking when he texted Ross Taylor on Sunday? Why had he done it? What would he tell Taylor when they met? He wasn't sure of anything.

Seeing the vibrant city of Chicago—not the corner of Third and Marion in Seattle—gave him hope for something better. Today, he would try to set it all aside.

Getting from the Sheraton to the cruise boat proved to be easy—a one-block ride in his wheelchair along the waterfront, a short elevator ride down to the river level, and another fifty feet to the boarding ramp.

Getting to Wrigley Field presented a different challenge. The ballpark was on the Red Line. The nearest accessible subway station was Chicago Avenue, a bit too far for Lucas Sims. He used an Uber to take him from the river to the station. An elevator took him to the mezzanine level where he bought his tickets. Another elevator took him to the platform and the trains.

Nothing like the Chicago subway system existed in

Seattle. The experience was all new to Lucas. Especially the noise. The activity was fast paced, with people going in all directions, herding each other along like cattle. He became confused. It was all he could do to find the northbound track. Fortunately, people tended to give room to a man in a wheelchair.

Lucas finally made it to the south end of the station where his train would arrive. After five minutes of waiting on the platform, a rumble sounded from the tunnel just to his right. The rumbling grew into a roar, and Lucas felt it through his chair. The ear-piercing squealing made by the train's wheels completed the assault on his hearing. Almost deafening.

The eight-car train roared past him into the station and slowed to a stop. He wheeled himself onto the last car, found a spot reserved for wheelchairs, and set his brakes. The remaining ride was uneventful. The train became quieter inside the car once they were through the turns. Before long, the train rose out of the ground, into the late-afternoon sunshine, and onto an elevated platform. Chicago's famous El. The ride became even quieter.

The trip took about half an hour. Lucas rolled himself off the train at the Addison Street elevated station— the stop for Wrigley Field. From the platform, he saw the famous ballpark. After an elevator ride down to the street, Lucas Sims, once again, found himself in a crowd of people. This time, they were all going to the same destination.

Lucas's ticket allowed him to wheel his chair into a special section for people with disabilities. He was almost on the field. He had seen at least three dozen major league baseball games but never from so close to the action. Although it would be another ninety minutes before darkness fell, the lights were on.

This is going to be great.

The Cubs were out of it after Oakland scored eight runs in the second inning. Nonetheless, Lucas thoroughly enjoyed himself. On the warm evening, he had downed a couple of hotdogs and beers. The two guys next to him—Chicagoans also in wheelchairs—kept him laughing at Chicago jokes.

When he arrived, almost four hours earlier, it had taken him barely twenty minutes to get from the train platform into the park. After the game, he had been in a slow-moving line for almost half an hour and was still a long way from the Addison Street station. It was at least another half hour before he finally rolled off the elevator onto the platform.

Extra trains were always waiting after games at Wrigley Field. Once he reached the platform, he quickly boarded the last car and began his trip back to his hotel. It had been a wonderful day for Sims. He hadn't felt this much happiness in three years. Or was it relief? He had visited an old friend, enjoyed the diversion of a river boat cruise, and cheered for his beloved Cubs. Most of all, he was two thousand miles from LeGrande Benefits, Jacques Levesque, and Perfect Score. And, thankfully, that would all be over soon.

It was after eleven o'clock when he got off the train at the Chicago Avenue station. When he exited the train, he was at the north end of the station. The elevator he expected on his left had three orange cones in front of it and a sign which read, "Closed for Repairs. Please Use Elevator at South End of Station."

Tired after a long day, Sims was annoyed at this inconvenience. Resigned, he turned his chair around and started the long trip to the south end.

Earlier in the day, there had been hundreds of people on the platform—getting on, getting off, or just waiting. Now there were only a handful. At last, he approached the elevator. Thankfully, there were no cones or signs, although this end of the station was deserted. As in the afternoon, he became aware of a rumble coming from the tunnel on his left, a northbound train. Once again, the rumble grew into a roar that vibrated his chair. Alone, he tensed and hurried his roll to the elevator.

Now he heard the squealing sound of the wheels. Metal on metal. He started to sweat. Whether from propelling his wheelchair the extra distance or from fear, he wasn't sure. While he was measuring the reason for his anxiety, two powerful hands grabbed both his arms and the frame of his wheelchair.

The train was almost in the station, its headlight dancing on the walls. Despite his iron grip on the wheels of his chair, Sims was unable to slow its skidding away from the elevator, toward the northbound tracks. Someone much stronger than he was in control. He twisted his head to see who had redirected his chair but could not. Sims tried again to tighten his grip. No use. Despite his effort, the chair skidded across the floor.

Terrified, Sims tried to propel himself from the chair but was unable to get the height needed to get over the armrest. He continued his forward momentum toward the tracks. The noise was deafening. He turned in the seat to try to grab whoever was pushing him but couldn't get a grip. He grabbed at the wheels again, only a few feet from the tracks. Now he was at the edge.

With one mighty effort, the two hands heaved Lucas Sims onto the tracks in front of the northbound train.

Chapter Thirty-seven

Wells Fargo Center
Seattle, Washington
Thursday, August 8, 2019

The moment Jacques Levesque had received word of Lucas Sims's death yesterday, he closed the offices of LeGrande Benefits out of respect. The people of LeGrande took the news of Sims's death as a terrible blow—especially under the circumstances. Initial reports from the Chicago police indicated that a homeless person attempting to rob Lucas pushed him under a subway train. He had been the most popular person at the company, and for the others, trying to continue as if nothing happened would be pointless. Today, the offices were virtually empty.

He sat in his office, thinking about how Sims's death was going to affect him. It would have a major impact on LeGrande Benefits. Sims had performed the role of *de facto* chief operating officer for years, even though Levesque never gave him the title. Sims knew every digital and manual system in the company and could perform every function by himself. He would be difficult, if not impossible, to replace. The few people remaining speculated among themselves about the future of the company. Could Levesque do the job alone? Could he find a suitable replacement? Could the company survive?

Nina Petaluma and Oskar Kungen were fiercely loyal to Levesque. He had helped them in their careers, and they would do anything for him. Notwithstanding the closed sign someone put on the office door, they were at work. Both offered their time and attention to helping Levesque navigate the company through the difficult period.

While Nina and Oskar tried to bring organization through the operational transition, Jacques Levesque contemplated a different transition. On his own for the first time since the fraud began, he felt uncertainty.

Lucas Sims had been the perfect partner in the crime for Levesque. He was desperate for help, and Levesque supplied help. In return, Sims applied his considerable talent to the development of Operation Perfect Score— to defeat an insurance company with insufficient safeguards.

Lucas first identified the weaknesses at Great Chicago—weaknesses which allowed Perfect Score to avoid detection by the Great Chicago auditors and exploit those weaknesses. Most internal frauds committed by administrators involve premiums, which were easier to detect. Lucas and Sims chose to work from the claims side.

Any scam involving claims left some sort of trail, which in hindsight, revealed the fraud. To make the search as difficult as possible, Sims selected the trail least likely to attract anyone's attention. He concentrated on terminated employees only.

The monthly reports sent by employers showed around one and one-half percent of all employees were terminated each month. Because LeGrande insured over one million people, an average of fifteen thousand were terminated every month. Lucas gambled they could submit fraudulent claims on a subset of this group, and it might be impossible to detect. The gamble paid off.

Initially, Operation Perfect Score selected five hundred of the terminated employees and created a fictitious claim for each of them—each claim between five hundred and one thousand dollars. In the first month, over three years ago, more than four-hundred thousand dollars was diverted away from Great Chicago into Levesque's personal account. No one noticed. The following month, they did it again. Same result. As their confidence in Perfect Score grew, Lucas increased the number of claims to almost eighteen hundred. Last month, they diverted over one-point-four million dollars, an annual rate of over seventeen million. And still, no one caught on.

Converting the fraudulent claims into untraceable cash proved to be a more difficult challenge. Again, Lucas Sims provided the solution.

From the data submitted by their clients, LeGrande possessed complete demographic information on over one million people. Lucas picked thirty names of randomly selected terminated employees and put together a profile of each. He included the real name, social security number, gender, name of spouse, and date of birth. He added "DDS" after each name to give them Doctor of Dental Surgery credentials. He substituted a UPS store address for the actual address and established an email account for electronic communication.

For a substantial fee, Felix arranged for drivers' licenses, social security cards, and identifications for each of the thirty names. The licenses with male names included Levesque's picture. Those with female names, Aubrey Reddy's. They now were in possession of credentials for thirty "dentists."

They posed as new dentists in town and opened thirty bank accounts in cities near where the bulk of LeGrande's clients were insured—each in the name of one of the fictitious dentists. When they told the bankers they were dentists and would make deposits of between twenty-five and forty thousand dollars per month, the bankers were always extremely enthusiastic to have them as new customers.

They used UPS store addresses so that no mail inadvertently went to the real person at their home. They used the new email accounts to receive bank statements and bank 1099s. Any mail sent to the UPS store would be collected periodically and shredded. Finally, the programming for Perfect Score prevented the claims system from sending 1099s. The IRS knew nothing.

Funds deposited to the bank accounts were transferred electronically each month to an account which Levesque set up and maintained privately. So long as no one picked up anything in an audit, Levesque was safe. So far, no one had.

Now, however, Ross Taylor and his partner Schlump

were poking around the LeGrande systems. Christine Bell made it clear to everyone that Taylor and Schlump were to be given access to all the raw data. Even so, they would still have to sort it in just the right way to unmask the scheme. More improbable would be their discovery of Perfect Score. If they did, it meant disaster. Lucas Sims could have created new diversions or red herrings, but Levesque couldn't. He could only stall if necessary.

Nina Petaluma walked into Levesque's office and interrupted his thoughts. She wore a business suit as always—today, black. "What can I do to help, boss? Everything is covered right now, and we'll be okay until everyone comes back on Monday after the funeral."

On more than one occasion, Nina stepped up and proved to be a more than capable team member. She would do anything to help Jacques Levesque.

"Thanks, Nina. I appreciate your help. You can do one more thing for me. Ross Taylor is visiting here at the request of Great Chicago. After the tragedy with Lucas, his involvement is a bit of an annoyance. Is there any way we can keep him out of here for a while?"

She smiled. "Leave it to me. I'll see to it that he won't be around here for at least a couple of weeks. In the meantime, why don't you take this afternoon and tomorrow off? You've lost a good friend and being here won't bring him back. Oskar and I will hold things together here. Go home and be with Aubrey."

He thanked her, and she walked out of his office. It was time to go home but not until he made one more call. To Christine Bell.

Chapter Thirty-eight

Yacht Haven Marina
Lake Union
Seattle, Washington
Friday, August 9, 2019

Schlump settled into his usual spot in the center of the cockpit. He learned long ago how his weight affected the stability of Ross's boat. Besides, he liked his spot. Raised slightly higher than the rest of the cockpit, he enjoyed a clear view to his right toward the water and the skyline along south Lake Union. He wore his usual uniform of baggy black pants and a baggy black windbreaker.

Today was Schlump's turn to supply the treats, and he pleased the others by stopping at the Swedish bakery for almond croissants and a loaf of *limpa* bread. He knew all along that Kim didn't get up early to bake the *limpa*.

When he picked them up, the *limpa* was just coming out of the oven, and they still smelled wonderful, especially because no wind existed to disburse the aroma. The temperature already hovered in the high seventies, warm even for an August morning, and Schlump and the

Taylors were discussing Lucas Sims's tragic death over their breakfast.

"He's going to be hard for Levesque to replace. From what I learned about the company, Sims and *only* Sims knew the ins and outs of the systems. He put everything together." Ross Taylor sketched an organizational diagram of LeGrande Benefits for the others and drew a box with Lucas Sims's name in it just under Levesque's. "Not just the systems. He knew everything about everything."

Schlump finished the last of a croissant and unfolded a paper which he placed on the cockpit table. "You're not the only one who came to that conclusion. I went to the offices of Consolidated Group Benefits on Wednesday just before I learned about Sims's death. Rich Ellis, their CFO, and I were together when we heard the news. He gave me this. It's a copy of a letter he wrote to Jacques Levesque a couple of years ago concerning Lucas. It seems that, at that time, Lucas helped Rich Ellis solve a programming dilemma that was driving Rich crazy. Ellis wanted to let Levesque know how much he appreciated Sims's help."

Taylor read the letter and shook his head. "This is quite a tribute. Don't you wonder what he did for them—a competitor? I suppose we'll never know. By the way, I got this text from Lucas just before I left for Chicago." He read the text in which Sims asked to meet him offsite when he returned. "Sims called it important. I guess I'll never know what he meant by that either."

Kim had remained quiet until that point, taking in what the two men were saying. Now she said, "I've never laid eyes on Lucas Sims, but I'm getting a pretty clear picture of a highly talented individual who everyone respected, everywhere he went." To her husband she said, "Christine Bell called him the best CFO she ever encountered." She looked at Schlump. "Rich Ellis told you Sims had been invaluable to Consolidated."

They both nodded.

"And everyone at LeGrande acknowledges that Sims knew everything, that although Jacques Levesque brought in the business, Sims proved to be the heart of the company." She waited to let her words sink in.

"Then he wanted to talk to you offsite about something he called important," she said to Taylor. "Could he possibly have known something sinister that he wanted to share? Did one of his associates kill him? Maybe this was an orchestrated murder. If so, the stakes have skyrocketed."

Taylor remained quiet. The question required thought rather than a quick response.

After a moment, Schlump said, "Along that line, I've given a preliminary but careful review to the data I picked up at Argus and Consolidated. I'm convinced that neither of these companies has done anything out of the ordinary with the premium accounts. In my opinion, they're both clean. I've only just begun with the claims analyses however. That will take me through the weekend."

"That's just about where I am with LeGrande too," said Ross. "I'll be analyzing claims for the next two days. At least, we now know the problem isn't in Great Chicago itself. Winston Lester runs a clean shop, and I believe he's beyond suspicion."

"Ross, you and I have always agreed not to reach conclusions before we have all the facts," Schlump said. "But, if Christine's problem isn't within her company, it must be in one of the three big agencies. We've analyzed data from all three. They're all sending one hundred percent of the premium they collect, but something smells. These agencies are all making a ton of money on commissions and administration fees. Why risk embezzling more money? I know money is its own motivation. I get that. But it still seems stupid."

"Who are the owners of Argus and Consolidated?" Taylor asked.

Schlump opened his notebook. "The Fisher Family owns Argus. They have for over sixty years. They're one of the richest families in Kansas City, so they don't need money. Jack Hogan owns Consolidated. He's the only shareholder, and he's over eighty years old. He isn't motivated. Is Levesque the sole owner of LeGrande?"

"I'm not sure. Let me check the regulatory filings. I have them right here." Taylor looked through the documents Nina Petaluma provided to him. "Here. LeGrande Benefits, Inc., has five shareholders. One owns fifty-one percent and three own fifteen percent each. Jacques Levesque owns four percent."

The three exchanged looks.

"Well, what do you know," said Taylor. "He's not the owner after all. Come to think of it, he told me that the first time I met him. How did I forget that? He told me that the owners had rewarded him with a small stock position because of his success in bringing in new business."

"Who owns the fifty-one percent?" Schlump asked.

Taylor looked again at the regulatory document. "Gerhardt Bergmann. Anyone ever heard of him?"

No one had. Schlump volunteered to use his source to check out Bergmann.

Taylor looked over the water as he continued to ponder the mystery. "Levesque's the CEO; he runs the company, but he doesn't own it. He gets a good salary and bonuses, but maybe that's not enough for him. Maybe he's not as rich as we thought. Maybe he's stealing from Great Chicago. Maybe that's what Sims wanted to tell me. It's a tempting hypothesis, but things often aren't what they seem."

For a few moments, the seagulls squawking overhead accounted for the only noise.

Taylor asked, "Does the name Tino De Angelis mean anything to either of you?"

Both shook their heads.

"My father told me this story to teach me a lesson. I may be imprecise on my details, but it's a good example of things not being what they seem. But did my father learn something from the lesson? Apparently not.

"According to news reports, De Angelis enjoyed his reputation as a successful commodities trader in the sixties. He knew that financial institutions loaned money against soybean oil as security. He accumulated a great deal of soybean oil and kept it stored in tanks in New Jersey. Then he borrowed money from American Express using the oil as security. He used the loan proceeds to buy more soybean oil futures contracts intending to corner the market and then raise the price of the oil and make a fortune.

"When he went to American Express to borrow more money, they insisted on auditing his inventory before lending him more. They sent inspectors who verified the quantity of soybean oil De Angelis claimed to have by physically measuring the volume of oil in the tanks. They were satisfied and American Express loaned De Angelis more money."

By now, the other two were finished eating and were concentrating on the story Ross told.

"In fact, De Angelis put only a relatively small amount of oil in the tanks—the rest, water. Since the oil floated on water, the inspectors, who accessed the tanks only from the top, were fooled. By the time the authorities uncovered the scam, the lenders were out over one-hundred-seventy-five million dollars. And that was over fifty years ago."

The story Taylor told produced the desired effect. While all three were inclined to start focusing on Jacques Levesque, they saw the danger of following the wrong path.

"That's a great example of how you can think you know something when you don't. In the case of Levesque, we have our first hint, but we don't have anything pointing directly at him," Kim said, inserting herself again. "You've ruled out premium fraud so whoever is behind this whole problem has most likely manipulated a claims system in some way. Someone with a great programmer. Someone with a motive to steal. I say focus entirely on LeGrande. It's your best choice. You can always come back to the others later."

The two men listened to her intently and nodded.

"You're right, Kim. It's a good approach." Schlump turned to Taylor. "Maybe you should give Chris a call and let her know that we're going to concentrate on LeGrande exclusively for the next few days. You don't have to tell her why. No need to put out a theory if it turns out we're wrong. Just say it's the way we've scheduled our analysis."

"I agree," Taylor said. "From now on, you and I will work exclusively on LeGrande claims. You get to work sorting them in every way you can think of. Then think of some more ways. I'll do the same. We'll be looking for recurring data points—a name or address turning up frequently, a dentist receiving an inordinate number of claims payments, the same dollar amounts. And try Benford's Law. You might uncover a pattern of payments that go against the expected. If we find anything, we might just uncover a major fraud."

They heard a knock at the front of the boat. "Probably Liz just wanting to say hello," Kim said. She stepped out of the cockpit and walked forward on the deck.

"Message for Ross Taylor. Is he here?" A young woman in garish bicycling gear stood on the dock.

Kim signed a ledger, and the messenger handed her a small white business envelope from LeGrande Benefits, Inc. She returned to the main cabin and passed the envelope to Taylor.

He opened it. A note from Nina Petaluma, including her title at the top of the page, General Counsel and Chief Compliance Officer, LeGrande Benefits, Inc.

Taylor summarized it for the others. "Because of the tragic death of Lucas Sims, management thinks it best if we postponed our on-site examination of LeGrande for two weeks, until August twenty-sixth. If we need anything in the meantime, just contact her."

He tossed the paper onto the table. "I suppose her request makes sense. There will no doubt be a funeral, and they'll have to replace Sims. Still, two weeks?" He thought for a moment. "Let's just continue as we planned. If we need to get into LeGrande's office sooner, I'll call Levesque directly."

"Is there any way I can help?" Kim asked.

Taylor refilled their coffee mugs. "Where are you with your proposal to get a commission to write a magazine feature? Has anyone signed on yet?"

"I just received an email this morning from *Puget Sound Business Journal.* They're agreeable to my conducting and writing about an interview with anyone on the list I gave them. The fee will be good too."

"Great news. That's wonderful. You'll be back on page one again." Schlump joined Taylor in clapping for Kim. "Have you lined up the interview yet?"

"Not yet. I still have the same inquiries out but no takers—except, of course, the governor. But the *Journal* doesn't want anything to do with him. Still looking. But now that I have the *Journal's* commitment, I won't have any trouble scheduling a subject."

"How about Jacques Levesque?" Ross asked.

She smiled. "I already put him on my list. My career would soar if I got Branson or Woods or Senator Warren. Even Bill Gates again. But they've all been written about. There's nothing the public doesn't know about them. But Levesque is still a bit of a mystery. Yeah, everyone's heard about the guy with the basketball court, but not many people know much about him personally. He could turn out to be a great story. The *Journal* might even publish it across their national distribution. It could boost my stature as a writer."

"Levesque is the kind of guy who will eat up being publicized in a national business magazine. He'd no doubt research you before agreeing. When he sees who you've interviewed and written about and where your articles have been published, he'll conclude that you're a celebrity yourself. His ego will be stoked, and he'll do it in a heartbeat."

"Hardly a celebrity, but I could write something about him that appealed to a broad segment of the business public. Still, it might get in the way of the investigation you're conducting. He might smell a rat and shut you off to information that might otherwise trip him up. My going there could hurt you."

"You're right, it could. But, if you were to concentrate only on his personal life and the accomplishments he's most proud of, it could work and might help."

"How might it help you?"

"I'm not sure. He's not going to tell you anything about their operations—the place where a fraud could be going on. Maybe he'd show a part of his personality we don't already know. Maybe he'd reveal that he needed money."

Taylor continued. "What do we know about his lifestyle anyway? Where does he live? How does he live? Does he have any hobbies besides basketball? Does he seem to spend more than he earns? There's a great deal about Levesque we don't know. It's just possible that something could slip out. In any case, you'll have an interesting interview, and it will, no doubt, enhance your career. And we'll know more than we do now about Jacques Levesque.

"Schlump, could you get your guy Postiglione to put together a file on Levesque? It could help Kim if she winds up interviewing him."

Schlump agreed to do so.

Kim thought for a minute. "I'm in. I'll do it. How do you want to set it up? Should I call and introduce myself or do you want to make the introduction? He'll know I'm your wife soon enough anyway."

"It's better if I make the inquiry," Taylor said. "He's likely to suspect something either way. At least you could interview him knowing that he's aware of who you are. I'll call him this afternoon. Thanks for being willing to help us."

The three finished their coffee, Schlump swallowing the last bite of his third croissant. Kim and Ross were forced to hold on to their mugs as Schlump moved to the side and stepped off the boat, but they were used to it.

Today, he got off without help. "I know I've got to get serious about the diet, Ross. Yesterday, Trudy and I went to the zoo. The elephants threw peanuts at me. Let's compare notes on Monday. I'll buy dinner."

As Schlump walked toward the parking lot, Ross Taylor looked behind the *Pura Vida* to the west. The bells on Fremont Bridge were ringing, and the spans were beginning to open. With the bridge only about thirty feet above the water, most sailboats were required to wait for it to open before passing under. Now there were nine boats waiting to go north out of Lake Union. Although he couldn't see them, an equal number were probably lined up on the other side waiting to come south into the lake. Enough boat traffic took place that the bridge opened more than thirty-five times each day. He never tired of watching it go up and down or the boats passing under it.

After Schlump left, Taylor called Christine Bell and told her about their plan to concentrate on LeGrande. He didn't mention any suspicion. She accepted his plan.

Then he called Levesque, not sure what to expect. Levesque not only liked the idea of an interview with Kim, but the more he talked, he could hardly wait to hear from her and start planning. He expressed his great appreciation to Taylor for suggesting it to his wife.

When Ross told Kim the news, she decided to get right to work outlining her research plan. She moved into their shared office.

Taylor changed into his basketball clothes and headed to the court at Ninth and Denny to see if he could get into a pickup game. He needed the exercise.

For a second time, he didn't notice the black Lincoln parked up the block from Yacht Haven.

Chapter Thirty-nine

1521 Second Avenue
Seattle, Washington
Friday, August 9, 2019

The view from his condominium took even Jacques Levesque's breath away. The floor-to-ceiling windows on the southwest and northwest facing corner opened onto a panorama of beauty which included the entire Olympic Peninsula and the Olympic Mountains. On a clear day, he could look to the south and see Tacoma—to the north, Whidbey Island. Spectacular.

He lived there with Aubrey Reddy. It was a perfect size for them since Levesque refused to entertain in his home. To him, home existed for him and Aubrey. Their unit featured one over-sized bedroom which they shared. What the designers envisioned as guest bedrooms, they made into elaborate offices—one for each of them. The rest of the condominium was an open living area.

From the thirty-fifth floor, the street-level sounds of a big city vanished—all, that is, except for the horns of ships and ferries navigating inside Elliot Bay and the seagulls, which occasionally flew as high as Levesque's condominium. At that moment, there were three sitting on the open window track of his indoor/outdoor glass room, staring at Aubrey. Curled up on a plush, cushioned, lounge chair, she stared back at them.

"How are things going without Lucas?" she asked Levesque as he walked out to join her. Late afternoon, the sun remained warm, and they wouldn't be in the shadows until nearly nine o'clock.

He leaned down and kissed her. "As good as possible. It'll be a while before I can find someone I can trust the way I trusted Lucas. In the meantime, Nina and Oskar are carrying the load. We'll work things out."

She refilled their wine glasses. "Anything new with that guy Christine sent?"

"Ross Taylor? No. So far, he's just an annoyance. We've asked him to stay away for a couple of weeks because of Lucas's death, so I don't expect to see him any time soon. He did call me today though. Asked me if his wife could interview me. It turns out she's published several articles where she interviewed an important celebrity. She's actually interviewed Bill Gates and Paul Allen. Can you believe it? She's going to call me this weekend to set up interview dates. She's under contract with the *Puget Sound Business Journal.* That reminds me, I left my black phone on my desk at the office. That's the number she has. I'll have to pick it up in the morning." He dropped onto the lounge chair beside her.

He left something out. He now knew for certain that the investigator Ross Taylor and the Ross Taylor who beat up one of Gerhardt Bergmann's lowlifes were one and the same. Although Taylor couldn't connect him to

Meyerhoffer, he would have to be careful, nonetheless.

"That could be fun," Aubrey said.

This wouldn't be the first time an article about Jacques appeared in print, but they'd always been published in limited-audience insurance publications. And the writers didn't even come to see him. They simply asked him questions over the phone.

Aubrey kept her eyes on the birds. "So, this is that guy's wife?"

"Yeah. Apparently she's made something of a name for herself with her writing. She's been published in *Seattle Magazine*, *Alaska Airlines Magazine*, and a number of trade journals. Maybe even *Newsweek*. I'm not sure. She used to write a column at the old *Post Intelligencer*. You're right. It should be fun."

The two became quiet. The glass room where they were sitting was a modified patio. Instead of open sides, it featured bi-fold glass panels which opened from waist height to ceiling. The design allowed for year-around use. The lounge chairs were set at right angles so the two could look at one another and, at the same time, enjoy the view. A small glass-topped cocktail table separated the chairs.

Today there were five commercial container ships and three Washington State ferry boats competing for space in Elliott Bay. The container ships were no doubt waiting to unload at the Port of Seattle, just south of their high-rise building. From experience, Jacques and Aubrey knew that two of the ferry boats were coming and going between Seattle and Bainbridge Island. The third headed from Seattle to Bremerton.

Aubrey interrupted the quiet. "Tell me about the South of France, Jacques. You've told me before, but I love hearing you talk about it."

He sighed but settled comfortably into his well-rehearsed story. "France never meant anything to me until college. I knew I had been born there, but I didn't care. I knew nothing except Queens. Then I started researching France. I spent hours—I should have been studying—reading about and looking at photos and paintings of France—especially Paris, the Burgundy region, the Alps, and the Cote d'Azur. That's when I changed my name and determined to one day live on the French Riviera, the southeast coast of France." He sipped his wine.

"I've never been there, but I feel I know it like I know my home. It *is* my home. And one day I'll—we'll live there. I'm in regular contact with real estate agents in the area between Nice and Cannes on the coast. Properties on a hillside with views of the Mediterranean which you and I might find suitable are available starting around fifteen million euros which is equal to around eighteen million dollars." He threw these figures out as if they were pocket change.

Aubrey shook her head.

"Just yesterday, I looked at pictures of one magnificent estate on the Cap d'Antibes where the view extends all the way to Monaco. It has six bedrooms on three levels, all of which face southwest toward the sea. It also has an infinity pool with the same view. And if that isn't enough, the housekeeper and gardener are willing to stay with the villa if we want them. The property includes a small house where they live in exchange for their services and a small salary. The cost is around sixteen million." He was energized by the retelling.

Aubrey sat motionless, unable to speak. Her eyes sparkled, although he hadn't mentioned if he was talking in dollars or euros. It didn't matter to someone like her.

He continued. "Think about the scenic beauty for you to photograph. There's no place like it in the world. You could even start a business. Spend the first couple of years assembling your best work, find a local framer, and set up shop in the nicest small town you can find. An ideal situation. You wouldn't even have to spend too much time in the shop. I'm sure there will be young, local photographers anxious to learn the profession from you. You could manage things, spending just enough time on site to let the local customers get to know the artist."

Aubrey looked out the window as Jacques talked about the house and the photography studio. "It sounds incredibly romantic. Are we still going to France this fall?"

"Yes. The company's in decent shape. My bonuses have been good, and as you know, I've invested the money in diamonds. They've increased in value, so we ought to be okay. I'll give the owners reasonable notice so they can begin planning for my replacement. I'll have to stay on remotely for five or six months, but the transition should be smooth. You and I might even come back to Seattle a couple of times."

Even while he spoke to Aubrey, he thought along a different line. It was more than just bonuses he invested in diamonds. Much more. And he would not give any notice to the owners. There would be no transition.

And he'd never set foot in Seattle again. They could have made him rich at little cost to themselves, but they were cheap and didn't. Who cares if Great Chicago lost a few million? They could afford it. An added beauty of the situation occurred to him. Gerhardt Bergmann, that cheap scumbag, and the other owners of LeGrande might very well get stuck settling Great Chicago's loss. The thought of them holding the bag for millions made Levesque's smile widen.

Soon, he'd be in France, living in luxury, converting his diamond inventory into cash as needed. He knew he would probably have to take a hefty discount when he sold them, but he had been smart. He knew the discount was smaller on more valuable diamonds, and a couple of years ago, he began concentrating on only the finest stones he could find.

What he lost in value was the cost of doing business. There were no ownership records, and except for a few of his earlier purchases at retail jewelers, the diamonds were impossible for authorities to track. No evidence, no taxes on profits. When he did find a suitable home, maybe he'd find just the right seller and pay him with diamonds; the house would be his. No records. And by the time Great Chicago figured out what happened, as they of course would, he'd be in France and couldn't be extradited. The Perfect Score.

"Can we go to that chateau you told me about? We can stay there while we looked for a home. What did you call it?"

"We'll stay at the Chateau Saint-Martin as long as we need to, darling. As long as it takes us to find our perfect home. It's near the center of the French Riviera, no more than an hour drive to anywhere we might want to see. You'll love it. It's numbered among the finest of the luxury hotels on the French Riviera, possibly in the world." Even as he reassured Aubrey of his plans, he questioned if she still fit into those plans.

He had been with Aubrey Reddy for almost four years. He even thought he might love her, though that remained to be seen. He considered her a wonderful person and living with her was easy. The standard of living he provided for them proved to be more than sufficient for her. She made no added demands on him, and she even liked the business associates they were infrequently forced to socialize with. Occasionally, though seldom, they exchanged professions of love, and he knew she wanted to marry him. He would have to decide soon.

"Will we have enough money to do all of this? It sounds even more expensive than being here. Will you use those diamonds you've invested in?" she asked.

"Those will help us out. Plus, we have our investments, and I have the retirement plan. We'll be fine."

"There's nothing illegal about buying diamonds the way you do, is there? We don't have anything to worry about, do we?"

"Not a thing, darling. It's perfectly legal. Of course, there will always be a lawyer who will try to find a way to make things hard for someone else, especially someone with money, but I'm not worried about anything. I can't be extradited."

Aubrey Reddy breathed a sigh of relief. "I feel much better knowing that; I promise to stop worrying."

Levesque changed the subject. "Why don't I call the limo, and we can go up to the Palisade for an early dinner? We can look at the boats in the marina. Maybe we'll get an idea for a boat of our own in the Mediterranean."

In the instant he thought about a boat in the Mediterranean, he decided. He would go to France alone.

Chapter Forty

Yacht Haven Marina
Lake Union
Seattle, Washington
Saturday, August 10, 2019

"Our life is good. We've got it made," Kim Taylor said to her husband. They were at The Rudder enjoying a glass of wine together on their usual stools at the end of the bar. "We're living in a great city, living on a boat like we've always dreamed of, and working only when we feel like it. And we have enough money to carry us through our retirement years. We couldn't ask for much more."

Both were quiet as they contemplated what she said. Until losing his job a few years ago, Ross enjoyed a successful career, and they set aside a substantial amount of money for their future. Moreover, Kim's profession as a freelance writer paid her well. The sale of their home in Phoenix paid for their boat with quite a bit left over and neither worried about a full-time job.

He nodded agreement, leaned over, and kissed her.

"We do have it made, and you enrich my life. I love you, Kim."

She smiled in appreciation. "How about enriching my life? Let's take the dingy out for the afternoon tomorrow. The weather's supposed to stay clear and mild, at least until Monday night, so it should be a perfect day. We can look at boats here in the lake, then motor up to Ballard. I think the sockeye are still running at the locks, and we can have a fish lunch at Chinook's. Remember the last time we went up there in the dingy? That guy with a big salmon he landed that morning? Showing off for selfies, he fell in the water. Lost his fish to a seal."

Both enjoyed a good laugh as Crenshaw refilled their glasses and took their food order. The other bartender had called in sick, so he took care of all the customers tonight. He excused himself for not stopping to talk but he still took good care of them. Taylor knew he'd return with a joke later. He also noticed that Crenshaw no longer limped as badly as a week ago.

"I know we said we'd talk about anything but the Great Chicago assignment tonight, but I just wanted to mention that I spoke with Jacques Levesque this afternoon," Kim said. "I'm meeting him at his office Monday morning. No more about it tonight—you can brief me about him tomorrow." She took a drink of her wine. "Now, let's talk about something else—anything else."

"Okay." Ross was quiet for a moment, twirling his wine glass as if examining it. "Remember the other day when Liz told us she heard someone roaming around on the dock the night before? I can't explain why, but my first thought—it might have been Derek."

Kim's mood changed instantly. She and Ross grieved over this topic for so long that, to keep their sanity, they agreed to banish it from their discourse. Now, Ross brought it up. Life didn't seem so perfect after all.

Derek, their only child. A normal child, then a normal fifteen-year-old adolescent doing the things that fifteen-year-olds do. Until one day, he didn't come home. They received a handwritten note from him a week later saying he wanted to be alone, and he'd see them again someday. He said not to worry, he loved them, and please don't come looking.

Of course, they notified the authorities who conducted a search, but they never found a trace and not a word from him since. As grieving parents, they both fell into temporary depression. Somehow, they never blamed each other and kept their marriage intact. Though they both prayed, they never talked about him. He'd be eighteen now.

The private investigator still searched and every few weeks, gave them a report. So far, nothing. They decided to continue their lives and move on while never giving up hope.

"I'm sorry, sweetheart. It's as hard for me as it is for you. I just wanted you to know the premonition I felt the other day. I never stop thinking about him."

Kim understood and held no hard feelings. She loved Ross and knew he grieved just as much as she did. Once again, they were both heartbroken at the reminder. Both could see the signs when the other pondered the wellbeing of their son. It's why they agreed not to bring up Derek.

Even now, she didn't know whether to talk about him or change the subject. What could they say that hadn't already been said? What could they say to soothe each other's souls? She decided to change the subject.

"Let's plan a cruise, Ross."

His reaction told her that he wanted to move on to something else as well.

"We'll be done with our projects in a few weeks. We could leave right after the Labor Day weekend. You should be finished with Great Chicago and final editing on my article should be complete. Everyone else will be back home from vacations, and the harbors won't be crowded. Let's go to the Gulf Islands in Canada."

Their spirits immediately lifted at the thought. Before either could say another word, Crenshaw brought their dinners. They were engaged in serious talk, so he left them alone.

As they ate, Ross Taylor showed his enthusiasm for the idea and drew maps and made lists on bar napkins. "I love that area. We could leave here and spend the first night in Port Townsend. We can even spend a day or two there if we want to. It's a cool town. Then, we can sail into the San Juans. The wind is typically good north of Port Townsend. We could spend a night or two at Friday Harbor and maybe see some of your old high school friends. Check in on your parents. It could be a blast."

He sketched another map on the back of a menu between bites of food.

Kim felt the same excitement as Ross, and they forgot about the earlier discussion—at least temporarily. "If we went then, we might still be in time to see the last of the lavender blooming on San Juan Island. It's so beautiful. I'm ready to start provisioning now." All smiles again.

"We'll go through Canada Customs at Bedwell Harbor. That may be the prettiest place in all the islands—especially the resort we toured the last time we went there. You said the next time we were there, you wanted to check out the resort instead of anchoring in the harbor. Let's do that. We can stay there for a while, then cruise north into the Gulf Islands. I'm ready too."

They started making a list of harbors and anchorages to visit. As the list grew, they became more enthusiastic. "This will be a great cruise; the longest we've taken since buying the boat," Kim said.

Crenshaw arrived to pick up their plates, and in no hurry, he jumped right in. "A guy starts with a new primary care doctor. After two visits and exhaustive lab tests, the doc says he's doing 'fairly well' for his age.

"A little concerned about that comment, the guy asked the doc, 'That doesn't sound so good. Do you think I'll live to be eighty?'

"The doc asked him, 'Do you smoke tobacco, or drink beer, wine or hard liquor?'

"'No, and I'm not doing drugs either.'

"'Do you eat ribeye steaks and barbecued ribs?'

"'Not much. My last doctor said that all red meat is extremely unhealthy.'

"'Do you spend a lot of time in the sun, like playing golf, boating, sailing, hiking, or bicycling?'

"'Never.'

"'Do you gamble, drive fast cars, or have a lot of sex?'

"'Nope.'

"'Then, why do you even give a shit?'"

Half the bar heard the joke, and they erupted in laughter and applause, including Ross and Kim. They thanked Crenshaw for the service and the joke and gave him their credit card.

As they waited for the bill, Kim said, "Mrs. Fletcher stopped by while you were playing basketball this morning. We must have talked over coffee for two hours. She's such a nice lady. She brought homemade scones. Did you know she's been here for fifteen years? Her husband died, and because they enjoyed boating so much, she decided to move aboard their boat permanently and live here by herself. She's never taken the boat out of the slip, but she still services the engine every month just like he did.

"She told me there's supposed to be an eclipse of the moon on Monday evening. She wants to see it. She doesn't have a deck on her boat where she can watch it and asked if she can watch from ours. It's the perfect place—comfortable seating and a great view. She's been recovering from a hip injury, and our boat is easy for her to get on and off. We're going to be with Schlump, so I told her to come over anytime she wanted, and we'd leave the hatch unlocked if she needed to get in the boat for any reason."

Ross liked Mrs. Fletcher as well and often helped her with boat projects. Of course, she could hang out on their boat as long as she wanted.

As they started to leave, he said, "Hey, Crenshaw, you said you'd like to take a look at our boat. How about tomorrow morning, before you start your shift—say, around ten o'clock? We'll have the coffee pot on."

"Sounds great."

Finished at the bar, Ross and Kim Taylor walked back to the marina and the *Pura Vida*. An almost perfect evening. Almost.

Chapter Forty-one

Yacht Haven Marina
Lake Union
Seattle, Washington
Sunday, August 11, 2019

Taylor started early doing boat work. Kim stayed in bed. This time he cleaned the dingy for their afternoon cruise in the lake. He also tested the outboard motor and confirmed that the gas gauge indicated full. Everything ready. He gathered up his tools.

"Wow, she sure is a beauty." Crenshaw walked up the dock, and as promised, he carried a bottle of wine. He handed it to Taylor. "I took the liberty of selecting something I thought you and Kim might like. Thanks for inviting me."

"Thank you and you're welcome. You're still my hero. We'll enjoy this later."

"Any plans for today?"

"We're going to motor around the lake in the dingy this afternoon, go up to the locks, then have a late lunch. Chinook's. Right now, just enjoying Sunday."

"You've got the life we all want, Ross."

"Climb aboard and I'll show you around. Ready for coffee?"

Taylor never saw Crenshaw dressed in anything other than his navy-blue uniform and black apron. Today, he wore khaki shorts, a plain purple t-shirt, Oakley shades, and a Red Sox cap which covered his shaggy, medium-blond hair. Taylor noticed Crenshaw's muscular arms and legs and, for the first time, realized he never paid attention to Crenshaw's size. Although he stood a couple of inches shorter than Taylor, Crenshaw weighed as much and gave the appearance of a formidable man.

Kim poked her head out of the cabin and handed both men large mugs of coffee. "Hi, Crenshaw. You boys enjoy yourselves. I'm going to put in a couple of hours preparing for my interview."

She disappeared below the decks.

Although rain and wind were forecast for tomorrow, today was still sunny and calm. A low volume of Sunday morning car noise spilled off the Aurora Bridge overhead, and seagulls squawked near the houseboats. Otherwise, very little disturbed the morning quiet—perfect for touring a luxury sailboat.

"Let's start up here." Taylor walked toward the front of the boat, and Crenshaw followed. "You already know about sailboats so nothing I show you will be new to you. We chose this boat for two reasons. First, it's our home, and we wanted all the comforts we could afford. You'll see what I'm talking about in a minute. But we also want to cruise. We needed a safe, solid boat with all the systems necessary for long-distance passage-making. The *Pura Vida* is fifty feet long, made by a Swedish builder,

Hallberg-Rassy. It's four years old but like brand new when we bought it. All the systems are in great shape."

They walked around the deck. It had a sloop rig with a center cockpit, unlike other sailboats. What really separated it from the others were the fine-grained teak decks in the natural finish, the stainless-steel rod rigging, and the highly polished stanchions and deck hardware. Contrasting in appearance, the mast and boom were black anodized aluminum.

"It's awesome, Ross."

"It's built like a safe, but it's still quite fast. I know we'll feel comfortable if we decide to go long-distance cruising. Let's go below, and I'll show you where we live."

The interior impressed Crenshaw even more. After his first look, he said, "I've never seen a house this nice, let alone a boat."

"That's how we feel too. This is our main living area." Taylor showed the astonished Crenshaw the interior of the *Pura Vida*. "All the walls are light oak veneer. The framework for the dining sofa and the two armchairs is solid light oak. With the white ceiling, it gives us a light and open feeling."

As he spoke, Taylor reached into the navigation station and lowered the volume on the music. Frank Sinatra. "The light gray upholstery on the chairs and dinette is made of wool. So is the carpeting which covers the entire interior. This main area is for lounging, dining, and cooking."

Crenshaw shook his head and remained quiet.

"The galley has everything we had in our kitchen in Phoenix. Refrigerator, freezer, oven, range, microwave, dishwasher, and running water. It's all electric, and we use power from the marina. When we sail away from the dock, we supply the electricity with our generator."

Crenshaw opened the refrigerator and freezer, remarking at the surprising amount of cold storage space.

"Take a look forward. The designers made that a large sleeping area. Because we're here alone, we converted it to an office. Whoever needs privacy gets the office. Kim's there now."

Crenshaw peeked in the door. "This is nicer than my office was with Fidelity in San Francisco."

Ross continued the tour. "There's another sleeping area off to the side where another couple might stay. In a pinch, we can also use the dining sofa as a bed. So, we can have three people stay with us. The bathroom for this part of the boat is right here. It has a full shower for guests as well."

Taylor walked toward the stern of the boat. "Our bedroom is in the back. As you can see, there's a queen-size bed, two armchairs and places to store clothes. The bathroom is larger than the one in the front and, of course, has a full shower." It looked like a lived-in home with pictures and lamps on the nightstands and clothes hanging in open closets. A large, flat-screen TV folded up on hinges in the ceiling.

"Do you ever feel like you need more room?" Crenshaw asked. "I'm sure your house in Phoenix was large."

"It was. It took us a few months to get used to the confined quarters, but we're good with it now. All in all, we're in fairly good shape. Except for our personal treasures like Kim's music boxes, we don't miss much from our old house."

Crenshaw asked a few questions about the engine, generator, and other systems but mostly just admired what he saw. "It's incredible, Ross. Maybe it's not everyone's dream, but I know it's mine."

They walked up and sat in the cockpit. Their coffees were cold. Taylor said, "You're probably due at the bar soon so I won't break out the beer, but next time you have a day off, we can have a few and talk a bit. Let me know. I haven't forgotten your offer to work with me. I don't know just what it might be, but I'll think about it."

"Thanks, Ross. Great tour of a great boat. Thank Kim for me too. Enjoy the wine." Crenshaw jumped off the boat, waved goodbye, and headed toward The Rudder.

Taylor enjoyed the thought of working with Crenshaw.

Chapter Forty-two

Wells Fargo Center
Seattle, Washington
Monday, August 12, 2019

Kim Taylor was a beautiful woman. She looked much younger than her forty-seven years, and today she made an exceptional appearance. Still standing, she was a perfect mix of business elegance and casual confidence.

Jacques Levesque spent the weekend researching Kim, so he already expected all of that. Still, when he joined her in the library, she took him by surprise.

Her hair hung loosely around her face. She wore a simple but perfectly tailored black jacket and pants. Her seashell-white blouse featured a high ruffled collar which hid her neck, and ruffled cuffs peeked out from her jacket sleeves. She wore a limited amount of jewelry—diamond stud earrings and a three-carat diamond wedding ring set—and carried a small black leather handbag and a matching writing portfolio. Black Louis Vuitton ankle boots completed her ensemble.

She had arrived in the LeGrande library minutes earlier, and Oskar Kungen welcomed her. He made her comfortable in one of the overstuffed leather chairs and brought the coffee and croissant service, customary for important guests of LeGrande, just like Jacques had instructed. Kim Taylor more than qualified as an important guest.

"Good morning, Kim. Welcome to LeGrande and thank you for coming." He found it difficult not to come right out and tell her how attractive he found her.

"Thank you for having me," she said. "I've read and heard a great deal about you, and it's nice to finally make your acquaintance. I'm sure the editors at the *Puget Sound Business Journal* are excited to see the product of our meeting."

"Well, let's make it worth their while. We've closed the offices for a couple of weeks out of respect for one of our valued friends and associates, Lucas Sims. Maybe you know who he is. So, only Oskar, Nina, and I are here today."

In a phone call on Saturday, the two had agreed to a limited number of ground rules. Kim could take the inquiry wherever she wished. In return, he promised to be candid and unguarded with her. During the call, neither of them ever mentioned Ross Taylor's name.

Levesque filled their coffee cups, settled back in his chair, and suggested she begin. He looked forward to the experience.

The interview lasted over four hours with only one short break. It couldn't have gone more smoothly. She told him she considered it to be one of the easiest interviews she had ever conducted, while still being quite enlightening.

She explored his French heritage in detail, his growing up, his school years, his name change, and his business career. Of course they talked about his basketball court. He was sensitive about his name change and didn't want to her to suggest he denied his Jewish heritage. In the end, he gave her permission to use the information any way she chose.

There were times when he expected Kim to raise questions about the operations of LeGrande—questions suggesting that Ross Taylor put her up to it, but she never did. Her questions never strayed from the topics they agreed to on Saturday.

"I'm sure you'll want to see the basketball court. It's what I'm best known for. The rest of the place looks like any other business office."

They walked from the library around to his office and the court. He launched into a presentation about every aspect of the court in the most minute detail. The dimensions, the special windows, the people who came to play. He made it clear to Kim that he loved being known for it.

"This is quite impressive. Thank you for the tour and the description." Without prompting, she turned and walked back to the library.

"I believe that does it for me, Jacques. I have everything I need." She closed her writing portfolio and placed it alongside her handbag, preparing to leave.

"Do you want to continue this interview tomorrow?"

"No. We've covered everything I wanted to cover."

"Then, please be my guest for lunch. The Metropolitan Grill is right across the street, and even in the early afternoon, their steaks and martinis are the best in Seattle." For more than four hours, he had hoped to hear a yes to his offer. As he asked her, he lightly touched her hand.

"Thank you for your kind invitation, but no. I make it a practice to transcribe my notes and outline my article immediately after my interviews, while they're still fresh in my mind. Perhaps you noticed, I don't record my interviews. This has been a pleasure, and I'm sure we'll meet again sometime. Please thank Oskar for his hospitality as well." With that, she picked up her things, shook his hand, and left Jacques Levesque and LeGrande Benefits.

Watching her leave, Levesque's mood changed quickly. He knew he gave her a lot of material with which to create a great article. He felt confident that whatever she produced would be widely read and his reputation enhanced. And he knew she appealed to him. Still, he didn't feel good at all. Could he trust her? Maybe she only interviewed him to discover something to help Ross Taylor in his assignment? A Trojan Horse? He didn't have much time to decide.

What did Kim Taylor learn about him that she didn't already know? What kind of article would she write? Did she learn anything that might help Ross in his investigation? Did she consider him a criminal or any kind of threat?

Chapter Forty-three

Yacht Haven Marina
Lake Union
Seattle, Washington
Monday, August 12, 2019

At the same time Kim Taylor conducted her interview with Jacques Levesque, her husband made a discovery. He worked on and off over the weekend and sorted the LeGrande claims data in every way he could think of. There could no longer be any question. LeGrande Benefits was stealing from Great Chicago. Big time. He called Schlump.

"I've got it," he said when Schlump picked up his phone. "They're writing fake claims on terminated employees."

"How do you know?"

He explained everything he'd tried so far. "Nothing else worked. Then I noticed that claims on terminated employees were much higher than expected. In some months, twice as high. The same for every one of their clients."

"What do you want me to do, Ross?"

"Do the same thing at your end. Look only at the terminated employee claims. See what you come up with. We'll compare notes later today."

"I'll take care of it. Are you going to call Chris?"

"Not yet. I want to wait until you confirm what I found. We'll talk about it tonight, and if we're sure, I'll call her in the morning. You still want to meet at Tulio?"

"Sounds good. I'll see you and Kim at six o'clock. I'm hungry."

"You're always hungry."

"Yeah, but I'm lucky. I get to eat whatever I want and not worry about getting fat." Schlump hung up.

Ross Taylor pondered the situation. Insurance claims tend to occur in predictable patterns. In large populations, experienced actuaries can predict, within close tolerances, what claims will be incurred by age, gender, income, zip code, employment status, education level, time of year, and other metrics. Taylor sorted the claims data for LeGrande into these categories and looked for results that varied from the predicted norms. At first, none emerged, and everything looked normal.

He even thought of Benford's Law. Five years ago, he uncovered a claims fraud in his own company by employing the little-known accounting test. From his knowledge of fraud detection, he knew that the first digit of multi-digit claims dollar amounts tended to follow a predictable pattern. By far, the highest percentage of claims have a first digit of 1. The next highest percentage is 2. And so on. The first digit occurring least often is 9.

The criminals wanted to keep the claim amounts low enough to avoid suspicion yet high enough to be meaningful. They chose to submit all their fake claims between $500 and $700. When Taylor sorted the claims in his company by first digit, he found they didn't occur in the predictable pattern. Claim amounts starting with 5, 6 or 7 were far more frequent. It provided the clue he needed to expose the fraud and have the criminals arrested.

Unfortunately, no such luck with LeGrande. The LeGrande claims were distributed exactly as they should have been. Taylor decided to sort the claims between active employees and terminated employees. A remarkably simple sort but he struck gold.

The first thing he saw when he examined 2019 year-to-date claims was that LeGrande paid between fifteen hundred and two thousand more claims per month on terminated employees than expected. A large variance and not explainable. He went back and checked prior years. Beginning in mid-2016, the number of these claims started to diverge from the expected level. Initially, there were around five hundred more claims per month. Then six hundred. Soon the excess numbered more than one thousand.

If the reason for these claims couldn't be explained, it pointed straight at a fraud. Few things brought out the anger in Taylor as much as criminals who tried to defraud his companies—or, in this case, his client's. Now he had a breakthrough, the opening he looked for, and he felt energized. But he didn't have enough. He needed more. Christine wanted an answer.

Taylor started to feel stretched. He knew hundreds, maybe thousands, of the claims were fake. But which ones? Who got the money? And if Jacques Levesque orchestrated the scam, how did he get the money and what did he do with it?

Chapter Forty-four

Tulio Ristorante
Seattle, Washington
Monday, August 12, 2019

Kim had stopped for a salad at The Rudder on her way home from the Levesque interview, and Ross made an early-afternoon snack for himself on the boat. Now both were hungry for dinner. Schlump arrived early, and even as the waiter seated him, he ordered a carafe of the house Chianti Classico and a plate of ravioli. His appetizer. The others could fend for themselves.

"I forgot to go to the gym today. That's thirteen years in a row now." Schlump shook his head in mock disappointment.

Tulio enjoyed a reputation as a long-time Seattle favorite among Italian food lovers. The staff recognized Schlump as a regular, and at his instruction, they had set a larger-than-normal table for them upstairs in a corner near the front windows. Away from the noisier downstairs, they could talk without being overheard.

Under other circumstances, they might eat outside, but the rain began early in the afternoon and now came down in sheets. Seattle rain tended to be soft and intermittent, but tonight, it poured down in pellets with no sign of letup.

With their orders placed and their wine glasses filled, they launched into the reason for the gathering.

Ross Taylor started. "There's no way this could happen by accident. LeGrande is stealing from Great Chicago. They've rigged the claims system to issue fraudulent claim checks on terminated employees. They receive those checks and deposit them into their own account or accounts. They've done it for almost four years, and it looks like they've diverted around sixty million. The trouble is, we don't know which claims are bogus. During the past four years, LeGrande has paid almost one billion in claims, and we're trying to isolate around six percent of them."

Taylor tore a piece of garlic bread from the loaf in the center of the table. He wasn't the first, as Schlump sat on the other side. "Whatever they're doing is almost foolproof. It slid past Great Chicago's own audit and the audit from Stockholm Fidelity, their bonding company. Nothing either of them looked at seemed out of line. But they didn't look at what we looked at."

Their food and another carafe came, and the conversation shifted to how good everything tasted. Schlump always talked about food, and tonight, between bites, he compared Tulio to every other Italian restaurant he knew in Seattle.

Schlump used his bread to mop up the last of the sauce on his plate. "What now?"

"We double our effort to find out who's getting

the money. Sixty million dollars went to somebody in LeGrande—most likely Jacques Levesque. We've got to sort those claims again with a fine-tooth comb and figure out how they did it. The answer's there."

Everyone nodded. They were close, but until they could isolate the claims and positively identify them as bogus, they couldn't prove anything. They knew a great deal but weren't finished. Far from it. They hadn't recovered any money. The steep hill Taylor climbed only steepened.

"I'll call Christine in the morning and let her know what we've found. It's too late tonight. I know she'll be excited that we're onto something, but we don't have much more than a hunch. I'm a little surprised she hasn't called the local FBI office. If I experienced an unexplained loss the size of hers, I'd have called them in at the first sign of trouble. But that's up to her."

Schlump started to sense the same urgency Taylor felt. "You know, if Levesque finds out we're onto him, he'll most likely just take off. While we're trying to pin down the answer, try to encourage Chris to bring in the FBI. They can keep an eye on Levesque while we dig deeper."

Schlump looked at Kim. "Did you learn anything about Levesque today?"

"He's just like Ross described him. Smooth, handsome, and extremely confident. He even hit on me as I walked out. So, when I hear about what you've found, it's not surprising—especially if he wants more money. But as to learning something that could help you, no. Nothing. And we have no plans to meet again."

"Did he seem anxious, like a guy getting ready to pull a runner?" Schlump asked.

"No. He stayed pretty cool. Didn't seem like a criminal or worried about anything for that matter. If he's the guy, he sure doesn't show it."

They finished dinner, and Schlump paid the bill as promised.

Taylor wrapped things up. "All right. I'll call Christine in the morning. You get back to the claims, Schlump. Look for recurring data points—same name, same address, same dollar amounts. You know what I'm talking about. I'll do the same. It's there, and we'll find it. Kim will help me. I'll call you in the morning."

The drive back to their boat took longer than usual because of the rain. The two said little as Ross concentrated on the traffic. As they crossed the Fremont Bridge, red and blue lights flashed from the area near the Yacht Haven Marina. When they reached the marina, two Seattle Police cars and an ambulance were parked at the entrance.

Kim and Ross trotted down the slippery dock as quickly as possible with large golf umbrellas in the pouring rain and found four Seattle Police officers talking together near the *Pura Vida*. Two paramedics were inside the cockpit of the *Pura Vida* attending to someone. All six were in bright yellow rain jackets.

Liz sat on the dock sobbing.

"What's going on?" Taylor asked the officers. "This is our boat."

One of the police officers said, "We received a call

about an attack on this boat." He pointed toward Mrs. Fletcher. "This lady says that someone tried to hit her over the head with a club. She dodged the blow but got hit hard on the shoulder. She's in pain, and the paramedics are treating her, but she refuses to get into the ambulance. Says she's fine and won't come with us."

Taylor introduced Kim and himself and described Mrs. Fletcher as a neighbor who asked to use their boat in case the weather cleared so she could see the eclipse. The police officer identified himself as Officer Slack.

"Somebody shot Brutus, Ross!" Liz shouted between sobs. She couldn't control her sobbing. "Jim took him to the vet."

The officer tried with little success to take notes in the rain. "Why would someone come onto your boat and hit this lady? And shoot this young woman's dog?"

"I have no idea. She's a harmless old lady who everyone loves," Kim answered. "She's almost eighty years old."

Ross nodded. "As for Brutus, he must have seen whoever did this and gone after him. He knows everyone on the dock and who doesn't belong here."

"Is it possible someone thought they were attacking one of you?" Officer Slack asked.

Ross thought about it. "It's possible. There's nobody who's given us any trouble or that we're worried about. My work is investigating business frauds. My wife and I are working on a case which might uncover a substantial criminal operation. I suppose someone we're looking into might want to send a warning."

"Has anyone involved in that case threatened you or

your wife in any way, Mr. Taylor? Directly or indirectly?"

"Well, not me directly. But one of the senior executives of the company we're looking into got shoved under a subway train in Chicago last week. I have reason to believe he held information he wanted to give me. Possibly there's a link. Now that I think about it, Liz heard someone prowling around on this dock last week. Brutus, her dog, chased him off. We didn't give it much thought at the time, but maybe all these events are connected."

"Anything else?"

"You could also ask the bartender at The Rudder across the street. Crenshaw told me someone almost ran over him the same night someone was prowling on our dock."

The officer nodded and wrote something in his wet notebook.

Mrs. Fletcher stepped off the *Pura Vida* with her arm in a sling. "I don't want this thing, but they made me wear it. But I'm sure not getting in that ambulance," she said to everyone present. She seemed in good spirits and smiled at Kim and Ross. "Pretty exciting for a rainy night. Never did see the eclipse."

Officer Slack asked her more questions and made notes before allowing Kim to walk her back to her boat. He then spent time talking to Liz who, by now, had calmed down.

His work temporarily finished, he came back to Taylor. "We'll want to talk to you about this again, Mr. Taylor. So far, nobody can tell us much of anything. The older lady didn't see the attacker, and the young woman with the dog couldn't tell us a thing about what the attacker looked like because of the rain and wind. My partner checked for security cameras at the office, but they're out of order. Do you have a gun?"

Ross nodded. "I keep a loaded 9mm Beretta in the office on our boat."

"You might want to keep it handy. Just be careful. Here's my card. Call if you can add anything."

The officers walked up the dock. Kim and Ross boarded the *Pura Vida*. Too energized to go to bed, they sat together on the settee, Kim in her usual corner and Ross by her side.

"That scared me, Ross. I'm afraid—for both of us. And poor Mrs. Fletcher. This is no way to live. She might have been killed. Or you. Or me. What's going on here?"

"Someone meant this for one of us, not Mrs. Fletcher." He put his hand on hers as she nodded agreement. "I'm ready to kill someone, but I don't know who. Levesque? He's too smart. He'd expect the finger to point to him. Meyerhoffer? He's not smart enough. But you never know how people think. If I find out who did this, I promise you, that piece of garbage is going to pay, big time."

Chapter Forty-five

Yacht Haven Marina
Lake Union
Seattle, Washington
Tuesday, August 13, 2019

The rainstorm that started yesterday still raged. Ross Taylor stood in the dark on the deck of the *Pura Vida*, the light of the new day not yet having made its debut over the Cascades east of Seattle. He held his second cup of coffee in his right hand. His left hand warmed in his pocket, and a wave of his wet hair blew in his face. Raindrops ran off his foul-weather jacket.

Last night, he slept poorly. The attack on Mrs. Fletcher first unnerved then infuriated him. What dirtbag would hit a seventy-eight-year-old woman? What could possibly have been the motive? He lacked answers but not questions. Kim still slept, and he tried to walk softly on the deck so as not to wake her. They had talked about the assault and Mrs. Fletcher well into the night.

The morning started out unusually cool for August, and although he didn't mind the rain, he felt cold and decided to go back into the warm cabin. It was only six-thirty in Chicago, but Christine Bell would be awake and take his call. He took off his jacket, went into the office, closed the door, and reviewed his notes. Then he punched in her number.

"Hi, Ross. Pretty early for you, isn't it?"

"Yeah, but I thought you'd want to hear an update." Taylor didn't need notes for this call, but he looked at his notebook anyway.

"Schlump and I have looked at everything you've given us. We've sliced and diced the data every way we can imagine. We've interviewed your staff, and we've visited your three largest producers. I'm going to summarize everything, even if we've already discussed this with you. Then I'll give you the bottom line. Here's where we are as of this minute.

"First, we can rule out fraud from inside your company. Whatever is going on is not internal. That should give you a degree of satisfaction."

Christine remained silent.

"Schlump and I visited Consolidated Group Benefits, Argus Benefits, and LeGrande Benefits. For two reasons, these are the only producers we examined. Most important, they represent almost ninety percent of your business. That alone makes them obvious candidates for suspicion. But equally important, all three handle claims processing on the business. If one of them were engaged in a fraud, it would be much easier for them since they are processing claims as well as premium."

He continued. "We checked out Consolidated and Argus thoroughly. We examined their books, analyzed their data, and audited their systems. While we can't yet positively rule out fraud at one of those companies, we're fairly certain they aren't the source of the problem."

"Does that mean you suspect LeGrande?" she asked. "They're our largest producer, and our relationship with them goes back as long as I've been with Great Chicago. I'd hate to call them out and be wrong. I hope you're being careful how you deal with them."

"I appreciate your concern, Chris. I know how important they are to you. We're being as careful as we can, and I'm managing that relationship personally. They're not happy about our audit, but they've been cooperating fully. Jacques has given us access to everything we've asked for. It's been a little slower since Lucas Sims's death. He all but ran the entire organization, and no one else has his knowledge or talent. Because of his death, they asked us to hold off for a couple of weeks."

"Is that a problem?" Christine Bell asked from two thousand miles to the east.

"No and I understand, but one thing has come to our attention which we find interesting. At first, it didn't seem out of the ordinary, but as we examined the data more carefully, we began to be wary. It's why we're still looking at LeGrande."

Ross took a drink of his now-cold coffee. "As you know, when an employee terminates employment, their insurance normally terminates at the same time. But previously incurred claims for terminated employees often take weeks or even months to work their way through the claims payment system. Your actuaries are quite aware of that process, and the number of claims from terminated employees is predictable. Normally, only slight variations show up in the volume of claims for terminated employees from group to group.

"That's true with LeGrande as well. Only slight variations exist from employer group to employer group. What's remarkable is that, for claims on terminated employees, considerable variation exists between LeGrande's pool of business and the pools of business of Consolidated and Argus. And our sample data pools as well. Claims for terminated employees are much more frequent on the LeGrande business."

Ross paused and allowed her to absorb the information.

After what seemed to be an inordinate silence, she said, "This sounds potentially serious. How confident are you in your conclusion?"

"It's preliminary, but it's a major red flag. It's enough to make us drop everything else and concentrate exclusively on LeGrande. I assume you'll want us to go ahead with a detailed analysis. Schlump and I are doing nothing else. We should be finished by Thursday. We'll know everything by then."

"This is remarkable. Of course, I want you to move forward. It's puzzling but I'll save my questions for Thursday. Are you doing the same analysis for Consolidated and Argus?"

"No. We've already studied their claims for terminated employees. They check out. Their claims are almost the same as we predict for any other population. LeGrande is different. We'll see what we find, then go from there. I'll call you on Thursday with an update."

"Ross," Christine continued, "if this is fraud, our focus is on the money. We need to get the money back, not just identify who did it and how. Don't let up until you know where it is and how we can get it back."

"Will do," Taylor answered, but he didn't like that Christine would be satisfied if he simply found the money. He knew his need for justice would weigh on him if he couldn't pin it on LeGrande. Then he asked her the question which bothered him most. "Do you think it's time to alert the FBI? After all, if someone is embezzling from Great Chicago, it's a federal crime."

She remained silent for so long, Ross thought they had lost the connection.

Then she said, "I'm tempted. What you've told me is quite unusual. But just in case they have an explanation, such as a programming glitch, let's wait another couple of days while you finish the analysis. If you find that the data continues to point to fraud, I'll make the call."

"Okay, we'll wait. I just don't want what happened to me to happen to you."

"This is excellent work, and I appreciate it. Keep digging. Just be careful not to upset the LeGrande people unnecessarily. If it turns out to be a false lead, we have an important relationship to maintain. Jacques Levesque may not be the most pleasant person to deal with, but he has been a great producer for us for years. Do you need anything else from me today? Should I ask Winston to put his team to work on this?"

"No thanks, Chris. Schlump and I are far enough along in the process to get you an answer quickly. You should know, Winston has been great to work with. He's exceptionally talented and has assembled a highly skilled team. He's fiercely loyal to you. You have every reason to be confident in him."

She acknowledged the compliment.

"I'm not sure it has anything to do with our work for Great Chicago, but someone attacked a guest on our boat last night. The police think the attacker might have been after either Kim or me."

"That's terrible, Ross. Is your friend all right?"

"From what she tells us, she's going to be fine and, under the circumstances, has taken the whole thing extremely well. We're concerned because it's unlikely the attacker targeted her. The attack might have been planned for one of us, and if that's the case, I'm dealing with a major threat. I'm trying not to get too far afield speculating on who might be behind it, but I'm furious about it. If someone we're investigating is responsible, we've found the criminals. And if I get my hands on them . . ."

"You be careful, Ross, and give Kim my best wishes. I'll talk to you soon." Christine ended the call.

Taylor felt relief at having the call out of the way. Christine Bell now knew everything he and Schlump knew. More than ever, he believed they were looking at insurance fraud and should call in the federal authorities. The public thought this kind of crime had no victims other than giant, wealthy insurance companies, but there is no such thing as victimless crime. Ross knew that fraud meant every policyholder paid more in premiums because of the crime. Finding the source of the insurance fraud would satisfied him immensely, and if he found out who hit Mrs. Fletcher, he'd find a way to make it even more satisfying.

Everything pointed to Levesque. Still, anything was

possible. Could Lucas Sims have been behind the fraud? After all, he was a brilliant programmer and totally capable of setting it up on his own. Maybe Lucas did it, and Levesque knew nothing. Maybe Lucas died from a random act. But maybe not.

Though excited about the progress they were making, he still didn't have all the answers. Which claims were fake? Who received the money? What were they doing with it? When he figured that out, he'd know the mastermind.

It bother him that Christine postponed calling the FBI.

He typed notes from the call to Christine, then walked onto the deck. The rain had stopped, and the sun was breaking through the clouds on the horizon. Though still early, he called Schlump to report on the assault last night and the call to Christine.

Taylor thought he knew the endpoint of this investigation. He felt reasonably certain that Levesque organized the financial disaster Great Chicago experienced. What if Ross could explain the crime but couldn't prove it or, worse, not recover the money?

Did Levesque have something to do with the attack on Mrs. Fletcher? Or the death of Lucas Sims? Taylor boiled inside.

Chapter Forty-six

Yacht Haven Marina
Lake Union
Seattle, Washington
Wednesday, August 14, 2019

The events on Monday night were beginning to recede from Taylor's consciousness, and after a long day of analyzing data, he needed exercise this morning. Staying up late didn't help. There were several promising leads buried in LeGrande's terminated employee data, but the decisive factor still evaded him.

Now, in his basketball clothes, he drove to Green Lake. His cell phone rang.

Christine Bell got right to the point. "After talking it over with a couple of my directors, I decided to have a conversation with the local FBI office. I gave the FBI all the information you've been supplying me. They were interested and promised to investigate. They said they didn't hear anything from my report to lead them to jump right in. I agreed with them. They're going to arrange for a local agent in Seattle to contact you to set up a meeting."

"Thanks, Chris. I appreciate the heads-up. I don't have anything new to report since we talked yesterday. I'll let you know if I do. Did you notify Levesque?"

"Yes, I called him as soon as I hung up with the FBI. He understood and seemed to be okay with it. He blames you, you know. He believes you've got something against him and have stirred this up without any evidence. He's threatening to sue. Take it easy on this. Tell the FBI what you know but don't guess."

"I'll be careful. Thanks for the update." He turned his Toyota SUV around and headed back to the boat.

The phone rang again. No caller ID this time, and he didn't recognize the number.

"Hello. Ross Taylor speaking."

"Hi, Ross. It's Frank Walsh. How are you doing?"

"Fine, Frank. What can I do for you?" Taylor wanted to do nothing for Frank Walsh. His question was simply a civil way to respond. Hearing Walsh's name and voice disgusted him. Frank Walsh, chairman of the board of Arizona Life and Health Insurance Company, fired Taylor three years earlier.

"I've been keeping track of you, Ross. I hear you've been doing great work for some fine companies. How about coming back to Arizona Life? Chief executive officer, vice chairman, country club membership, double what we were paying you and a bunch of options. I can fly up to Seattle over the weekend, and we can work out the details over dinner. Bring Kim along. I know she'll be interested in what I have to say."

Taylor thought for a moment. "Have you resigned as chairman and sold all your stock in Arizona Life?"

"Hell no! Why would I do a thing like that?"

"Because until you do, I won't set foot within five miles of you or your company. You're a sleazebag, Frank, and if I ever hear your voice again, if I ever see your face again, I'm going to start the lawsuit that I've been contemplating for almost three years. The statute of limitations hasn't run out yet. And I may kick your ass while I'm at it."

"You can't talk to me—"

Taylor hung up. He hadn't spoken to Walsh in almost three years. The passage of time made him feel even better about the call. He couldn't wait to tell Kim.

Chapter Forty-seven

Yacht Haven Marina
Lake Union
Seattle, Washington
Wednesday, August 14, 2019

Less than an hour after he hung up on Walsh, his phone rang again. FBI Special Agent Dale Harrison called and asked to meet him. Harrison had been assigned to follow up on the information Christine Bell gave to their Chicago office, and he wanted to meet at Taylor's office. As a precaution, Taylor said he'd call him right back.

He made a quick call to Schlump and asked him to call Postiglione to verify Harrison was, indeed, an FBI agent.

When he was satisfied as to Harrison's identity, Taylor called him back and agreed to meet for lunch at The Rudder.

Taylor liked Dale Harrison the moment he met him. When lunch finished, they moved their conversation onto the *Pura Vida*, a more comfortable and pleasant environment than going to Harrison's office.

"We covered a great deal at lunch, Ross, and I have almost everything I came for today. I'd like to have a look at your data and understand your analysis, of course, and maybe make copies. From what I've heard from you and Christine Bell, if your suspicions turn out to be correct, LeGrande and possibly Mr. Levesque are guilty of several federal crimes."

Exactly what Ross Taylor wanted to hear.

"Any use of the US Postal Service in the commission of this type of crime is a federal offense, as is use of the phone, wire transfers, or internet. And if there have been any monetary transactions using funds they obtained illegally, such as opening new bank accounts or making any purchases, it becomes what we commonly refer to as money laundering. Because of the dollar amounts involved, we've changed our minds. This is a serious matter, and we have already put our resources to work."

"What's next?" Taylor asked.

"That's all I need for now. We'll keep you posted on our progress. I'll probably want to talk to you again after we've reviewed your data. I'd like to know a little more about the kind of work you do, and if you don't mind, I'd love to talk about your boat. I have a small runabout myself, but I've always wanted a larger boat to cruise with my family."

Harrison made his feelings clear; he loved Taylor's boat. The two men sat in the cockpit and talked while soaking up the afternoon sun. Everyone who lived near Seattle lived for days like today. If every day was like this one, there'd be thirty-five million people living here. But every day wasn't like this one, so only four million did.

"What made you and your wife decide to live on a boat instead of in a house like most of us do?"

Taylor had anticipated Harrison's first question.

"Not an easy decision, by any means. Kim and I were like you; we've owned small boats and lived in houses. But we wanted to cruise. We've traveled to at least thirty countries and have a well developed spirit of adventure. We used to talk all the time about what this life could be like. Deciding to do it proved to be tougher than talking about it. Believe it or not, the biggest obstacle turned out to be what to do with everything in our house."

Harrison raised his eyebrows.

"We looked at a house full of furniture, closets full of clothes, and a garage full of cars and equipment, and we couldn't imagine being without any of it. Besides, what would our family and friends think? Moving from a big house onto a boat. We'd be weirdoes.

"Of course, looking back, we didn't need any of the stuff in our house. After our massive garage sale and donations to the Salvation Army, we didn't miss a thing, and we still don't. We have a small trailer in the parking lot. We keep the things we just couldn't part with and our out-of-season clothes in it. But, for the most part, what we have on the boat is everything we own.

"Now our family and friends envy the freedom we have. We've come to appreciate the time we used to spend simply maintaining our home and our possessions. Now, even though there's always boat work to be done, we have all the time in the world to do things together. Our lives are much simpler. And northwest Washington is a great place to have time to spend on enjoyment."

Dale Harrison could hardly conceal his envy.

"We all know people who live their whole lives in the same job without getting any enjoyment. Doing the same thing every day. Going through the motions. I loved my work, and my job gave me satisfaction and many rewards. But both Kim and I knew we wanted something else, more adventure. When they fired me, we decided to take the risk."

Harrison leaned forward as if listening to a suspect. "Why did you choose a sailboat? Why not a cabin cruiser with all the room they have inside?"

"We spent a great deal of time on that question too. We like big cruisers, and we looked at new ones in the fifty-foot range. The main living saloons were always spacious with large windows, and the galleys are open and accessible. Cruisers are nice, but we're adventurers. The idea of being limited to protected cruising areas didn't appeal to us. In my experience, big cruisers aren't as hospitable out in the open ocean. They bob around like corks and are somewhat limited to protected waters. Sailboats, on the other hand, are much heavier and tend to cut through the water rather than ride on the top. In my opinion, they're stronger and more comfortable. We saw ourselves as the kind of people who might just decide to sail around the world someday, and only a sailboat qualified. So, here we are."

"You're a lucky man, Ross. I'm sure a sizable portion of the population wished they were in your place right now. I'm sitting here thinking about my big house full of things, closets full of clothes, and a garage full of junk. Your story sounds pretty appealing."

Taylor got a couple of soft drinks for the two of them. At lunch, Harrison showed a clear aptitude for the insurance business, and Ross gave him an overview of the Great Chicago matter. Taylor spread out his data, offering email copies of anything Harrison might want.

"Any time there's money involved," Ross Taylor said, "someone will want to take a shortcut to get it—legally or illegally. Sometimes, in our business, we're our own worst enemies."

"How so?"

"Take the idea of what we call Third Party Administrators. Insurance companies hire these organizations to help with back-office functions because they can do it cheaper. We usually refer to them as TPAs.

"Typically, TPAs prepare billings for the insurance company's clients and collect the premiums. The TPA then pays commission to the brokers and sends what's left over to the insurance company. Also, the TPAs are likely to pay claims. These are all important functions and good TPAs do them well."

Listening carefully, Harrison asked, "Doesn't that give the TPAs a great opportunity to steal money?"

"You bet it does. It's the biggest source of insurance fraud from outside the companies. That's why I said we were our own worst enemies. We keep hiring them. Part of the problem is that these TPAs have competition. They are forced to price their services as low as possible. Sometimes, this leaves them short of capital, and the temptation to *borrow* it from the insurance company is compelling. The borrowing usually takes the form of delaying sending the premiums to the company. The

TPA uses a portion of the premium to fund operations and remits the proper amount using part of the premium from the next month. Like a Ponzi scheme. The cycle continues until the TPA is behind by more than it can cover up."

Energized by Harrison's concentration, Taylor continued. "Companies are often far too liberal in allowing the TPAs to hold funds. In some cases, they don't require payment until forty-five days after the TPA collects them. This can be unbearably tempting to a TPA with a cash flow problem."

"Don't the insurance companies audit these guys?" Dale Harrison asked.

"Yes, they do, but it's typically not frequent or thorough enough. This kind of fraud is quite easy to detect—if the company sends good auditors. Often, they don't, and the TPAs pick up on that pretty fast. LeGrande is a TPA for Great Chicago. If it turns out that we're correct about what they're doing, it's a perfect example of the auditors not doing their job."

"Have you ever been a victim? Do you think this is the kind of fraud being perpetrated on Great Chicago?" Harrison asked.

"Three times in my companies and four others with client companies," Ross answered. "I've been lucky because we resolved all of them positively for the insurance companies, although in different ways. Of course, one of them did cost me my job, even though I solved the problem."

"Do you mind telling me about one?"

Chapter Forty-eight

Yacht Haven Marina
Lake Union
Seattle, Washington
Wednesday, August 14, 2019

"Not at all. Just a minute." Taylor went below to get two more drinks. The temperature had risen steadily since the two men left The Rudder.

When Taylor returned, he began his story. "Even though this took place a few years ago, I remember the details of one scam quite vividly. It involved a guy who functioned both as a broker and an administrator—just like LeGrande. I'd tell you his name but he's back in business, and I don't want to start any trouble for myself. You can find out who I'm talking about easily enough."

Harrison nodded.

"Are you familiar with credit life insurance?"

Harrison shook his head.

"Credit life insurance is sold to customers who borrow money from banks and consumer loan companies. When their loan is approved, the loan officer will suggest the customer buy a life insurance policy to pay off the loan in case of the customer's death.

"The premium is added to the loan and is financed along with the loan. The borrower's monthly payments are slightly higher as a result. Borrowers are thrilled just to get the loan and hardly consider the question of life insurance. They simply agree. Or they believe it's a requirement, which it's not, and just sign the application."

"Is this a legitimate form of insurance?"

"Absolutely. It's legitimate, and it provides valuable protection for certain borrowers. If a borrower with credit life insurance dies, the loan is paid off, and the surviving family no longer must pay the loan obligation. Having a home mortgage paid off through credit life insurance can be a life-altering event if a family loses the breadwinner."

Taylor warmed to his audience. "The scam took place about twenty years ago. Our company performed due diligence on this broker/administrator and determined he maintained a spotless record during his insurance career. He operated solely in Illinois and specialized in credit life insurance programs for three large Illinois bank chains and consumer credit companies. We contracted with him to sell our credit life product to his clients. As part of the set-up process, we gave him compact discs which included our rates. He, in turn, passed them along to his bank clients. Those rate CDs contained the premiums the banks charged their borrowers. Remember, this took place almost twenty years ago, so we were still using discs. Today, it's all internet-based, and we have a different set of risks.

"Anyway, the bank sold credit life insurance to some of their borrowers, collected the full premium from the borrower as part of the loan and remitted the premium to our broker/administrator. As our administrator, he aggregated the premiums from all his clients and remitted them in bulk to us—just like LeGrande does for Great Chicago. The process worked smoothly, just as it does for almost all such relationships—just like it does for LeGrande."

Special Agent Dale Harrison nodded his understanding. "How did he defraud you?"

"As soon as we provided him with our rate CDs, he produced new ones, on a computer in his basement, with rates that were about twenty percent higher than we charged. He gave his bogus CDs to the lenders and destroyed ours. Those were the rates the lenders charged and remitted to our administrator.

"The administrator remitted premiums to us based on our rates and kept the difference. Our auditors focused on the administrator. He left no trail because he sent us exactly the amount of premium due for each customer. Because everything balanced, our auditors never looked at what the administrator collected from the banks."

"So, in reality, the administrator stole from the bank customers, not you. Correct?" Harrison asked.

"Exactly. Over three years, before we caught onto him, he overcharged borrowers by more than eight million dollars. Our problem turned out to be a little different than most frauds. We didn't lose any money. Neither did the banks and finance companies, but they overcharged all their borrowers big time." Taylor took a long drink.

"We chose to pay all the borrowers back with our own funds and go after the administrator. Not as easy as it sounds. We were forced to examine the record of every customer who purchased credit life insurance and reimburse the excess premium charged. There were thousands of them, and the administrator tried to hide the files. It took us two years to straighten everything out."

"Did he go to prison? Did you get any money back?" Harrison asked.

"We were lucky in that by reimbursing the borrowers, we avoided major lawsuits from the lenders. We were lucky with the administrator too. We involved the local police and FBI just before he took off. They arrested him, and we recovered almost everything he stole. It could have been a lot worse."

"I understand the crime; it's pretty straightforward," Harrison said. "How did you figure out what went on if your auditors didn't catch it?"

"We didn't suspect a thing. The lenders were selling a high volume of credit life insurance—even at the higher rates. Everything seemed to be going along fine, and we liked the relationship. Then one of those events took place which no criminal can ever predict.

"One of our employees, who is based in Illinois, took out a car loan and bought credit life insurance at one of our client banks. Because he knew something about credit life insurance, he thought his premium seemed higher than he expected. He asked one of his colleagues about it. The colleague recognized it as being excessive. Next thing you know, the auditors are looking into it, and within days, we were onto the fraud. You just never know where the tip-off is going to come from."

"Amazing, Ross, and not unlike our work. We never know when a break is going to come our way that answers everything we've been asking."

He stood up and Ross did likewise. Meeting over.

"I've got to get back to the office. Thanks for everything, and I'd love to come back when this is all over and see the inside of your boat."

Taylor agreed. "I'll get back to you soon."

As Harrison stepped off the boat and they were saying their goodbyes, Taylor's phone rang. He went below deck to answer. Officer Slack of the Seattle Police.

After brief greetings, Slack got right to it. "We sent a detective back to Yacht Haven yesterday. He found a closed-circuit camera in a building across the street from the marina. There's a somewhat blurry picture of the guy we think assaulted Mrs. Fletcher and shot the dog. Unfortunately, not enough detail to identify anyone. But we may have caught a break."

Taylor heard Slack shuffling papers in the background.

"We followed up on the story about a guy getting pushed in front of a subway train in Chicago. The Transit Authority cops have closed circuit footage of the guy they believe pushed your contact onto the tracks. We looked at it and think it's the same guy. Same exact build, same exact dress, and the same exact movements. And it gets better. There's been an unsolved murder on our books for a little over four years. A guy tied to a rope, thrown off the back of a ferry. The closed-circuit cameras caught some footage of that one too but not enough to make an identification. We can't prove it yet, though we're sure it's the same guy. We think we know his name. I'm going to pass this along to Special Agent Harrison as well."

Taylor remained silent.

"I'm telling you this first, so you can watch out for yourself. If these crimes are related, you could be a target. Second, I want you to think hard about anything you might have forgotten to tell me. We want to find this guy, and you may be the key."

"If I remember anything more, I'll call you immediately, Officer Slack."

The two hung up simultaneously.

Ross Taylor could best be described as perplexed. He and Schlump were on the verge of breaking this financial crime wide open for everyone to see. At the same time, there were serious crimes being committed outside the fraud—murder, assault—and he might be a target. And Kim.

His phone rang again. "What have you got, Schlump?"

"I figured it out, Ross. I know how they did it. I know where the money went. I'll show you everything when I see you, but trust me, I know the accounts the money went into. The only thing I don't know is how they get it out of those accounts. I don't know how it gets into his pocket."

"That's great. Don't worry. I may be onto how they get it out. I just need a few more hours. We're close to shutting down LeGrande forever." Taylor wanted to do a final analysis and sleep on everything before going to Harrison. He knew from experience not to act until he was certain. "Can you meet me in the morning for breakfast and show me what you've got?"

They agreed to seven-thirty at The Rudder to put the final nail in Levesque's coffin.

Chapter Forty-nine

Fifteen Twenty-One Second Avenue
Seattle, Washington
Wednesday, August 14, 2019

Aubrey Reddy normally slept well. Most nights, she and Jacques went to bed around eleven, and she didn't wake up again until around seven-thirty. Tonight she couldn't sleep. After midnight, she still rolled around trying various positions, but nothing helped. She couldn't explain it; she felt no discomfort and nothing bothered her. Then she thought she heard a voice.

She peered over at the other side of the bed. No Jacques. She didn't think anything more of it and tried to sleep again. For a second time, she thought she heard a voice. After staying in bed for several more minutes, she got up and tiptoed silently to the half-open bedroom door. The voice became louder. She slowly opened the door and listened in the hallway. Now she could hear Jacques's voice more clearly. It sounded as if he were talking on the phone in his office. She sneaked down the thickly carpeted hall to the partially open door to his office. She felt her pulse racing.

Wide awake now, she knew she shouldn't be listening in on his call. She'd never done this before, but she couldn't help herself. She moved as close to the opening as possible without being seen, not making a sound.

"I agree," he said. Then, silence.

Aubrey leaned closer to the door opening, hoping to hear more. She heard footsteps as Jacques came toward the door. As he did so, his voice became louder and terrified her. He might discover her snooping.

He closed the door, and relieved at not being caught, she pressed her ear against the wood to hear him better.

His voice sounded as if he were fifty feet away, but she could still hear him. After a long pause, he said, "You're right. That Taylor guy is getting too close. It's only a matter of time now. Let's wrap it up. I have one more diamond to pick up—almost eight carats. That'll be the end of it. We'll meet here and split things up. Okay? How does a week from Friday sound? We'll all leave together."

Aubrey's heart pounded now. Finally. They were going to leave, and she felt elation.

Then Levesque said, "Okay. I'll see you in my office at five o'clock on Friday, August twenty-third."

She tiptoed quickly back into the bedroom. Who could he have been talking to? Who else knew about the diamonds? Lucas was dead, and she thought that only he knew. When would Jacques tell her they were leaving the country? Still, she could hardly contain her joy. In a few days, her dream of going to France with Jacques would come true. So little time to prepare, barely a week. Incredible excitement nearly overwhelmed her.

Back in bed, she pretended to be asleep when he

returned. She wanted to throw her arms around him but decided not to. Tomorrow, she'd ask him about the new plan. She needed to start packing and preparing to leave.

Chapter Fifty

The Rudder
Lake Union
Seattle, Washington
Thursday, August 15, 2019

The boat was quiet. Kim had left early for an interview in Olympia. Alone below deck, Ross paced within the close quarters of the office and the main cabin. Up most of the night analyzing the LeGrande data, he now felt certain he reached the same conclusion Schlump reached. Everything finally came together a couple of hours ago. He knew how Jacques Levesque skimmed the funds.

The rain, which had started during the night, had stopped though clouds remained. The wind must have been out of the north because he heard the float planes fly over the boat as they took off from the south end of the lake. Other than the occasional sound of the planes, silence.

Schlump met him at the boat, and they walked together to The Rudder. A short walk, they soon stood inside the entrance.

"Do you have reservations?" the hostess asked.

"Yes, we do have reservations," said Schlump, "but we'd like a table anyway."

The hostess paused for a moment, unsure of what to say. Ross helped her out. "We'll be happy to sit wherever you put us. Thank you."

The hostess seated them and gave them coffee and menus.

"Hungry, Schlump?"

"Pope a Catholic?"

They ordered. The Rudder didn't have a separate menu for different meals. They made everything on their menu available during all the hours they were open. Ross ordered a veggie omelet and a side of bacon. For Schlump, two Bacon Blue Burgers, fries, and a side of chicken strips.

"Don't you know how much weight that kind of eating can put on you?"

"I don't care, Ross. I live to eat. Besides, it makes me harder to kidnap."

A server Taylor didn't recognize refilled their coffee mugs. Schlump started in on his report. "We knew they rigged the system to pay bogus claims on certain terminated employees. It turns out, the employees were selected randomly. No employer ever became suspicious of those claims. Apparently, no one cares about terminated employees."

Taylor understood and nodded.

"The claims were paid directly to a fake dentist. In this scam, the names of the people for whom claims were submitted were real people, but the dentists were made up using random names and social security numbers from employer data. That way, a legitimate name and a correct social security number were always connected. The banks had no reason to question the accounts, and the auditors would never think to audit the dentists."

The server brought Schlump's chicken strips. "Thought you'd like these while the rest of your order is coming."

His smile said everything. But even while eating, he wanted to present his findings.

"I gave this part of the project to Michelle, my new assistant. She's great. She's the one who discovered the link to the fictitious dentists. And if that's not enough, Trudy loves her. She's even stopped trying to clean up my office. Last week, she went down to Orange County in California to visit her sister and left Michelle in charge. She wants me to find more work so I can afford to hire her full-time.

"Another nice thing. With Michelle around, I've got time to go to my regular Wednesday night poker game— my first time in almost two months. I won six hundred dollars last night.

"Anyway, Michelle found an abnormal number of checks from LeGrande that were direct deposited into accounts at thirty banks in the names of the fictitious dentists. Most likely, Levesque himself or Lucas opened each of the accounts. Maybe even his girlfriend, since some of the accounts have female names. They probably posed as dentists and described the account as a "clearing account" for insurance claims or some such thing. The banks won't tell me anything, of course."

Ross Taylor came to the same conclusion overnight, but he let Schlump continue uninterrupted.

"They opened boxes in UPS stores in the same towns as the banks and gave that box number as the address of the dentist. My guess is, that way, any correspondence, bank information, or tax information for the dentist came to the UPS box. Pretty shrewd. No mail went to the actual address of former employees or their employers to raise questions."

Schlump took another bite and spoke with his mouth full. "We're still left with the question of how they're getting their hands on the money. We can see where the fraudulent checks are deposited but how are they getting the money out? And what are they doing with it?"

The last pieces of the puzzle. Until the FBI tracked the money in the thirty dentists' accounts, the questions couldn't be answered.

"You're right. This fraud could get as high as fifty to sixty million dollars, maybe more," Taylor said. "That kind of money is hard to hide. For as long as this scam has been going on, if the money is in a bank, we should find a long paper trail and records—some kind of evidence. Swiss banks used to be the place for this kind of money, but they've changed their laws."

He paused to consider the next steps. "The FBI is going to have to figure this part out. We don't have any authority to look at any bank records except LeGrande's, and we've already been through those. Christine doesn't just want to know who did it; she wants her money back."

"What's next?"

"You've done great work, Schlump. We've got

almost everything. I'm going to alert Christine, then call Harrison at the FBI. We can show them enough detail on specific claims to prove that Levesque's company has been engaging in fraud for more than three years. By the time an audit is concluded, I'll wager that it will explain almost all, if not all, of the deficiency Great Chicago has experienced. This should be enough for Harrison to move in on Levesque. We'll have to cross our fingers the money's still around."

While they were waiting for the bill, Schlump said, "My guy checked up on Gerhardt Bergmann—the majority owner at LeGrande. He's a bad actor, Ross. He's a former enforcer for the East German Stasi. Definitely has dirty hands. He came here about twenty-five years ago with a group of his old comrades. He's involved in other businesses around Seattle in addition to LeGrande. One of them is a bookmaking operation. He could also be a part of the fraud although he doesn't have nearly the incentive Levesque does. He's making a ton of money. But if Levesque is doing this behind his back and has put LeGrande in jeopardy, Levesque has more to worry about than us and the FBI."

They agreed that things were getting more complicated the further they dug. Taylor paid the bill, and they walked out into bright sunshine. The clouds were gone.

"'I've got to loosen my belt," said Schlump.

"That's your belt? I thought it was the equator."

Schlump ignored him and walked in the direction of his car.

Ross added, "I'll call you later. Thanks for the good work."

Delighted that Schlump's work confirmed his own, Taylor returned to the *Pura Vida* and called Christine Bell's private cell phone. She didn't answer. He left a message describing what he and Schlump suspected and recommended she bring the FBI up to date as soon as possible. He then called her office phone.

Her assistant told Ross, "I'm sorry, Mr. Taylor. She's not in the office, and she's not going to be available for at least a few days."

Taylor left a message anyway, urging her to call back soon. If they were right about Levesque masterminding a fraud, a real risk existed that Levesque would take off when he first suspected they were closing in on the truth.

Chapter Fifty-one

Fifteen Twenty-One Second Avenue
Seattle, Washington
Thursday, August 15, 2019

Aubrey slept as soundly as ever, secure in the knowledge that she'd soon be in the South of France with the love of her life. A dream come true. She had waited a long time for this and forced herself to overcome doubts.

Jacques had already left for the office, so she went for a quick run along the waterfront. Today looked like a perfect day, scattered cumulus clouds set against a clear blue sky. She felt exhilarated. She ran for almost an hour, all the while imagining herself with Jacques on the shore of the Mediterranean.

When she entered their building, she called him. No answer on his cell phone. She rode the elevator to their floor, made a large mug of coffee, and walked into Jacques's office.

When he traveled or was away, she often sat in one of his leather armchairs and read. Although their offices were the same size and enjoyed the same view, his office always seemed more comfortable and lighter.

She walked around to the side of the desk where he sat, settled into his chair, and looked around the desk. It was mostly neat but stacked with a pile of unorganized papers on the left side. For no good reason, she started to organize the disarray and noticed his white phone hidden among the papers. Not the first time he left one of his phones at home. No wonder he hadn't answered. She'd call his office and let them know she would bring it to him.

She touched the screen of the phone, and it opened. She had never used his phone and expected it to be secure. Apparently not. She opened his phone log and immediately noticed an incoming call at 12:16 a.m. last night. The call she overheard. She made a mental note of the number.

After organizing the pile, she stood to go back to reading in her favorite chair. She noticed a paper on the floor and picked it up. A computer printout of an airline reservation. For Jack Levy. One-way from Seattle to Paris. Friday, August 16, eight o'clock tomorrow evening. Didn't he say August twenty-third in his call last night? She looked for the other printout—the one with her name on it. She didn't see it. It must be mixed in with the other papers. Not there either. She began to get a bad feeling.

Her coffee turned cold, but she didn't care. She had been staring at the same spot on the wall for several minutes, barely able to think. He was leaving her and going to France without her, and he planned to stiff the person who was at the other end of last night's call as well. Who had he been talking to? She simply sat in the chair stunned.

Jacques's phone rang. She answered it, hoping he had an explanation.

"Hi, darling," he said. "Glad you picked up. Can't explain how I forgot the phone. Must have been preoccupied with something. Can you bring it to the office later? Then we can have lunch at the Met."

Aubrey loved the Metropolitan Grill, but this morning, she felt overwhelmed and preoccupied. "Sure. And sometime today, can we go to your box? I'd like to put my jewelry there until our travel plans are settled. It won't take a minute."

Jacques told her to meet him in the lobby of his building at noon, and they could stop at the bank before lunch.

Aubrey rode an Uber to Jacques's office at the corner of 2nd and Marion. She looked stunning this morning in a dress by Alaia and her favorite grain leather Dolce & Gabbana shoulder tote bag. She didn't always dress that way, but on special days like today, she indulged herself. Rather than climbing the stairs, she took the covered escalator to the lobby and met Jacques just before noon. She gave him his phone, and they walked through the lobby to Violet's desk.

"Good morning, Violet," Jacques said. "I'd like to get into my box."

Today, Violet wore all black—long-sleeved turtleneck shirt, jeans, and platform shoes. "Absolutely, Mr. Levesque. Good morning, Miss Reddy. I hope you both are well this morning." She broke into a broad smile. "I just got such great news. I passed the civics test! All I have left is the interview. I'm so thrilled."

In her excitement, her normal Estuary English dialect became more pronounced than usual.

"Congratulations, Violet. You're almost an American," Jacques said.

Jacques and Aubrey signed the bank's forms and followed her to the safe deposit boxes. Aubrey stepped to one side while Jacques and Violet inserted their respective keys into the lock. After they completed the process and Violet had left, Aubrey put the jewelry she brought into the box. "Thanks, Jacques. I feel safer now. Let's go have lunch."

Chapter Fifty-two

Wells Fargo Center
Seattle, Washington
Thursday, August 15, 2019

Jacques Levesque had been preoccupied during lunch with Aubrey and spoke much less than normal.

For her part, Aubrey performed her role perfectly.

Levesque finally said, "You seem quite happy this afternoon. Energized. Normally, you aren't this bubbly."

She smiled, exactly how a woman in love with the man across the table should act but she said nothing. All the while, she knew Jacques planned to disappear from her life in a matter of hours, and she loathed him for it. She had given him every opportunity to tell her they would leave together tomorrow but he had not.

After another of the long pauses in conversation, he said, "I'll be working late tonight, dear. Then I've got to make a quick trip up to Port Ludlow in the morning."

Ira Stone lived in Port Ludlow. For Jacques to go there on the day he planned to leave the country must mean that Stone acquired an exceptionally valuable diamond for Jacques.

"I'll pick up a float plane and be back by early afternoon." In the past, when Jacques heard from Ira Stone, he couldn't stop talking to Aubrey about the purchase he planned to make. And, after completing the purchase, he couldn't wait to show the stone to her and explain all about it. Today, no hint.

Aubrey nodded and smiled again. This was the last time she'd ever see Jacques Levesque. She'd be in bed when he got home, and he'd be gone when she got up. Three days ago, she might have been crushed at the thought after investing so much of her life and her emotions in this man. Now, she saw him as scum—a dirtbag and a criminal. In a brief time, she went from unconditional love for him to total hatred. Time for her to protect herself.

"This has been a wonderful lunch, darling. We should come here together more often," she said. "But it sounds like you're busy. Go back to the office to your work. I have errands to run myself. I'll be asleep when you get home, and you'll be gone early, so I'll see you tomorrow night. Maybe the Mariners are at home."

She stood up from the table, kissed him on the cheek, and left the Met to get on with her afternoon plans.

Chapter Fifty-three

Puget Sound Region
Washington
Friday, August 16, 2019

The overnight rain had stopped, although the clouds were dark enough to warn it might return at any minute. Jacques Levesque wore a dark gray, Zegna, hand-tailored, business suit and black Ferragamo, oxford shoes. He seldom dressed in such high fashion, but he knew later that day he would be flying first-class from Seattle to Paris. He had a great deal to accomplish between now and his evening flight.

The Uber driver dropped him off at the entrance to the Kenmore Air terminal at the south end of Lake Union. Levesque carried a small leather duffle bag holding two extra shirts and ties, a fold-up umbrella, his wallet, his passport, and airline ticket, as well as the cash required for today's transaction. A nonscheduled charter to Port Ludlow, the float plane's propeller turned as it awaited his boarding. The pilot planned to wait while he conducted his business then return the same afternoon.

After his lunch with Aubrey yesterday, Jacques had

returned to his office for a final search for incriminating documents and files. He found nothing. He left his office for the final time, secure in the knowledge that, by the time the authorities worked everything out, he would be safely out of their reach, basking in luxury in the South of France.

The flight to Port Ludlow took barely more than half an hour. While in the air, he thought again about the wisdom of coming here on the day he planned to leave the country. Could one more diamond be that important? Even one this size? He decided, yes, this diamond was worth it. Ira Stone just obtained the diamond yesterday and planned to fly to Vancouver that afternoon because another buyer also wanted the gem. Stone gave him no choice. The plane landed just east of the harbor at Port Ludlow and taxied across the water to the tie-ups reserved for float planes. Ira Stone waited at the end of the pier.

"Glad you could come up, Jacques," Stone said. "Any other day, I'd happily come to your office, but I need to head north in a couple of hours. Thanks for accommodating me."

The two men exchanged pleasantries as they drove in Stone's car to his home. The rain continued to hold off.

Port Ludlow was a pleasant community of upscale homes, owned mostly by retirees; its harbor area was one of the most beautiful in Puget Sound. Many found it a welcome change after hectic business careers in the larger cities. Among them, Ira Stone.

Even among the pricier homes in Port Ludlow, Stone's stood out. All brick, built in the Tudor style, it was situated on a hilltop lot of approximately five wooded acres. An eight-foot-high brick wall surrounded the property. In addition, an unobtrusive but effective electrified shock, camera, and alarm system topped the wall, discouraging intruders. The only entry through the wall was via an unattended iron gate. It opened as the two men approached. Two Doberman Pinschers roamed the grounds. The dogs appeared to be unconcerned with the car's arrival.

"They have been trained to ignore me and any other guests," Stone said, "unless they hear a certain command. If they hear that command, they will come quickly."

Levesque sensed he was being watched. He spotted two men—one standing outside the house near a water feature, the other at a window inside the lower level of the house.

Stone led Levesque into a four-thousand square foot home, beautifully designed and furnished—the home of a wealthy man. From the ground floor windows at the front of the house, an expansive view of the harbor at Port Ludlow stretched before them with the entrance to Puget Sound to the northeast. Cargo ships could be seen in the distance.

On any other occasion, Levesque would want to see more of the house. Today, he was on a tight schedule. He followed Stone into an office to the right of the entryway.

"Please be seated, Jacques. I'm sure you're anxious to see what I've acquired for you." Stone opened his desk drawer and extracted a small envelope. From the envelope, he removed a paper parcel. He unfolded the paper to reveal a magnificent diamond. "It's a Trip X."

Even from where Jacques sat four feet away, this stood out as the most beautiful and most valuable diamond for his collection. His breath caught.

Ira Stone motioned toward a rectangular object the size and shape of a small book with a three-inch diameter semispherical red button on the top. "If I press this button, my associates and my dogs will come to my aid. I'm confident there will be no reason for me to do so, but I thought I'd explain, just in case you were curious."

Jacques heard and understood him, but he remained captivated by the gem. He needed it for himself. "Please describe the diamond to me, Ira."

"Certainly. This beautiful diamond is a round, ideal cut, eight carat, D color, of flawless clarity. As you will see when you look closer, it's perfect."

Levesque almost passed out. He could barely concentrate enough to react to what Stone said. The diamond dazzled him like nothing he ever saw.

"Care to hold it?" Stone asked.

Now Levesque's hands shook—first unnoticeably, then more so. He slowly reached for the stone. He picked it up with his fingers—not trusting the tweezers—and held it nearer his eyes.

Stone reached over, handing him a loupe.

Levesque didn't claim to be a skilled jeweler, but over the past few years, he developed an ability to make a reasonable evaluation of a gem. He looked inside the stone. Perfect.

"The price?" he asked in a voice unlike his own.

"Eight-hundred thousand dollars. Today only. It's a great price. I'll get a little touch, but you're getting a bargain."

Levesque was prepared for the response. His bag contained every dollar of cash he could raise. This purchase would leave little for his new beginning in France. Of course, that's what his diamonds were for.

Calm began to return. Time to do business. He handed over eighty packets of ten thousand dollars—each containing one hundred circulated one-hundred dollar bills. He knew Ira Stone's requirements. Levesque settled back in his chair as Stone counted the money by hand. It took almost two hours.

Stone then handed over the diamond to Levesque. "*Mazel Tov*, Jacques. You have made an excellent acquisition."

Levesque nodded, as much to himself as to Stone. "The day may come when I might want to sell this or a portion of the other diamonds you've sold me. What do you suppose the market will be like?"

"My friend, buying diamonds is the easy part. But as you know, selling them can be problematic. Markets can be hot one day and cold the next. It depends on where you are in the world. For stones such as you have acquired from me, it will be easy to find a buyer in Antwerp, not so easy in Morocco."

"What about France?"

"It should be good. There is an active diamond market in Paris. But the best advice I can give is to anticipate. Sell when the prices are high, not when you need money. If you wait, you may be forced to accept an unreasonably low price."

The meeting ended. Everything went perfectly. The men walked out of the office and directly to Stone's car.

The eight-minute drive to the marina went by in silence. When they arrived, they shook hands and said their goodbyes. Stone returned to his car.

Levesque arrived right on time. As the pilot started the float plane's engine, Levesque called Felix to arrange for him to meet at the Kenmore Terminal. Felix could drive him to the bank to pick up the diamonds, then take him to the airport.

Felix didn't answer. Jacques called Oskar. Oskar didn't know Felix's whereabouts either.

Oskar then told Levesque that a man who identified himself as Special Agent Harrison from the FBI visited the office. Harrison had asked to see Jacques and made an appointment to visit with him tomorrow afternoon.

Jacques Levesque felt uneasy, his stomach tied up in knots. He rarely experienced unease, but he did now. Only about four hours remained before his flight to Paris and safety. No one knew his plans. He wondered if the FBI was looking for Felix too. Levesque understood Felix's fear of the authorities. He suffered from severe claustrophobia as well, and Levesque knew that Felix couldn't last long if the FBI started to interrogate him—especially in a small room. But why should the FBI even know about Felix? Maybe he worried about nothing. He called Felix again. No answer. He made one more call, to arrange an Uber to take him to the bank and then to the airport.

The Uber waited for him at the Kenmore Terminal. He tried Felix once more. No answer. Not good. He'd have to get in and out of the bank quickly.

The drive downtown was unremarkable until they

approached the Wells Fargo Center. Levesque asked the driver to come in on 2nd Avenue and wait for him while he ran into the bank. Fifteen minutes at most. Then he noticed a large commotion between Madison and Marion. It looked like the homeless and their supporters were rallying. Hundreds of people milled around, and hundreds more walked toward them. Jacques told the driver to wait at the base of the escalator. He left his leather duffle bag on the rear seat.

A light mist had started to fall again. He pushed a path through the crowd onto the escalator and stepped off at the lobby floor. He worked his way through the demonstrators, into the lobby, and across to Violet's desk. Today he got in and out of the safe deposit box vault in eight minutes, not even opening his wooden box.

It was finally happening.

Chapter Fifty-four

Yacht Haven Marina
Lake Union
Seattle, Washington
Friday, August 16, 2019

Ross Taylor still couldn't prove how Levesque disposed of the money. He'd been skimming from Great Chicago for years, and he hid the funds someplace. It was one thing to solve the mystery that plagued Christine Bell and quite another to recover the money. Of course, once the FBI came into the case, they could force the banks to confirm Taylor's suspicions and reveal where the money went. In the meantime, Levesque could get away.

His phone rang.

"Is this Ross Taylor?" The voice sounded tinny and in a location with echoes like a tunnel.

Male or female? He couldn't tell.

"This is Ross Taylor."

"I have information about LeGrande Benefits which might interest you," the voice said.

"I'm listening."

"Jacques Levesque has been embezzling money from

Great Chicago Insurance Company. He's leaving the country tonight. You should also check into the murder of Lucas Sims. Look into a man named Felix Contador. Contador is also responsible for drowning a man off the end of the Bremerton Ferry."

"Who is this please?" Taylor asked.

"That's not important. What you need to know is that he will undoubtedly go to the bank in his office building this afternoon. It's in his interest to stop there before leaving."

"Where does he keep the money?" This might be exactly the missing piece of the puzzle if the caller told the truth and wasn't just sending him on a dead-end hunt.

"There is no money."

"What do you mean there's no money?"

"Just find him and you'll find out."

"Where is he?" he asked the anonymous voice.

"I don't know. But if he hasn't already been to the bank vault, he'll be there soon. His flight is at eight o'clock tonight."

Bank vault. What could be in the bank vault? Taylor waited, expecting the call to end. It did not.

"He uses the money to buy diamonds and keeps them in a safe deposit box at his bank." The line went dead.

Ross Taylor finally knew the answer to his last question. Now, if he could just get to the diamonds before Levesque took off, he'd have everything.

Did the person on the other end of this call really know something? Why did the person call him? How did they know about his involvement? It certainly sounded real. He'd call Harrison at the FBI and alert him. Then he'd call Christine.

His phone rang again. "Ross?" the voice asked.

This time Taylor recognized the voice. "I was just going to call you, Dale."

"We just received an anonymous call from someone fingering Jacques Levesque for murder and embezzlement."

"That's what I wanted to call you about. I just got the same call. Do you think it's for real? Do you think the voice knows what he's talking about?"

"We're not even sure it's a he. We're working on identifying the caller, but, yes, we think it's for real. Did your caller mention the bank in Levesque's building?"

"Yes."

"That's where we're going now. If he goes there or to his office, we'll get him. We'll see that he doesn't get out of the country. We already have the airport covered. One way or another, we'll get this guy. Do you know anything about this Felix?"

"Never heard of him," Taylor said. "I can tell you he's not part of the LeGrande staff."

If Levesque masterminded all of this and the FBI got their hands on him, Taylor wanted to be there, to be a part of everything. It would be enormously satisfying watching that self-important creep brought to earth. Especially after what happened to Mrs. Fletcher and might have happened to Kim.

After hanging up with Harrison, Taylor called Christine to fill her in on the news, but she didn't answer her private phone. Her office assistant told him she was away at a business conference, and she didn't expect her to be back until Tuesday morning.

Taylor left a brief voicemail for Kim, telling her he was on his way to Levesque's office, and he'd explain everything when he came home. He jumped off the boat and sprinted up the dock to his car.

He finally knew everything. Levesque stole from Great Chicago and used the money to buy diamonds. Not bad. Impossible to trace. No ownership records. No bank records. Easy to hide. Levesque could carry fifty million dollars' worth of high-quality diamonds in a coat pocket onto an airplane.

Taylor's excitement built. As he drove away, all he could think of was getting his hands on Levesque. The trip to the Wells Fargo Center normally took fifteen minutes with no traffic. Not today. Friday and rush hour. He couldn't let Levesque get away.

Chapter Fifty-five

Wells Fargo Center
Seattle, Washington
Friday, August 16, 2019

The time had finally arrived. Jacques Levesque was about to escape to the South of France and live the life he had always dreamed of. At last. His grand home with a view of the Mediterranean. The finest food and the finest clothes. He would enjoy the company of beautiful women and have more than enough money to do it all. And he would be safe from the authorities. He had never been so exhilarated.

He carried the small wooden box holding his treasure safe and secure inside the breast pocket of his suit jacket. It was inconspicuous there. His heart pounded in anticipation. He thought about going up to the office one last time—just in case he had forgotten something. No, he had everything he needed. Nothing more could be done to cover his involvement in the embezzlement. The FBI or Taylor would figure it out eventually, but by the time they did, he would be safe in France. He couldn't get away from this place fast enough.

All he had to do was walk the two floors to the street where his Uber driver waited. He stepped out of his office building for the final time. What had been a large crowd fifteen minutes earlier had tripled in size and had turned into a mob. The homeless and their supporters were milling around everywhere, and protesters with loudspeakers roamed the streets below, yelling. They packed the stairs, making them impassable. The escalators were filled with people going in both directions, but at least they were moving. Levesque pushed his way on.

The crowd boiled with hostility, and Levesque stood out in his designer suit. People jostled and shoved him. He pushed back but lost his balance. Instinctively, he reached for the box in his pocket, gripping it securely in his right hand. As he did so, a homeless man fell hard against him from behind. At the same moment, a screaming woman in front of him turned and thrust her arms toward him, knocking the box from his grasp. The lid to the box popped open, and the diamonds flew out in all directions.

A cry escaped Levesque's throat. He tried to grab the diamonds, but the crowd prevented any movement. The escalator deposited him at the first landing where he fell to the ground. He crawled to pick up the diamonds, but feet scattered them in all directions. *This can't be happening.*

He scrambled on his hands and knees, making an animal sound somewhere between crying and squealing.

When people noticed the diamonds, fights broke out.

Levesque's heart pounded, and the pressure of the mob smothered him. Air rushed from his lungs. Dizziness swept over him, and he became disoriented.

He felt detached from himself, a separate person. He vomited. He thought he was dying.

He dragged himself to his feet, his clothes torn and covered with vomit. His face, knees, and hands were bleeding. He couldn't think. He didn't know which way to turn. He looked around but didn't recognize anything. He struggled to control his breath, forcing short puffs of air in and out. He knew he had to get somewhere quickly, but he didn't know where.

Later, he retained no memory of getting on the escalator and going back into the building. Nor did he remember the elevator ride to his floor or staggering into his office.

Oskar saw him first. "My god! What happened, Mr. Levesque? What can I do for you? Do you need a doctor?"

Without waiting for an answer, he ran off to get help.

Levesque couldn't speak. He lost control of his legs and collapsed into a chair near the basketball court. His mind had ceased working. Numbness came over his body. He urinated all over himself. He didn't notice Ross Taylor sprint into the office.

Taylor ran up to Levesque. "Looking mighty sharp there, Jack Levy. Planning to do some traveling? First class?"

Taylor smiled as he looked at the beaten mess that resembled Jacques Levesque. He hadn't seen what happened to Levesque but he seemed not to care. "Now it's my turn, you piece of crap."

Levesque jumped up and shoved Taylor. Then he cocked his right fist.

Taylor grabbed Levesque by his jacket and jerked him off balance, at the same time, stepping to his right. He stood nearly as tall as Levesque, and in that instant, Taylor shifted into the street-smart, tough guy who lived inside his civilized demeanor. He delivered the first punch—a short, powerful left hand to Levesque's stomach. In Jacques's weakened condition, the blow folded him up. "That's for going after Kim."

Taylor followed that up with a hard left-hand punch to the side of Levesque's head. Jacques Levesque dropped to the floor like a stone.

"That's for Mrs. Fletcher."

Taylor prepared to pick him up and hit him again when a strong hand pulled his shoulder back.

Dale Harrison said, "Don't get yourself in any trouble, Ross. We'll take it from here. Believe me, he'll get worse where he's going."

Harrison's team made a quick pass through the offices to make certain no one tried to remove any information which might prove valuable in a prosecution. A careful search would come later. Harrison kept watch over Levesque.

Slowly, Levesque pulled himself onto the chair. No one helped him. By now, Oskar had returned with a wet towel and tried to clean Levesque's face. It proved to be pointless. A small group of LeGrande employees gathered to watch in amazement.

Levesque looked at Taylor, then at Harrison. His face drooped and quivered in resignation. He began to sob. He knew they knew. Through his tears, he looked at his hands, his right hand clenched into a fist. He slowly opened it and saw a large diamond. The diamond he had acquired from Ira Stone an hour and a half ago.

"Special Agent Dale Harrison, FBI. Jacques Levesque or Jack Levy, you're under arrest for insurance fraud, fraud by mail, fraud by wire, money laundering, kidnapping, conspiracy to murder, attempted murder, and more." Harrison handcuffed him, searched him, then took the diamond.

Levesque threw up again.

"Where are the diamonds?" Taylor asked.

Levesque couldn't answer because he couldn't stop retching.

Harrison said, "We stopped at the bank before coming here. The attendant told us Levesque had been there earlier but had only been in the vault for a couple of minutes. If he picked up the diamonds, they're not here."

Still staring at his shoes, Levesque croaked out, "I lost them. That's all I've got left." He pointed to the stone in Harrison's hand.

Despite having his face washed, Levesque remained a mess. His clothes were torn. His pants were soaked in urine. He was still bleeding and covered with vomit.

"Do you think you'll find the diamonds?" Taylor asked Harrison.

"I don't know. The bank told us he walked straight from the vault out the front door. They've got to be nearby."

"At least Christine will be thrilled that we got him. I can hardly wait to call her. I can't remember the last time I felt so energized." He picked up a nearby basketball.

He dribbled five times, changing hands and going between his legs as he did so. Then he took off toward the basket. He took three long strides, leaped into the air, did a 180-degree twist, and stuffed the ball backward with both hands. He landed with his hands thrust high in the air.

"How do you like that, Jack? That's how to dunk. You're a loser, Jack, in every way."

Part III

Chapter Fifty-six

Seattle Times
Seattle, Washington
Saturday, August 17, 2019

Prominent Businessman Arrested
Charged with $50 Million Embezzlement
Insurance Community Shocked

Seattle, August 17, 2019, Associated Press—
FBI agents arrested a prominent Seattle insurance
executive yesterday afternoon at his office in the Wells
Fargo Center. Jacques Levesque, 47, also known as Jack
Levy, was taken into custody around 4:00 p.m. The FBI
charged him with insurance fraud and conspiracy to
commit murder, as well as other crimes. Levesque is the
well-known chief executive officer of LeGrande Benefits
Insurance Agency.

According to Special Agent Dale Harrison of the
Seattle office of the FBI, "Levesque has been under
investigation in connection with financial deficiencies at
Great Chicago Insurance Company for which LeGrande
Benefits sold policies and administered premiums and
claims."

Levesque also faces charges in the murder of Lucas Sims, a wheelchair-bound, former chief financial officer of LeGrande. Closed circuit television surveillance cameras in the Chicago subway revealed a man pushing Sims in his wheelchair in front of an arriving subway train earlier this month. Police also seek another, yet unnamed, individual in connection with the murder.

Charges accuse Levesque of misappropriating funds and purchasing diamonds with the proceeds. Moments before his arrest, witnesses saw Levesque being accosted by homeless demonstrators on the escalator outside the Wells Fargo Center. They said Levesque carried a small container that was torn from his grip. Those witnesses described a mad scramble as dozens of people rushed to grab diamonds which spilled from the box. Upon later examination, the diamonds turned out to be fake. Authorities had no explanation except to say the investigation was ongoing.

Chapter Fifty-seven

Town of Vence
South of France
Thursday, August 22, 2019

The luxurious hotel with incredible scenic beauty and world-class cuisine long ago exceeded any expectations of the two guests. They dined like royalty in the most exquisite of settings. They marveled at the display of nature's serenity. For five days, they savored every sight, aroma, and sound. They hiked through flowered fields and bicycled to nearby towns. They agreed that staying in this beautiful, tranquil corner of the French Riviera, and one of the most beautiful in the world, was never to be forgotten. They were guests at the Chateau Saint-Martin & Spa in the small French town of Vence.

Today, they enjoyed a leisure awakening in their respective villas. Later, they planned to enjoy a mid-morning lunch outdoors at the L'Oliveraie—a magnificent olive garden set apart from the main hotel. They'd sit at the same table they enjoyed on their first day at the Chateau—under the shade of a three-century-old olive tree. The olives were not yet ripe. In the afternoon, they scheduled a ride in the limousine to a secluded beach in Cap d'Antibes to lie in the warm Mediterranean sun for the first time since their arrival.

For now, they enjoyed coffee and a pastry in a private corner of the Spa Saint-Martin as they awaited their massages. Since arriving earlier in the week, the two discussed only the beautiful chateau and spa. By agreement, nothing else. They were there to enjoy the setting and experience and to avoid the subject they knew they would eventually address.

As if reading each other's thoughts, they understood that time had arrived.

"Do you mind telling me when you first got an inkling that Jacques planned to leave you high and dry?" Christine Bell asked. The aroma from the nearby lavender fields filled the air.

Aubrey Reddy could hardly wait to answer. "I always hoped he'd fall in love with me and marry me. I loved him from the first time I met him. But I never felt comfortable with his honesty. I wanted to trust him, but almost from the beginning, I didn't. He gave me nice things. He took me to fine places and made promises to me. Still, he always acted distant—treated me more like a business associate than a wife. I set aside money for myself, but I kept my hope—especially when he confided his plans to me."

"How did that happen?" Christine asked.

Aubrey told Christine how Jacques revealed his plans to her three years ago. "Of course, I could barely contain my happiness. He had it planned almost to the week. But,

Chris, I'm dying to hear when he brought you into the scam."

Christine breathed in deeply. "It's time you know the truth. I thought of the whole thing in the first place, not Jacques. At first, I loved my job with Great Chicago, even though I could see I'd never get rich. I was underpaid as a woman. Even my stock options only gave me about three million dollars after taxes. Nice money but nothing that could be called real wealth. I wanted more. Then, when one of those clowns on the board started feeling me up when we were alone in the elevator, I'd had enough. And my husband could barely conceal his desire to dump me for another woman. So, I planted a seed with Jacques. How would he like to make real money—tens of millions?"

Large cumulus clouds drifted overhead causing bright sun, then shade, to compete for the women's attention.

"From the beginning, I assumed that Jacques's activities involved some form of scam, but I never connected those activities with the problems you faced. Levesque told me your company experienced great losses, and you were at risk of losing your job, your pension, and your stock options as a result. Now, it turns out, you organized the entire thing. How did it work?" Aubrey asked.

"He couldn't have done it without my involvement. I knew that. Although sales and schmoozing came naturally to him, he had no clue where to begin with the complicated programming that was necessary to hide the scam. But Lucas Sims did.

"Jacques already knew about Lucas's trouble with

the gamblers although he never let on. The principal shareholder of LeGrande Benefits is a tough East German by the name of Gerhardt Bergmann—not Jacques. Bergmann is also the money man behind a large illegal gambling operation in Seattle. Bergmann knew Sims owed big money to the gamblers and told Jacques about it. He and I agreed that we should bring Lucas into the fraud but, at first, didn't know how to do it. Lucas took great pride in his integrity and couldn't bring himself to do anything illegal. So we set up a fake abduction to scare Lucas into taking part. Jacques hired Felix to arrange everything."

"Fake abduction? What do you mean?" Aubrey asked.

"The gamblers never abducted or threatened Lucas. No way. Those are serious federal crimes with long prison sentences. Instead, we put on a show. Felix hired a large man to pose as an enforcer for the gamblers. In reality, the man performed as a stage actor at Seattle Rep. He wanted to earn some extra money. We planned to force Lucas to voluntarily come to Jacques for help. We couldn't have Jacques trying to recruit Lucas directly.

"It worked perfectly. Well, almost. Lucas fell for it, but the actor saw through what Felix did and demanded more money. Felix drowned him behind a ferry in Puget Sound."

"We saw it, Chris! Jacques and I were in our car on the ferry. I never knew what we witnessed until this minute. Jacques must have wanted to make sure Felix went through with the killing. Now that I think of it, Jacques may have even taken pictures to have something to hold over Felix. You know, though I could never prove it, I've thought from the time it happened that Jacques also might have something to do with Lucas's death. All of this adds up."

They looked at each other in quiet disbelief.

Christine continued. "Lucas fell into line just as we hoped. He developed what he called Operation Perfect Score. It allowed LeGrande to divert claims payments to their own accounts and disguise the transactions in such a way as to be almost undetectable. At first, we worried the auditors might figure out what we were doing. We took a huge risk. But it worked. It fooled Winston Lester's group and the bonding company's auditors. Operation Perfect Score remained undetected."

Christine reached across the table and took a scone from a basket, breaking off a small piece. Her now-cold coffee was an inadequate accompaniment. "But I still needed to run my company in a way that kept our internal auditors off-track. That's where Winston came in. Winston Lester was absolutely faithful to me. After all, I helped him when everyone else abandoned him. I led him to conclude that our losses were just bad luck and things were due to turn around. He never suspected my involvement. He still doesn't know. A more conscientious CFO might have attacked the problem from the beginning.

"By the time Winston became alarmed, Jacques and I were in possession of almost fifty million worth of diamonds. When the board threatened me with my job, I suggested to Winston that it might be a fraud within the company. He agreed to examine us, and for five months, he concentrated on internal operations. Of course, he found nothing, but it gave Jacques and me more time."

Aubrey shook her head in astonishment as the story unfolded. "So why did you bring in Ross Taylor? With his reputation for uncovering fraud, he's the last person you should want poking around in your company business."

"You're right." Energized at finally telling the complete story, Christine kept talking. "In most cases, I'd never bring him in. But the pressure my board piled on me kept adding up. I feared if I didn't act quickly, they'd fire me, and I'd lose any ability to control the situation. I thought that by bringing in the foremost authority on insurance fraud, I could stall the board until Jacques and I could wrap things up. I deliberately didn't tell Taylor about Winston at first. It worked. When Taylor learned about Winston's background, he turned his attention to Winston and away from Jacques."

She paused for a minute while a waiter silently refilled their coffee cups. "What I'd like to know is how you linked me with Jacques? After all, as far as you knew, he could have been stealing from anybody. Why suspect Great Chicago?"

Aubrey took her turn to explain. "It didn't occur to me until a little over a week ago. I overheard him talking to someone late one night. The next morning, I found one of his phones under a stack of papers on his desk after he left for the office. I saw your number. If he hadn't forgotten his phone that day, he'd have been here now instead of us. I'd never have guessed."

"I remember now," Christine said. "I called the number I usually used, but he didn't answer. Because I was anxious to speak to him, I called the other number I knew."

It was all coming together for Aubrey as well. "He was always forgetting his phones, including his secure red one that was only available to two or three people. Even I never had that number. You reached him on his white phone, the one I usually called him on. For some reason, he never secured that phone. Seeing your number, and based on what I had heard, I knew he planned to take off alone. I still thought you were the victim. You were the first person I called. I've always liked and respected you and your accomplishments; I knew your future was at stake."

"I appreciate that, but more than anything else, I want to know how you got the diamonds from him."

"That part took some inventiveness, but everything came together perfectly." Aubrey went on. "After overhearing his call, seeing his phone log, and finding his airline reservation, I became convinced that he planned to dump me on the sidewalk, screw you out of your share, and leave for France.

"That morning, I told Jacques I wanted to put my jewelry in his safe deposit box. On two earlier occasions, we went to his bank vault where he showed me his diamond collection, so it wasn't the first time."

Aubrey looked off in the distance as if contemplating her next words. "But he didn't know everything. Last week, I obtained my own safe deposit box in the same vault. It was the key to getting the diamonds."

She stretched languidly. "When I did gopher work for the better-known Seattle photographers, candid photos became my specialty. I hid a miniature camera in my leather tote bag and took pictures of people wearing glamorous clothing in unposed settings. The fashion editors loved them. Candid photos became the single part of my career as a photographer in which I succeeded.

"When Jacques and I went to the bank that morning, I wore my leather tote bag with the concealed camera. While he and the attendant were using their two keys to open the box, I took high resolution close up pictures of the keys. That afternoon, I printed enlarged pictures of the keys and took them to the engineering manager in our building. He's always looked me over carefully, and I knew he'd jump at the chance to do me a favor—maybe get his hands on me. Ten minutes later, we were in his shop."

"Did he suspect anything?"

"Nothing. I told him the keys were for two antique cabinets in our apartment. Using my safe deposit keys as templates for the correct dimensions, he fabricated new keys in his shop while I waited. He may have known they were safe deposit box keys, but because I was standing close to him, occasionally rubbing against him, he said nothing and took his time."

Christine shook her head.

"I still needed to make one more stop before going back to the bank. Not necessary but I thought it might buy me a little more time. I stopped at a magic shop in the Pike Market. They sold fake diamonds for stage use. The fakes were very convincing. I bought their entire inventory.

"I went back to the bank the next morning and asked to access my box. The attendant and I opened my box, and she left me alone. After she left, I used the two new keys and opened Jacques's box. I replaced the diamonds in Jacques's wooden box with the fakes. In and out in less than five minutes, and my bag held almost sixty million dollars in diamonds. I knew that if Jacques looked carefully in the box, he wouldn't be fooled. I just hoped he'd be in a hurry when he made his run.

"I still needed to make two calls. I wanted Jacques to pay for what he did to me and to you. I downloaded a voice-disguising app to a burner phone and called the FBI and Ross Taylor. Furious, I told them Jacques's plan to leave that night, and I was sure he'd stop at the bank to pick up his diamonds."

By then, their coffee cups were empty but neither woman noticed.

"But why didn't you just cut me out and keep it all?" Christine asked.

"Believe me, I thought about it. But there's enough for both of us. Even after selling the diamonds, we should each have over twenty-five million. That's enough for me. And besides, I thought how ironic it would be if you wound up with half of the diamonds while he's sitting in prison."

The two women just smiled at each other. Two successful American women from ordinary backgrounds, who outwitted auditors, investigators, insurance company executives, and a shrewd criminal to become multi-millionaires in the South of France.

Multi-millionaire *criminals* in the South of France.

"Have you thought about where you'll settle, at least temporarily?" Aubrey asked. Staying in such an idyllic, peaceful place such as the Chateau Saint-Martin, she'd given no thought to the question herself. Soon she would have to decide. It turned out, Christine already had.

"First, I'm going to a place called Eze Village," Christine said. "I've read that it is one of the most beautiful places in the world. I've spent so much of my life in big cities and offices, I'm ready for something peaceful. It's less than an hour from here. After that, we'll see."

Two men approached their corner of the spa. One wore the uniform of a law enforcement officer. The other wore a business suit. He said in French-accented English, "Christine Bell and Aubrey Reddy, I am Commissaire Galois of the French National Police. You are under arrest."

The world dropped out from under the women. They could forget about a peaceful retirement on the French Riviera. Almost before it began, their planned future ended.

Christine tried to speak, but no words came out.

As he placed them in handcuffs and escorted them to a waiting police van, the commissaire informed the women of the rights they were entitled to in France. He then advised them that the process of extradition to the United States had already begun. He introduced them to a third man they didn't recognize.

"This is United States FBI Special Agent Dale Harrison. You will ultimately be placed in his custody. Until that time, he will be assisting us."

Aubrey Reddy's legs became so weak, she had to be held upright by one of the officers. When he placed her in the van, she sobbed uncontrollably.

A fourth man stood quietly off to the side of the police van. Aubrey Reddy didn't know him, but recognition showed on Christine Bell's face.

"I solved your problem, Chris," Ross Taylor said.

Chapter Fifty-eight

South Pender Island
British Columbia, Canada
Friday, August 30, 2019

Ross and Kim Taylor soaked in the hot tub on their patio. Each held an almost empty glass of Dom Perignon champagne. Before this early evening, neither of them ever tasted Dom Perignon. They were still uncertain as to whether they enjoyed it. At that moment, however, it made no difference. Everything seemed perfect.

Four days ago, Ross returned from France and began the process of putting the LeGrande/Great Chicago matter behind him. Local law enforcement held Jacques Levesque without bond in a Seattle jail cell. Christine Bell and Aubrey Reddy remained in custody at the office of the commissaire in Nice, France, during the processing of their extradition to the United States. Special Agent Harrison stayed in France to help manage the extradition procedure. The FBI's legal attaché in Paris told Harrison to plan on the two women being in federal custody in the US within days.

On the flight home from France, with his lucky charm facing him on the tray table, Taylor had begun mapping out the cruise he and Kim had been looking forward to. His assignment with Great Chicago completed, he'd thought about their first destination. At the same time, edits for Kim's article for the *Puget Sound Business Journal* were complete, and the people at the *Journal* were thrilled to learn the interview took place only four days before the arrest of the subject. They planned to rush it into publication.

Now Ross and Kim could enjoy life again as they wished.

As quickly as they could bring provisions aboard the *Pura Vida*, Ross and Kim left Lake Union and sailed north. They spent the first night in a marina in Port Townsend. Instead of staying in the San Juan Islands as originally planned, they left Port Townsend before daybreak. Due to little wind, the boat's engine allowed them to cover the remaining forty-five miles quickly, directly into Canada where they cleared customs and immigration. They decided, en route, to visit Kim's family and friends in Friday Harbor on the way back.

Now, they were in an idyllic place on South Pender Island called Bedwell Harbor for the Labor Day weekend, though not for the first time. Through the years, the anchorage ranked at the top of their list of harbors in southern British Columbia. Wanting the comfort of a large bed, they rented a cottage at the Poets Cove Resort and Spa. In addition to the champagne, which they arranged to be waiting for them on arrival, their cottage included a fully stocked kitchen and wine bar. Best of all, it featured its own private patio and hot tub. Set apart from the other cottages, theirs afforded a dazzling sunset view. And, they could see the stern end of the *Pura Vida*, safely tied up in the resort's marina. Their phones were shut off.

"Can we stay here forever, Ross? Why don't we buy this cottage?" Kim asked. "It's for sale. We don't need anything more. Our boat is here. We could sail to all the islands. And we could always come back here when we wanted to be on land. We could stay here forever—we have everything right here. A nice dinner? We can just walk up to the resort dining room. It's perfect, and we're together. I love you, Ross."

At that moment, Ross couldn't imagine a single objection, and he loved Kim more than ever. He put his arm around her, drops of water splashing on them as he did so. "I love you too, sweetheart. It sounds like a wonderful idea."

They refilled their champagne glasses and soaked quietly.

Kim interrupted the silence. "How did the police find the diamonds?" she asked, the Jacques Levesque matter surfacing again.

"You won't believe this." Ross laughed and shook his head. "They taped bags of diamonds to the bottom of dresser drawers."

Kim laughed out loud. "Are you kidding?"

Ross shook his head. "Nope. All they had to do was put them in a safe deposit box, and law enforcement probably would never have found them. But they just divided up the diamonds and held onto them. When the police came in with search warrants, they found them within minutes."

"Unbelievable." Kim sipped her champagne.

Later, after dinner in the resort dining room, they were curled up on their patio sofa in floor-length robes and soft slippers, sipping a final glass of wine. The evening temperature remained mild. During dinner, they talked about living here permanently and little else.

Now, despite their excitement about Bedwell Harbor, their conversation gravitated back to the subject of Levesque. "Why do you think Aubrey tipped you off about Levesque?" Kim asked. "She could have taken the diamonds and disappeared. Even if she gave Christine half, she might never have been caught."

Ross had pondered the same question since the police identified Aubrey as the caller. "She wanted lover's revenge on Levesque, pure and simple. She felt hurt then angry. For years he promised to marry her and settle in the South of France. Now, he planned to leave her behind."

Ross stared out over the marina and the water behind it. "She called Chris because she admired and respected her. She knew Levesque was double-crossing Chris but didn't know why. And she had no idea Chris participated in the theft. She told her Levesque kept some diamonds in his box, but that's all I know about the call. Someday, we may learn the whole truth—maybe at her trial."

"Have you ever heard of anything like the way she got the diamonds from Levesque's box?" Kim asked.

"How Aubrey switched the diamonds bordered on

genius. He never suspected a thing. Then she met up with Christine, and they were on their way to France before Levesque even went to the bank to pick up the fakes. Can you imagine if Levesque had eluded the police and escaped to France with the fake diamonds? He'd have found himself broke in France and a fugitive from justice in the US—if some diamond broker didn't kill him first.

"But Aubrey made a simple but fatal mistake. According to the French authorities who questioned her, Aubrey said that, for years, Levesque told her that when he accumulated a sufficient value in diamonds, he planned for the two of them to relocate to France to live. He described France as a refuge for them, because even if someone thought their activities were illegal, they could not be extradited back to the United States. Aubrey Reddy believed him.

"When Levesque dumped her, she went to France comfortable in her understanding that, even if caught, she couldn't be extradited. Whether overly confident or merely ignorant, she used her own credit card to buy her airline ticket and reserve the rooms at the Chateau Saint-Martin & Spa. It took the French police little time to locate her."

Ross continued. "Levesque lied to her as he lied in so many other ways. Aubrey, though highly intelligent, tended to believe things unquestioningly—a simple, uncomplicated woman. Levesque told her the truth—for him but not for her. Born in France, even though he spent only eleven days of his life in the country, he enjoyed protection by virtue of his French citizenship. She did not.

"The FBI explained it to me this way. A treaty exists between the United States and France which addresses what happens when a French national commits a crime in the United States and flees to France where he is captured. Among other things, the treaty says that France isn't required to turn over its own citizens. In fact, French law prohibits it. Levesque enjoyed the protection of the law. He said it to Aubrey often enough that she believed she enjoyed it as well. When the French OPJ officers arrested her, she didn't believe their authority extended to her. Too late, she learned the reality. No protection against extradition. Same thing with Christine. They're coming back to Seattle to face trial."

"I still can't believe Christine's involvement," Kim said. "We've been with her so many times. I've always admired and liked her."

"Me too. I never thought of her as a suspect, especially because she hired me to find the answer. But, in hindsight, there were hints. First, she directed us to Argus and Consolidated. Nothing pointed to either company, so the work Schlump and I did with them wasted our time and theirs. By doing so, she diverted us away from LeGrande.

"In addition, shortly after she and I agreed that I should audit the administrators, she told me about Winston Lester's background. That trained my focus on him and away from her and LeGrande. I wasted time in Chicago while the crime took place in Seattle.

"She hired me to determine if Great Chicago was being defrauded, not to find out who did it. She emphasized that every time I spoke with her. She didn't want us speculating as to who Levesque might have been collaborating with. And, at least at first, she didn't seem particularly interested in getting the money back.

"Looking back, it always seemed as if Jacques Levesque anticipated our inquiries. We'd come to LeGrande's office, and they were always ready for us. Bell warned Levesque so that he could misdirect us. Then, when we started to get closer, she came to Seattle to see Levesque personally.

"Finally, toward the end, I could never reach Christine. She should have wanted to know everything. I left messages on her phone and at her office, but it always took her hours, even days, to respond. We reported our progress to her by email and voice mail and told her our suspicions. Even then, she expressed reluctance to call in the FBI. She, no doubt, warned Levesque and planned her own disappearance. When Aubrey told her about Levesque's plan to stiff them both, she altered her strategy and connected with Aubrey."

"You did great, Ross. The scheme Levesque and Christine put together exceeded any you've come across. Lucas Sims created the most complex set of programs that you've seen, but in the end, they couldn't disguise what they were doing. And, of course, we can't overlook Levesque's greed. If he had been satisfied keeping his promises to Sims, Christine, and Aubrey, they might have pulled the whole thing off. But he wanted it all."

Taylor nodded, thinking about the climax in France. "You should have seen when the police brought them to the van. They could barely walk. Their faces lacked any of their normal shape or color. I barely recognized Chris, but she recognized me instantly, and I felt extraordinarily satisfied."

Kim moved closer to Ross. "Do you know what happened to that guy Felix? He killed Lucas Sims, didn't he?"

"That's what Aubrey told me and the FBI. If it's true, I suspect that Levesque will implicate Felix eventually. It might cut a few years off his prison time. As to where he is, the police are still looking. No one has seen him for weeks. I'm sure he'll turn out to be the person responsible for Mrs. Fletcher as well."

As he spoke, Kim brushed a stray hair away from his eyes. Their heads had become increasingly sweaty.

"But even if his sentence gets shortened," he continued, "Levesque may have a worse problem to worry about. There were four other owners of LeGrande. Levesque only owned a small percentage. Those four owned a business earning them upwards of ten million a year. When the story about Levesque and the embezzlement becomes public, the insurance department in Olympia will shut them down, and Great Chicago will sue the owners for any costs Great Chicago incurred. There won't be anything left. They'll be forced out of business. That won't go over well with the owners and don't be surprised if they find a way to make Levesque pay for it. Schlump's friend Postiglione says they're dangerous people and capable of anything."

"Lucas was a sad case, wasn't he?" Kim said. "Bad fortune as a kid, then gambling, then breaking the law. Lost his money, his wife, children, and his life."

"You're right. So much talent, and he winds up under a subway."

Kim shook her head. "Aren't you glad this is over? It

turned out great for us. Great Chicago has most of its money back, and you're safe. You worked your tail off and were in danger more than once, but it's nice to have it behind us and have time for ourselves again."

"Yeah, it's turned out great for us," Ross said.

Chapter Fifty-nine

South Pender Island
British Columbia, Canada
Friday, August 30, 2019

Great indeed. Great Chicago paid him his consulting fee of $80,000 plus expenses. More importantly, the contract he signed with Great Chicago promised him a bonus of $250,000 if he solved the mystery. One day after he received his consulting fee, he received a FedEx envelope containing the bonus check.

Two days ago, he had received a call from Winston Lester at Great Chicago. By then, Winston had begun the slow process of getting over the shock of learning the truth about his friend and mentor Christine Bell. She masterminded the sixty-million-dollar fraud and almost cost him his reputation and job.

"Ross," Winston said, "all of us at Great Chicago appreciate the work you did for us. As you know, for reasons that are obvious now, we were unable to find the underlying cause of the problem on our own. We have you to thank."

"I wish you nothing but the best," Taylor said.

"On a personal note, the board at Great Chicago has named me interim CEO. I can hardly believe it. I hear you had something to do with that too."

Taylor could hardly believe it either. He was thrilled by Winston's good fortune. "Congratulations, Winston. You earned the opportunity, and I'm sure you'll do well."

"There's one other thing. We want you to know the diamonds are back in our possession, and they've been appraised by two reputable dealers here in Chicago. Both are willing to redeem them, and it looks like we'll recover about sixty million dollars. We expect to receive the funds in three days. As soon as we do, I'll wire you one point two million dollars. Our contract promised you two percent of any recovery if due to fraud, and we're happy to pay you. You earned it. Just give us wiring instructions, and I'll take care of the rest."

After the call ended, it was Taylor's turn to be stunned. He and Kim were compensated well during their careers but never close to this level. They could scarcely believe what happened.

After two days, they still couldn't. As they relaxed in the silence on their patio, he remembered his arrangement with Schlump. He had already paid him his hourly rate and the one hundred thousand dollars bonus as promised. He asked Kim, "How would you feel about giving Schlump an additional hundred thousand for his part in the solution? He certainly made a big contribution."

Kim agreed immediately. "As soon as we're back in the United States, we'll transfer the funds."

"Sweetheart, can we talk about Derek for just a few minutes?" Ross was breaking one of their promises, but he felt compelled. "We've always done everything we could to find him. We've never spared any expense." He paused to get control of his feelings and put his arm around Kim. "We've just received a windfall we didn't expect. Let's get more people involved in the search. I've been thinking, I'll bet Dale Harrison knows experts who are among the best in America at locating missing people. We've got nothing to lose."

Kim kissed him. "I can't think of a better use for the money. It'll be hard for us to relive the experience and build new hopes, but that's nothing compared to what finding him would mean. I'm in."

They sat together in silence. Ross was relieved they had discussed the topic of Derek without coming apart emotionally. Then, as if knowing it was time to change the subject, he stood and refilled their glasses, turned on the Seattle jazz station, and returned to sit next to her.

As she sipped her wine, Kim said, "You know, Ross, the word is going to get out quickly about how you were responsible for figuring things out for Great Chicago. You're going to be in demand. Maybe we should hang around here for a few more weeks or a month before heading back to Seattle. It's the absolute best time of year to be here. We can enjoy the time together, and you can consider how you want to spend the next phase of your life. You could even write a novel about your experiences."

"Or we could move to North Dakota." Ross tried, without success, to look serious.

Kim rolled her eyes and threw a pillow at him. He made a theatrical duck to avoid the pillow, and as he did so, glass shattered behind them, and something slammed into a wall in the cottage. A small hole appeared in the patio door. At almost the same time, they heard a muffled snap. A gunshot?

"Get down! Crawl inside!" Ross shouted. "Get behind the wall."

Another shot scattered more glass and thudded nearby.

Within seconds, they were inside the cottage and out of view. Ross reached up and turned off whatever lights the switch controlled. Then, he crawled around and turned off the remaining lights. They were in total darkness.

"What's happening, Ross?" Kim crawled on the floor behind a sofa.

"I don't know." His breathing quickened as his pulse pounded at an abnormal rate. He didn't feel fear as much as extreme anxiety. "Stay where you are."

Avoiding the windows and slider doors as much as possible, he crawled to a side window from which he could observe the marina. He slowly moved his head so that he could see out from the lower left corner of the window. He thought the shots came from the direction of the marina, but because of the darkness, he could see no unusual movement. As if nothing happened.

He didn't remember hearing a gunshot, only the bullets breaking the glass, the thump into the wall, and a soft snapping sound. A sound suppressor? Was someone still out there?

Chapter Sixty

South Pender Island
British Columbia, Canada
Friday, August 30, 2019

First Ross Taylor felt fear. Then anxiety. Now fury. He needed to calm himself. But someone had shot at them, and he planned to do something about it. He crawled to Kim's side. "I'm going to get dressed and settle this. I promise I won't put myself in any unnecessary danger, but I want you to call the front desk. Tell them what happened and have them contact the RCMP. They'll come soon and take over. Lock the door behind me. You'll be safe here." While talking, he pulled on jeans, a windbreaker and running shoes.

Kim knew better than to try to talk him out of going. "Be careful."

As he grabbed his binoculars and sprinted out the back of the cottage, she yelled after him, "I love you!"

Taking a path behind the main hotel, he stayed out of sight of the marina and remained hidden from view. Though nearing midnight, Friday night band music covered any noise he made. The sound of the band playing in the lounge floated over the entire resort grounds with speakers placed every fifty feet or so to extend the music.

The path led behind the hotel, across the entrance road, and to the fence line at the north boundary of the resort. He turned left at the fence, his route taking him behind the resort pool and to the water's edge. He still saw no one.

The boat dock at Poets Cove Resort was roughly eight feet wide and extended away from the shoreline approximately 200 feet with boat slips on both sides. Normally, each slip was occupied, and tonight being the start of a holiday weekend, there were no vacancies. A packed marina. At its far end, the dock took a ninety-degree left turn and extended another 150 feet with slips on both sides. From the air, the entire dock looked like an inverted L. By using his binoculars from his vantage point on the shore, Taylor could see every boat. No unusual movement, and nothing suspicious going on. It meant checking out each boat individually.

Taylor thought it impossible for the shot to have come from the right side of either the main dock or its extension. Other boats obstructed the sightline. If Taylor figured correctly, he stood a better chance of finding the sniper by staying to the right and out of sight. There were foot-level and overhead lights every eight feet along the dock, so he placed his binoculars on the ground and stepped into the water at the northern edge of the harbor.

He could walk for a short distance because of shallow water, but soon, as the water deepened, swimming was his only option. The water cooled him but didn't give him chills. Even though the late-summer sun set hours earlier, his windbreaker kept his upper body warm. That would soon change as the water deepened.

Taylor observed that a number of the boats were open fishing boats. They offered no concealment to a shooter. On several larger cruisers, groups of people were singing and laughing. They were equally unlikely to conceal a shooter. But there were also boats which were dark and quiet, and which afforded a sharpshooter an excellent sight line into the cottages, especially those on the outer dock extension.

He decided to swim between the boats on the outside of the extension, then look across to pick out the boats most likely to conceal a shooter.

Until that moment, Taylor never thought about what action to take if he found the shooter. He thought about his Beretta 9mm on the *Pura Vida*. If he could reach his boat without being seen by the shooter, his probability of success increased. But getting aboard the *Pura Vida* forced him either to climb onto the dock and then into the boat or climb onto the boat from the swim platform. Either way, everyone in the marina, including the shooter, could see him. The Beretta was not an option.

He swam quietly to the row of boats on the outside of the dock extension. He used protrusions from the boats to propel him through the water to the dock. When he reached the dock, he pulled himself up until only his eyes and the top of his head were visible to anyone. He saw no one and likely no one saw him. He looked across to the other side of the dock. None of the four boats closest to him offered any type of cover or concealment to a sniper. He dropped back into the water and moved down four boats, pulled himself up to eye-level on the dock floor, and looked across. Same thing. He moved down again. Same result.

By now, Taylor neared the end of the dock extension. Only three more boats on the inside of the dock. Once again, he made his way between boats to the dock and pulled himself up to eye level. For the first time, he began to feel the effects of being in the cold water. He forced the thought out of his mind. In his new position, he could look to his right and see the end of the extension. His eyes long ago adapted to the darkness and what he saw gave him an immediate adrenaline rush.

A muscular man of medium height, dressed in all black and wearing a black balaclava, leaned almost motionless against a dock piling. In the dark, he blended in with the background and became all but invisible. Taylor could barely make out an object in his right hand.

A light wind blew into the harbor from the south. Small wavelets danced across the water's surface. They made lapping sounds against the dock pilings though they weren't large enough to cause any motion to the boats. Downwind of the man, Taylor took comfort in knowing the breeze supplied just enough noise to cover his sounds as he worked his way closer to the end of the dock. He passed behind four boats and stopped. Now, even in the dark, he could clearly see the man and the thing in his right hand. A pistol.

Taylor knew this couldn't have been the shooter. His handgun probably couldn't hit the cottage from this distance, let alone a small target. That meant someone else lurked nearby.

He noticed a boat tied up at the end of the dock along the outside. Unlike the fishing or pleasure boats that filled the marina, it lay low in the water and measured forty to fifty feet in length. Taylor didn't know a great deal about high performance speedboats, but this one looked like it could outrun anything.

Once again, he swam silently to the dock, now only about fifteen feet from the man in black. Except for his head, the man hardly moved and continued to focus his attention on the marina, probably watching out for Taylor. He also guarded the speedboat.

From his new vantage point, Taylor's view of the boat improved dramatically. The speedboat was long, narrow, and built close to the water. When new, it may have been painted in the bright, shiny colors of a racing boat. Not now. All black with a matte finish, it became almost invisible in the dark. Its design placed the cockpit near the stern leaving a long, flat foredeck. The cockpit provided a shooter with an excellent gun rest on the foredeck and an expert, with the proper rifle, should have no difficulty hitting a target on the shore.

It faced directly at the cottages.

Taylor no longer noticed the cold as he contemplated his next moves. Still no sign of the RCMP. He knew if these people took off, they would disappear forever. He must do something.

Chapter Sixty-one

South Pender Island
British Columbia, Canada
Friday, August 30, 2019

The man in black appeared to be a guard. Guarding what? Most likely, a second person hid in the cockpit of the speedboat. The sniper. If Taylor targeted the sniper, the guard would respond instantly to rescue his partner. Taylor discarded that choice.

The sniper probably sat or lay in a prone position looking for another shot. If Taylor targeted the guard, he might overpower him and be able to disappear into the water before the sniper could disengage himself to help. Time for action. He decided to focus on the guard.

The footlights on the dock and the overhead lights on the pilings were out; no doubt shut off by the shooters. Inadvertently, that gave him an advantage. Attempting to remain silent, he moved around the sterns of the remaining boats on the extension, slipping to the end of the dock. There were two vertical pilings—one at the exact spot where Taylor held on. The other, eight feet away where the guard stood.

Taylor waited, motionless. One minute. Two minutes. Three minutes. The guard, extremely disciplined, barely moved. Four minutes. The guard shifted his weight slightly. Stretching his arms, he moved across the dock to the corner where Taylor hid. If the guard glanced down, he could look right into Taylor's face. Instead, he focused his attention on the approaches to the boat. His feet were now within Taylor's reach.

With one powerful lunge, Taylor lifted himself up, hooked his right arm around the guard's legs, and grabbed an ankle. As gravity pulled him back into the water, he yanked the guard's feet out from under him. The guard didn't have a chance to react. He fell face first onto the dock, striking his head. His gun dropped at his side. Taylor pulled him, unresisting, into the water and swam under the dock to the other side.

Taylor's intuition proved to be correct. Someone moved aboard the speedboat. At the commotion on the dock, a man appeared. He stepped out of the cockpit carrying a short-barreled rifle fitted with a sound suppressor. The sniper. The man noticed the guard floating motionless, face down, a short distance from the dock. He looked around for the source of the attack.

From his vantage point on the land side of the dock extension with the shore light at his back, Taylor's eyes saw and recorded everything.

The man appeared to be much smaller than his guard, though his body looked trim. At first glance, he seemed considerably older with gray hair and, like his partner, was dressed in all black, though not wearing a balaclava. Taylor stood at least six inches taller and outweighed the man by more than twenty pounds, but the rifle made him a formidable adversary.

The sniper scrambled back into the cockpit of the boat. He was about to get away. Still no RCMP.

The boat's dock lines were still firmly secured to the dock cleats. As powerful as the boat might be, the lines were one-inch, double braided nylon, and the boat couldn't move until they were untied.

Taylor swam free of the dock and under the speedboat to its outside.

The sniper set the rifle down and started the engines. The twin engines rumbled to life. Even with heavy muffling, they roared with power.

When Taylor heaved himself onto the foredeck, the sniper reacted to the list of the boat in response to the added weight. He leaped to the rear of the cockpit and cast off the aft dock line.

Taylor crawled along the foredeck toward the cockpit, cutting off the man's access to the forward dock line. Taylor vaulted over the windshield into the cockpit.

The man punched Taylor in the forehead, surprising him with the power of his punch. Before Taylor could recover, the man hit him again, this time aiming for his throat. If that punch had landed squarely, Taylor probably would have been killed. Instead, it was a glancing blow that knocked him to the floor of the cockpit.

The man turned toward the dock and jumped out of the boat, reaching for the forward dock line. As he kneeled to untie the rope, Taylor hauled himself to the side of the boat and climbed onto the dock. Despite his pain, he gathered his strength to land a solid kick to the older man's ribs.

The man pulled himself to his feet and went on the attack. He punched Taylor again, this time in the stomach.

Taylor's boxing experience took over, and he avoided the damage the punch might have caused. He let go with two quick left jabs to the jaw of the old man.

The jabs staggered the sniper, but he shook them off, charging Taylor. When he head-butted Taylor, the two men fell onto the edge of the dock floor, grasping for the other's throat. The old man showed skills and strength of someone thirty years younger. The sniper took a firm grip and twisted the collar of Taylor's windbreaker.

Taylor's hands flailed for purchase on the dock floor, and he felt the aft dock line. He grabbed it and wrapped it around the old man's neck. As he tightened the pressure, his opponent's hands release his windbreaker. The old man fought to escape. They fell off the dock.

As they rolled into the water, Taylor took a deep breath. He tried to hold the man under water, but his strength was fading. The old man continued to struggle to free himself from the rope, inhaling water and clawing at Taylor's eyes.

Taylor saw bright colors, heard a loud roaring noise, and felt his arms start to twitch. He was almost out of strength.

Finally the man went limp. It was over.

Taylor kicked his way to the surface and gulped in air. The sniper did not, remaining suspended in the water.

Chapter Sixty-two

South Pender Island
British Columbia, Canada
Saturday, August 31, 2019

The RCMP arrived seconds after Ross Taylor dragged himself out of the water. He sat on the dock with his back to a piling, regaining his breath and composure. In his lifetime, the thought of killing someone never entered his mind. Now there were two men floating in Bedwell Harbor because of him. Even though they had tried to kill him, the shock of taking a life filled him with a profound feeling of sadness. The officers quickly assessed the situation and, at least for now, believed his story. But because questions remained for them to answer, they insisted Taylor accompany them to their barracks.

In little more than an hour, the police identified the two men. Taylor didn't know either of them, but he recognized the names. According to the officers, both were killers.

"There's a great deal of information about the older man. It made him easy to identify. Oberst Horst Brundt, more recently known as Gerhard Bergmann, whichever you want to call him, is a former East German Stasi officer. You did what the underground resistance in the Federal Republic of Germany and Poland were unable to do for almost fifteen years during the 1970s and 80s," said the younger of the officers.

"He shot at you with an old .223 caliber SSG 82 carbine with an 8-power scope. I won't be surprised if we find it's the same weapon he carried as an enforcer," another RCMP officer said. "With his skills, even with the sound suppressor, he could hit a golf ball from that distance. You're a lucky man that you ducked at precisely the moment you did."

He looked at his notebook. "The other guy's name is Felix Contador. Seattle police and the FBI want him for two murders, assault, and other crimes. We found him about fifty feet from the main dock, also drowned. Seems like there's a lot of that going around tonight. These were bad guys, Mr. Taylor. It could have turned out worse."

Ross Taylor thought the same thing. Bergmann obviously wanted revenge for the imminent collapse of LeGrande Benefits and the loss of the substantial income it brought to Bergmann and his associates. After all, Bergmann served as a Stasi officer and was no stranger to revenge. How Felix Contador fit in remained unclear. The RCMP said the Seattle police wanted him for murder, but why did he work for Bergmann?

For the next three hours, Taylor repeated his story, giving the RCMP every detail he could about the shooting and his battle with Bergmann and Contador.

After the official part of taking Taylor's statement

was over, the young officer said, "If either shot were successful, there'd be no chance of our finding them. That boat is a Cigarette Marauder 50 GT S. It will go over one hundred and fifty miles an hour. They'd have been back in Seattle before we could get out of the harbor. Some days are better than others."

The second RCMP officer told Taylor he was free to go, although they might have to call him back. "You and your wife are safe. We'll drop you off at the resort. Have a drink and get to sleep. I'm sure it's been a long day."

The wall clock showed three in the morning, but neither Ross nor Kim felt like sleeping. A little more than six hours had passed since they had heard the sound of the first shot. It seemed like days.

They drank wine, sitting on the couch covered by a blanket, but they were in new accommodations—a three-bedroom villa. The manager even comped the charges for the next three nights.

Ross replayed the entire experience for Kim. She listened intently as he regaled her with every detail.

"I can see Bergmann sending someone after Levesque, but why you?" she asked. "You didn't ruin his business."

Ross shrugged. "I doubt an ex-Stasi would take such subtleties into account. I caught Levesque, and when he went down, the business that Bergmann owned went down with him. He pursued revenge wherever he could find it. But now, it's over."

She pulled up the blanket, wrapped it around them up to their necks, and snuggled closer to him. "You've been through a lot tonight—the last couple of weeks.

You're still cold from the water. Maybe we should just enjoy each other."

After a long pause, Ross said, "I love you, sweetheart. You're right. Let's drop this for tonight and just enjoy being safe and together. We're going to be here for the next three nights. Why don't we take advantage of all three bedrooms?"

Kim's smile told him she liked the idea.

"By the way, I brought you something from France." He reached into his suitcase and handed her a wrapped package. Under the ribbon, a card said, "To my wonderful wife, Kim. Something to enjoy on the boat. Love, Ross."

She unwrapped the package—a highly polished, Italian music box with three red roses inlaid into the walnut case. "Oh, it's beautiful, Ross. Thank you."

When she opened the music box, it played "You Raise Me Up." They listened and held each other, finally setting aside the events of the evening.

They turned out the lights and went to bed.

He didn't look at his phone. Had he done so, he'd have seen eleven new voicemail messages.

####

Coming Soon

Follow the Fortunes

S ome criminal financial geniuses never get caught. The question is: will Oliver Quist?

A shrewd insurance executive, who is not above ordering the murders of his enemies, finds himself up against an equally clever fraud expert. The two match wits in a thrilling, murderous, high-stakes, financial crime which will resolve the question.

Quist, a highly successful health insurance marketer, has fashioned a scheme to redirect millions of dollars in customer reserves into his offshore account at the expense of his Belgian reinsurer. Quist will stop at nothing, including murder, to achieve his goals and disappear with the money. So far, everything is going his way.

But the reinsurer is suspicious and has engaged Ross Taylor, former insurance company executive and now the nation's leading expert on insurance fraud, to dig into and untangle the complex web of relationships and intrigue. Utilizing a blend of yet unproven metaverse technology and old-school street smarts, Taylor and his team confront mysteries, roadblocks, and a deadly psychopath as the opposing forces race to outwit each other.

While confronting his own doubts, will Taylor overcome Quist's guile? Will murder and extortion be avenged? And will his eclectic crew—a four-hundred-pound actuary, a bartender, a feature writer, and two twenty-somethings—be equal to the task?

Even Taylor could not predict the outcome.

About the Author

Rick Lindstrom is a former insurance company chief executive officer whose financial thrillers highlight fraud and other crimes against insurance companies. *The $50 Million Perfect Score* is his breakout novel, with his second and third being prepared for release.

Rick gained practical knowledge of financial crimes firsthand. He held executive and board positions with several well-known insurance companies and has consulted with dozens more. True crimes and criminals from his investigations form the basis of his stories.

Born in Chicago, he attended Northern Illinois University where he received a bachelor of science degree plus graduate studies in mathematics. He has lived in ten states and spent time in fifty. Professionally, he was a Registered Principal with the NASD (now Financial Industry Regulatory Authority) and achieved the Chartered Life Underwriter designation from the American College of Financial Services.

Rick is inspired and supported by his loving wife, Kim. Her experiences as both a business-savvy nurse and health insurance executive have contributed to his stories and his success.

Rick and Kim share an enthusiasm for Western Washington, the home of his main characters, as well as the setting for his first novel. They also enjoy traveling, sailing, golf, photography, and their grandchildren. They spend their time in Arizona, Southern California, and the San Juan and Gulf Island archipelago.

www.ingramcontent.com/pod-product-compliance
Lightning Source LLC
Chambersburg PA
CBHW021436240626
47153CB00001B/174

* 9 7 9 8 9 9 0 6 2 4 0 1 6 *